Her Last Moment

A Jake Cashen Novel

Declan James

One

She was dead the moment the killer reached for the doorknob and turned it. He knew. This was going to be the hardest part. The unknown. If he'd had to break one of the panes of glass to get to the lock, she might have heard it. She would have known what it was. Her instincts would have kicked in.

But everything happened the way it was supposed to. The way he trained and imagined, choreographed in his mind.

At least up to that point.

He slowly opened the door with his left hand, keeping a vice-grip on the knife, holding it flat against his chest.

He took the last step up into her kitchen. A galley kitchen, the realtors called it. Long and narrow. She had new tiled floors and white granite countertops. Those had been expensive. An extravagance. Something she *had* to have but hadn't been grateful enough when she got them, probably.

She was a taker. A narcissist. The worst kind of woman who had no idea how her actions impacted other people. Tonight, she would learn the consequences of them. She had taken the last thing that didn't belong to her.

The killer made a sharp turn from the kitchen down the bedroom hallway. Hers was closed. He heard the shower running, just like he was supposed to. A sliver of light from under the door spilled out onto the white carpet runner in the hallway. Everything else was in shadow. Including him.

She was singing. Bright. Cheery. She had a good voice. A rich alto with a smoky quality. She probably fancied herself the star of every karaoke night at the local hillbilly bar. Yes. She'd be the type. The one who wore cowgirl boots, tank tops that barely covered anything, and too short skirts then got indignant when men ogled her.

He waited. Steadied his breath. The water shut off. He pressed his back against the wall, staying in the shadows as he crossed into the living room. From there, she'd have to pass by him as she came down the hall. There was nowhere else to go.

Sweat dripped down the back of his neck. His leather gloves creaked as he squeezed the knife tighter to his chest. He turned, looking out toward the front of the house. She had a big bay window there tucked under her arched ceilings.

There was nobody out there tonight. By morning, they were calling for up to a foot of snow. It was already starting to come down. In another hour, any tracks he'd made coming in or out the back door would be obliterated. It was as if God Himself were willing to cover his tracks.

He heard the soft whir of a blow-dryer. It was nine o'clock at night. Was she styling her hair before she went to bed?

His blood turned cold. Or was she expecting somebody? A late evening tryst to add to the sins she'd already committed.

Then the dryer stopped. He heard a drawer shut. The light changed. Footsteps. She was heading out into the hall.

He took a breath. Let it out. He wondered if he'd get scared just before. It wasn't like that though. Instead, it was a rush. A primal power he'd never known he had.

The bedroom door opened. In the shadows as he was, she couldn't see him. She kept right on singing as she vigorously rubbed her half-dried hair with her towel. She wore a pink robe tied loosely. He could see the curve of her breasts.

She reached the end of the hallway and felt along the wall, maybe looking for the light switch.

It happened so fast. Instinctively. Almost easily.

One step. One swing of his arm and the knife cut into her back on the right side. Not soft like butter. Sharp as the blade was, skin, muscle, tendons, they're tougher than you think they are. But he struck out, snakelike, then pulled the knife out. Before she could turn. Before she could really even react, he struck again. Almost the exact same spot on her back on the left side.

It would have been enough. He wouldn't know until later, but his initial blows had punctured both of her lungs.

She never even got a chance to scream. She turned then, facing him. Her eyes filled with shock. Confusion. He wondered if she even had a chance to feel the pain. A moment later, he knew she did.

She staggered forward, reaching for him. He sidestepped her, not letting her touch him. She clutched her chest, then grabbed the wall, digging her nails into the plaster, smearing her own blood across it in a wide arc.

She made the most awful sound. Gasping for air that wouldn't easily flow. Her lungs betrayed her. She couldn't fill them. She couldn't scream.

And that was the point.

He existed outside himself for a moment. Curious. Almost welcoming her fight. Then he realized what she was after. The bedroom. Her nightstand. It's where she would keep her service weapon.

He reached out and grabbed a fistful of her hair, dragging her back into the living room. She flailed her arms, trying to get to him. A surge of strength came to her.

He let go of her and raised the knife again. This time, she faced him as he brought it down. She got her arms up in time. His blow went wild, cutting into her forearms. She made a guttural sound. Eyes wild, she lunged at him. With strength she shouldn't have, she came at him, using the only weapon she had, her entire body. She managed to drive her shoulder into his chest. He put his arms around her and flung her off of him, tackling her. They went down together, crashing into her glass coffee table, shattering it into a thousand pieces.

It wasn't supposed to happen like this. He was losing control. She clawed at him, trying to remove his ski mask. Her nails stung his flesh, ripping into his neck. He grabbed her wrists and wrenched them high above her head. Her robe fell open. She was covered in blood. Now, so was he.

Her bottle of wine rolled on the floor, spilling yellow liquid and mixing with her blood.

She tried to reach for her cell phone. He kicked it away with his foot. When he turned back to her, she had the bottle in her hand. "No!" he shouted.

She swung her arm wildly, backhanding him in the jaw with it. The blow rattled his teeth. He tasted his own blood. His ears rang and for a moment, he couldn't see as blood ran into his eyes.

When he got his bearings, she was gone. Her phone was gone. But that sound.

Her ragged, rattling breaths as she tried to draw air that wouldn't come. He got to his feet. He took a step forward.

She would go to the bedroom. Of course she would. Even now. He took a slow step forward.

"Where do you think you're going?" he said through clenched teeth.

She crawled down the hallway, dragging herself forward with her elbows.

A fighter, he thought. He could respect that. That's when he saw the cell phone in her hand. New adrenaline rushed through him. Had she managed to use it? How could he be so stupid? So careless. It was all slipping away.

She stopped moving. Whatever adrenaline she had began to drain along with the last of her blood. He was careful not to step in it. He'd been so careful of everything. Down to the paper booties he wore over his shoes.

She reached her bedroom door and tried to drag herself over the threshold. Part of him wanted to let her. Let her get an inch from the thing she sought so desperately. Her gun. But he'd been careless one too many times.

"I don't think so, honey," he said. He reached down and grabbed her by the ankles. She no longer had the strength to kick. She just stretched her fingers out and tried to dig them into the floor as he pulled her back into the living room.

He flipped her over onto her back and straddled her.

"Shhh," he said. "It's almost over. I know it hurts. It won't for very much longer."

She was still pretty to him. Dark hair. Big green eyes. Perfect skin.

"I'll stay," he said. "Just a few minutes more."

He let her see his eyes through the mask. He'd like to think they were an odd comfort to her. No matter what brought them to this, he understood what it meant to take a life. She had to die, but maybe not alone.

He thought it made a difference there for a moment. Peace came into her expression. Her eyes softened. He even thought she was trying to smile.

"That's it," he said. "You can let go. I'm right here."

That's when she betrayed him. Her face turned hard. She swung at him, digging her nails into his neck. She pulled at his mask. Got a fistful of his hair.

He staggered back. Shocked. Then he remembered the knife.

Rage poured through him. He raised his arm one last time and delivered the final blow. He slashed her across the neck, just deep enough to sever her right jugular vein. He tore the cell phone from her other hand. She was still there. Still watching. He smiled at her, then smashed the phone against the wall, shattering it.

Even after all of it, he would have stayed with her. But light flooded the living room, blinding him.

Headlights. Someone had turned into the driveway.

He called her a vile name. A four-letter word even he didn't like to say. But she deserved it. It's what she was.

She convulsed. Tried to stop the blood. It was too late. It had been too late the moment he walked in. The last he saw of her, she was clawing at the ground. He was right though, it wouldn't be long. Her pain would soon end.

He left her there and ran back through the kitchen, out the door, and into the snowy night.

He felt guilty for just that one moment. He really hadn't meant for her to die alone. But she'd given him no choice. As the newly falling snow covered his tracks, he disappeared into the night.

Two

"Let's go! Let's pick it up!"

Jake clapped his hands together as three of his sophomore wrestlers jogged by him on their second lap of stairs. He had them running through the gym then up and down the stairs on either side of the second floor behind the bleachers. Twenty laps. Half of them were wearing plastics, trying to sweat off the pounds they'd gained from overindulging at Christmas.

He felt for them. He did. But he was glad it wasn't him anymore. He still had nightmares about cutting weight, sleepwalking into the kitchen and Grandpa Max finding him there stuffing his face with cake.

One by one the wrestlers ran by him, sweat dripping down their faces. His nephew, Ryan, led the pack. In three weeks, he'd turn eighteen. In six weeks, he'd wrestle his final state championship tournament. If he made it that far.

Jake stopped and let the kids run by him while he leaned down to tie his shoe. They were worn. Some of the plastic piping on the sides had cracked off. But twenty years ago, he'd worn the same ones when he won his own state championship ring. He had a newer pair of wrestling shoes at home. This close to the state tournament, it felt like bad luck to wear them though. Even if it wasn't his time anymore.

"They're too slow." Out of breath, red-faced, and drenched with sweat, Ryan rounded the corner and stood by Jake's side. He slapped each of his teammates on the back as they ran by.

"How many more?" Ryan asked.

"Five more laps," Jake said. "Then a cooldown. St. Iz might out-wrestle some of them, but none of my guys are gonna get winded in the third period."

"None of your *team*, Coach Jake!" Ashley Polhemus whizzed by. At 106 pounds, she was a contender for a state title herself.

"Sorry, Ash," Jake said. Ashley was currently running circles around the lower classmen.

"How are you feeling?" Jake said to Ryan. Over the summer, Ryan had his right knee scoped to fix some torn cartilage.

"Strong," he said. He thumped his abs. Ryan had put on ten pounds of muscle in the off-season. He currently wrestled at 144 but wanted to bounce up a weight class so he could face Blake McManus again, the kid from St. Iz who'd beaten him two years in a row. But that was an argument for another day.

"How much longer?" Toby Bugg, one of the freshmen, whined as he dragged himself up the steps.

"Twenty more laps if you ask again!" Ryan yelled.

"Is this even legal?" Toby asked. "It's a snow day, Coach Jake."

A withering look from Ryan, his team captain, and Toby kept on running.

"Come on," Jake said. "Let's head downstairs. Make sure we don't have any stragglers. I haven't seen Travis or Kirby in a few laps."

"Oh, I'll kill Trav if he's slacking off."

Jake and Ryan waited for three more wrestlers to race by before heading down the stairs. As they made it to the lobby in front of the gym entrance, the doors swung open, letting in a cold blast of air and swirls of snow.

A trick of the wind, maybe. Jake went to the storm doors to shut them. Deputy Dan Tuttle walked in. He didn't immediately see Jake, but something was wrong. Tuttle looked like he'd been crying.

"Tuttle?" Jake called out.

Tuttle turned. His face went slack when he saw Jake. He practically lunged for him. Jake got his arms up just in time. Tuttle seemed ready to collapse.

"Is he okay?" Ryan asked.

"Tuttle, what's up?"

"Jake," Tuttle sputtered. "Detective Cashen. Um. They've been trying to get a hold of you. For over an hour. I went to your house. Your grandpa told me you were here. You weren't answering your phone."

"I'm off today," Jake said, though instinct told him in about five seconds that would be irrelevant. The hair on the back of his neck stood on end.

"My phone's in the locker room," Jake said.

Tuttle nodded. "You gotta come. We've got ... Hammer's not ... we aren't ..."

"Tuttle, get a hold of yourself," Jake said. "What's the matter with Sergeant Hammer?"

"Nothing," Tuttle said. "It's ... God. Jake, it's Mary. You've gotta come. They're securing the scene, but you gotta come."

"Tuttle, I'm off duty today. Detective Rathburn is on. Is she trying to get a hold of me?"

Tuttle shook his head. If it was possible, his face turned even whiter. "No. Jake. No. You don't understand. Mary's the one ... she's ... Jake ... God. She's dead, Jake. She's dead. Somebody killed her."

Jake felt a whoosh inside of his head. Time seemed to slow down. Tuttle wasn't making sense. Mary Rathburn had just been promoted into the detective bureau. He was still training her. She was ...

"Uncle Jake?" Ryan said.

Jake turned to Ryan, adrenaline coursing through him. Tuttle's disjointed words coursing through him. Mary. Dead. Crime scene.

"I have to go," he told his nephew. "You take over. You finish practice."

"He's saying Mary Rathburn is dead?" Ryan asked.

"Never mind," Jake said. "Not a word of what you heard. You understand?"

Ryan nodded. Jake handed Ryan the keys to his truck. Then he followed Deputy Dan Tuttle out into the snow.

The plows had been out early, but six fresh inches of snow had fallen since Jake started practice this morning at seven a.m. Mary Rathburn lived in the western part of the county at the end of a long street. It was quiet out here. Jake had picked her up a couple of times when her car wouldn't start. In the country like this, she had no neighbors close by. Just three at the other end of her street.

Tuttle drove skillfully through the snow and ice. Two patrol cars blocked the end of Mary's road. Jake recognized deputies Stuckey and Bundy. They each gave him a solemn nod as Tuttle drove slowly past.

"Nobody's been in or out since ..." Tuttle started. "Since Sergeant Hammer called."

Two more patrol cars parked at an angle in front of Mary's driveway. He saw their tire tracks in the snow. Nothing else. With the rate of snowfall, Jake already recognized one major problem.

Tuttle parked. As he got out, Jake saw Sergeant Jeff Hammer sitting on Mary Rathburn's front porch step, the overhang protecting him from the snow. Beside him, Lieutenant John Beverly patted him on the back.

"You found her?" Jake said to Hammer.

Hammer started to get up. He didn't make it. Instead, he keeled over sideways and dry heaved. That's when Jake noticed a melted patch in the snow where Hammer must have lost his breakfast earlier.

A tremor ran through Jake. Jeff Hammer was a seasoned cop. Whatever happened in that house, it was by no means his first crime scene.

"She drives that piece of crap car," Hammer said. "It's not reliable in this kind of weather. I told her I'd pick her up."

"We all take turns picking her up," Jake said, more to himself than Hammer.

"I knocked," Hammer said. "I called her and told her when I was leaving. She didn't answer. I sat in the driveway. Called her when I got here. She didn't pick up. So I came up here and knocked. Nothing. Then I opened the front door."

"It was unlocked?" Jake asked.

Hammer nodded.

"Who's inside?" Jake asked.

"Nobody," Lieutenant Beverly said. "We've been waiting for you."

"Good." Jake reached into his pocket. Tuttle had gloves and booties in his kit in the car. Jake put them on. He steeled himself, then walked through Detective Mary Rathburn's front door.

The smell hit him immediately. That metallic tang of blood. Sickly sweet death. Whatever happened, the body had been lying there for a while.

The house was a hundred years old. A one-and-a-half story, craftsman-style home. She had a dining room off to the right side. In front of him was Mary's living room. She had two couches along the north wall and a glass-topped coffee table in the center. Shattered. Shards of glass were everywhere. Jake spotted a broken wine glass halfway under one of the couches.

He took a step forward, cautious about going any further. He saw her then. His heart lurched.

Mary Rathburn. Young. Pretty. At thirty, she was going to be one of the youngest deputies to ever make detective. The only woman, too. Jake had handpicked her after she'd proven herself invaluable in two separate investigations.

She lay on her side in a loose fetal position. Barefoot. Smeared with blood. Blood streaked the hallway leading into the back bedrooms. It pooled beneath her. From here, Jake could already see what was likely the mortal wound. A slash across her neck. She'd bled out. Her robe might have been white or pink originally. Now, it was dark crimson, soaked with blood.

"God," Jake said. His stomach roiled. He knew how Hammer must have felt.

"God. Mary."

He wanted to go to her. His protective instincts kicked in even though rationally, he knew she was dead. But this wasn't some random victim. This was his colleague. His friend. He took a breath. Closed his eyes. Said a quick prayer. When he opened his eyes again, she was no longer any of those things. Neither was he. He was Detective Jake Cashen of the Worthington County Sheriff's Department. Former Special Agent of the Federal Bureau of Investigation. Whatever Mary Rathburn had been to him, now, he knew what she needed.

"Jake?" Beverly came in behind him.

"Nobody else comes in or out," Jake said. "I need to talk to Hammer. Has anyone searched the bedrooms? Mary's got a little boy. Kevin. He's four years old."

"Nobody else was in the house," Beverly said. "She's alone."

Jake nodded. He stepped closer, careful not to contaminate the scene. He put a hand out, cautioning Beverly to stay where he was.

Mary's eyes had pearled over. She stared at the wall. Her left hand was curled beneath her, her right arm stretched out with her fingers curved into a claw as if she'd been scratching at the ground.

She fought, Jake thought. The shattered table. The broken wine bottle. The streaks of blood running along the wall and down the hallway.

She fought.

Jake knelt down, getting as close to Mary's body as he dared. He wouldn't touch her.

"I need BCI out here," he said. "Now. I need two more deputies blocking the road from the other end. Has anyone tried to talk to her neighbors down the street?"

"We've been waiting for you," Beverly said again. "We've been trying to call you, Jake."

He nodded. As he was about to rise, something caught his eye. There was a pattern in the blood on the floor. Jake pulled his small flashlight out of his pocket.

"Christ," Beverly said. "What is that?"

Jake shone the light in the space at the tip of Mary Rathburn's outstretched hand.

Letters, perhaps. A number? Mary Rathburn had fought for her life. But as she lay dying, she'd tried to write something. A message. It hit Jake like a thunderbolt, nearly knocking him backward off his feet.

She knew. Of course, she knew Jake would be the one to read it. In her last moments on earth, Mary Rathburn had written him a message using the only weapon she had left. Her own blood.

THREE

When Jake walked into the sheriff's station, Meg Landry was the first to greet him. Her face drawn, dark shadows beneath her eyes.

"Jake," she said, her voice cracking.

He knew what she wanted. Of course, she'd heard the dispatch call. She most certainly understood what Jeff Hammer had discovered. And yet, until Jake himself got eyes on it, he knew she couldn't let it be real.

"We need everybody," he said. "All units. Pull everybody in. Command. Everybody."

"Everyone's already on their way," she said. "I've got people volunteering on their day off. Retired officers are calling asking what they can do to help. Darcy's cleared out your war room. Lieutenant Beverly's about two minutes behind you."

"Good," he said. Jake's ears rang as if the overhead fluorescent lights had become amplified somehow. Each of his senses seemed to heighten. He fixated on a tiny spot of lint on Meg's lapel. A crooked black line beneath her right eye where she'd maybe applied her makeup hastily or in the car. That wasn't like her.

"Jake," she said. He hadn't realized he'd gone frozen for a moment. She put a hand on him.

"Five minutes," she said. "Just you and me. Before we go in there. Tell me ... everything."

He walked across the hall with her. That buzzing sound hadn't left him. He knew his heart rate wasn't normal. Blood roared between his ears as the adrenaline had yet to dissipate. He wanted to run. He wanted to hit something.

Meg closed her office door and turned to him.

"Please, Jake," she said.

Jake shook his head. "She's dead. Mary's been murdered."

She dropped her chin. "You're sure? I mean, there's no chance that ..."

"She was murdered. Stabbed probably multiple times. Slashed through the neck. She bled out, Meg. Her living room floor is pure red."

Meg's eyelids fluttered. For a second, he wondered if she'd stay on her feet. Meg reached for her desk, then sat on the edge of it.

"Okay. Okay," she said.

"BCI's on the way," he said. "The ME just pulled in as I was leaving. I wanna get back out there."

"Of course. Like I said, everybody's starting to file into the war room. They're waiting for you. What do you know so far?"

"Nothing," he said. "No sign of forced entry. Both her front and back doors were unlocked. She was coming out of the shower."

"Do you think she was ..." Meg couldn't bring herself to say it.

"I can't tell you whether she was sexually assaulted yet," he said. "She was half naked, but I told you, it looked like she was coming out of the shower."

"Do you have any sense of when this happened?"

"Hammer said he was picking her up to bring her in."

Meg nodded. "She drives that Tracker. She can never get it to start when it gets cold like this."

"Yeah."

Meg stood up and came to him. She put a light hand on Jake's arm. He didn't mean it, but he jerked away. Even that, the smallest touch, made his nerve endings burn.

"Jake," she said. "I have to ask you this. Mark Ramirez called me too. He's on his way to the scene. He asked ... that is ... he offered. You'll have his help, you know that. The full resources at your disposal. He understands Mary is one of our own. But he's offering to have BCI take the lead if you want him to. Maybe ..."

"Maybe what?" Jake snapped.

"I'm just putting it out there. If you feel like you're too close to this. Hell, I'm too close to this. Mark is offering ..."

"No," Jake's voice boomed. "No way in hell I'm stepping aside on this one. It has to be me."

He turned away from her. He'd gone rigid as granite. His nails cut into the flesh of his palms.

"Okay," Meg said. "I understand. But you understand I had to ask."

Jake whipped around to face her. "She wants me."

Meg cocked her head to the side. "Who? What do you mean?"

"Mary," Jake answered, his voice barely more than a whisper. "She knew. Dammit, Meg. She knew."

"What are you saying?"

"She didn't die quick. There are signs of a struggle. She fought like hell. And she knew."

"You think she knew her attacker?"

"I don't know yet. I'm saying *she* knew what was happening and what I'd need. God. I trained her! Taught her how to process crime scenes. What to look for. Where we'd find the best evidence. That scene out there? Mary Rathburn was becoming a skilled homicide detective. Even as she was bleeding to death, she knew what I'd be looking for. She scribbled something in her own blood. Something she knew I'd be the one to read."

If it was possible for Meg Landry to go even whiter, she did. Jake took out his cell phone. He'd snapped just one picture. He turned the screen so Meg could see it.

"What does that say?" she asked. "W? I can't make it out."

"W/M," he answered. "White male. That's the number five next to it. She was trying to write down his height. His physical description."

"It's barely legible," she said.

"Not to me. She's using the same shorthand I do."

Meg closed her eyes. "All right."

"It's too soon to make assumptions," he said. "But Mary was trying to tell me something. Me personally. You think she didn't realize I was the one who'd end up walking through that scene?"

"Of course," Meg said. "It's just ... it's too horrible to think about yet."

"Well I have to."

There was a knock on Meg's door. Darcy Noble, the main civilian dispatcher, poked her head in. Tears streamed down her face. "They're all ready for you in the next room. Oh Jake, I'm so sorry."

She came into the room. Darcy walked into Jake's arms and squeezed him tight. He comforted her. It was all he could do.

"Come on now," Jake told her. "We don't have time for that. Mary needs us at our best. You understand?"

Darcy nodded and wiped her tears. "I'll put a fresh pot of coffee on."

"Good. And keep it coming."

He knew it would at least make Darcy feel better to have a tangible task. He still had his arm around her as they walked down the hall and into the war room. A dozen solemn faces greeted Jake as he entered. Each of them looked to him for answers. For a leader. For someone to make sense of what had happened to their sister, Detective Mary Rathburn.

They were all there, crowded into the 12x12 room, lining the back wall when the chairs were all taken.

Lieutenant Beverly stood at the front of the room. He patted Jake on the back as he came to join him, then Beverly stepped aside.

"All right," Jake said. "I know the rumor mill has already spread this thing throughout the department. So let me say it officially. Mary Rathburn is dead. She was stabbed to death. It was just as brutal as I'm certain you've already heard. That's what I know. And the rumors end right here. Right now. You have a question about something that happened out there. You come to me directly. You hear anyone else gossiping about either Mary or my crime scene, you come to me. The information on this investigation is going to flow one way through me. Nobody talks to the press unless I know about it and approve it beforehand. And I'll make it real simple. I have no intention of approving any media interviews. Sheriff Landry is going to be the only person talking to reporters and even then it will be through her office through scheduled press conferences. Okay? I cannot afford any leaks on this one. Mary ... can't afford any leaks. Are we clear?"

The men and women in the room all nodded. Many of them were in tears. He couldn't afford those either.

"What do you know, Jake?" Deputy Morse sat in the front row. Prior to Mary being pulled up to work in the detective bureau, she'd worked field ops with him. Jake hesitated. Though he'd just warned everyone not to leak details of the case, he knew the best way to prevent that was to share as few of them as he could. At the same time, Mary was one of them. Just as he was, they were still trying to process the horrifying loss of a friend. A colleague. A woman many of them, including Jake, had relied on to help bring them home safely at the end of their shifts.

"I mean ... it was a homicide? There's no doubt?" someone called out.

"There's no doubt," Jake answered. "So what I need to know from all of you, those of you who knew Mary socially. Who hung out with her on weekends ... I was only just getting to know her. So I need your help. Your insights. Even if you think it's nothing. You come find me. You let me know."

"Has anyone found Kevin?" Deputy Amanda Carter raised her hand. Jake knew she had a young daughter about the same age as Mary's son.

"He wasn't in the house," Jake said.

"It's Shane's weekend," Deputy Morse said. "That's Mary's ex. Shane Edwards. He gets visitation every second weekend a month. I don't know where he lives. Or even what he does. But that was their arrangement."

"It was nasty," Deputy Carter said. "Shane and Mary never had the best relationship. Their divorce and custody fight got pretty ugly. Judge Lacey just gave her full custody right before Thanksgiving two months ago. They'd been in court over it for two years."

"Anybody got an address for Shane Edwards?" Jake asked.

"He lives on Wyman Road. I went with her once when she dropped Kevin off," Deputy Carter said.

"Write it down for me," Jake said. "Anybody know where Shane works?"

"Most of the time he doesn't," Morse said. "For a while, he was just doing odd jobs. Stuff where he got paid under the table. That's part of the trouble Mary had with him. He hides his income so he can keep child support low. Mary was even talking about hiring a private investigator to try to track all that down."

"He's been working for Pete Gansett over at his body job for the last few weeks," Deputy Carter chimed in. "At least that's the last I heard."

"Anybody know the name of the PI she hired?" Jake asked.

The men and women looked around the room at each other.

"It might have been Ike Schumer," someone called out.

"I don't know if she actually hired him," Morse added.

"Thank you," Jake said, writing everything down. He knew Ike Schumer. He was probably the least sleazy of the local private investigators around town. Had Mary asked him for a recommendation, that's the name he would have given her.

She hadn't asked though. And in the last ten minutes, he'd learned more about Mary's life than he ever had. She kept it away from him. She was strictly professional when he worked with her.

"She was off-duty yesterday," Jake said. "Does anybody know how she spent her day? Did anyone talk to her? Do we know if she was seeing anyone?"

"She went on a few dates with one of the firemen," Beverly said. "Mike Simmons, I think. That was a few months ago though. No idea if they're still involved."

Jake wrote down Simmons's name.

Deputy Birdie Wayne and Sergeant Jeff Hammer walked in. Hammer's eyes were still red-rimmed, but he'd pulled himself together. Jake knew Birdie was off-duty today as well. She'd been home when Jake and Ryan picked up her nephew, Travis. She'd waved to him from the driveway.

"I'll need to talk to Simmons," Jake said. "And anybody else you can think of. Was there anybody internal Mary might have been seeing? From the department?"

Everyone looked around at each other, but nobody spoke up.

"I'm not judging anybody," Jake said. "I'm just trying to build a picture of what was going on in Mary's life. If you know something, say something. But only to me. Got it? I meant what I said. No gossip. No leaks. It's what Mary deserves."

Jake's phone buzzed with a text. It was Mark Ramirez from the Bureau of Criminal Investigations. He'd just arrived at the scene.

"All right," Jake said. "I've got to get back out there. Thanks for your initial thoughts. It gives me a few places to start."

"Anything, Jake," Beverly said. "Anything you need. Any time of the day or night. You just ask."

"I appreciate that, Lieutenant. I really do."

"All right!" Meg shouted. "We're clear on our initial marching orders. It's a mess out there. We're under a level three snow emergency. That's gonna make certain things harder today. Everybody watches out for everybody else. Now let's let Jake go to work for Detective Rathburn, okay?"

Jake slipped his phone in his pocket. Birdie followed him out into the hallway.

"Jake," she said, sprinting to catch up with him. "Are you okay?"

It occurred to him she was the first person to ask him that. He honestly didn't have an answer. Birdie didn't press.

"Listen, I might know something. Can we go to your office? I know you told everybody to zip it. It's just ... people can't spread rumors they don't hear, right?"

"Right," Jake said. He and Birdie waited while the entire Worthington County Sheriff's Department filed past them in the hallway. Then they stepped into his office and closed the door.

Four

"I don't know what to say."

Birdie stood with her back to the door, holding on to the knob behind her. Jake felt like he had a jackhammer inside his head. He took a seat at his office desk and started rummaging through the drawers. He knew he had a bottle of ibuprofen in there somewhere.

Birdie came in further. She grabbed a chair from the small break table they kept in the detective's office and pulled it up alongside Jake's.

"Jake," she said. "I saw Mary. About a week and a half ago at Wylie's. She was having drinks with someone."

"A date?"

"I don't know. I didn't recognize him. Average height. Five eight. Light blond hair. Medium build. I'd be able to recognize him if I saw him again but he didn't stay long. He got up and left and Mary came up to the bar alone. I was sitting in a corner booth. I wouldn't have really paid much attention to any of it but someone approached her."

"What do you mean?" Jake found his bottle of ibuprofen. He downed four pills and washed them down with the last of the lukewarm water in a bottle on his desk. He crushed the thing and arced it over his head, hitting the wastebasket dead center.

"Another guy came up to her. He sat on the stool next to her. Mary wasn't sitting. She was paying her tab. She had her purse over her shoulder and I think she was getting ready to leave. This guy? He was drunk. Swaying in his seat. When Mary tried to leave, he grabbed her arm."

"Who was he?"

"Didn't recognize him either. But five ten, five eleven. White. Muscular build. Dark brown hair. He was wearing a canvas jacket and motorcycle boots. She jerked away from him. That's what initially caught my attention. He started yelling at her. Saying how she better do the right thing. At that point, I slid out of the booth. I just wanted to be close enough in case this guy started making more trouble."

"Did he?"

"He said that boy needs a daddy. You're turning him soft. She told him to mind his own business, or something to that effect. She threw a twenty on the bar and started to walk out. He followed her. He wasn't steady on his feet. Repeated what he said. That boy needs his daddy. You aren't gonna get away with bleeding Shane dry."

"Did Mary seem upset by it?"

Birdie shrugged. "Not really. She acted like he was more of a nuisance. Waved him off. But he kept coming. Karl was working the door. He saw this guy following her. He stepped in his way.

Wouldn't let him pass until Mary was out the door. After that, the guy just dropped it. Went back to the bar. The bartender wouldn't serve him. He swore a little. Karl stayed close. At that point, the guy left. Staggered out the front door. Mary was long gone by then."

"You don't know who it was?"

"I'd never seen him before. He's got to be some friend of Shane Edwards, Mary's ex."

"Shane's the first person I want to talk to," Jake said. "Did you ask Mary about it?"

"The next day," Birdie said. "I saw her at the beginning of my shift. I'm not sure if she knew I was at the bar that night. I asked her if everything was okay. She was nice about it, but she more or less told me to mind my own business. I think it embarrassed her that anybody else saw what went down."

"Did you hear this guy threaten her?"

"No. It wasn't a direct threat. Just that same thing over and over. That boy needs his daddy. And him saying she wasn't gonna get away with it. Mary didn't argue with him. She's ... she was smart enough not to try to reason with some drunk in a bar."

"And you think you could pick this guy out if you saw him again?"

"I know I could. Both the guy harassing her and the guy she was sitting with before that."

"I appreciate this," Jake said. "Did anyone else in the bar see what you saw?"

"Other than Karl? I don't think so. The guy I was with didn't even pick up on it until I came back to my table and told him where I went."

"The guy you were with?" Jake said. "You wanna tell me who you were with who didn't see the need to go with you when you decided to confront some five foot eleven drunk in the bar?"

"I didn't confront him. There was no need."

Jake needed something stronger than ibuprofen.

"What do you know about Mary's custody problems?" Jake asked.

"Jake, you spent almost every day with Mary. Are you telling me she never talked to you about it?"

"No. Other than I knew her ex was a bum. She didn't bring that stuff to work."

"Are you okay?"

"I'm fine."

"Jake ..."

Birdie kept her eyes laser-focused on him.

"I'm fine!" he repeated.

"I want to help if I can. Anything you need."

"You already are. Can you write down everything you just told me? I need details. The physical descriptions. Who else might have witnessed it."

"Of course."

"I need to find Shane Edwards." He got to his feet. "I sent two deputies to his house. Told them to text me the minute they had their hands on him."

"Jake," Birdie said, louder this time.

"What?"

"Connie. Mary's mother."

The words hit him like a blow to the chest. Mary's mother. Connie Rathburn. Not long ago, he posed for a picture with her and Mary as Sheriff Landry pinned her detective's badge on her.

"Would you like me to?" Birdie asked. "I know her a little. Connie was friends with my mother. With your mother too, if I remember right."

Jake nodded. "I can do it."

"Let me. Jake, Connie knows me. She's made a point of checking in on me since Ben died. She still keeps in touch with my folks from time to time. She ... she asks about you a lot. I know ... Jake, she loved that Mary was going to be working with you."

"Mary's her only child," Jake whispered. "And her old man passed away after a stroke a few years ago. She's alone."

"I know. I'll go now. Before this gets out. And you know it will."

"Yeah. Go. And Birdie ... hurry."

She nodded. Birdie reached for him. She meant it as a comforting gesture, but Jake turned to stone. It was too much. Too soon. He knew if he gave into even a second of sentimentality, he might turn a corner he didn't want to.

Birdie seemed to understand. She withdrew and stepped away from him.

"Tell her," Jake started. Hell. What could Birdie or anyone else tell Connie Rathburn that would make any of this bearable?

As if she could read his mind, Birdie gave Jake a sad smile. "I'll tell her you're going to do your very best for Mary."

Jake clenched his jaw. "Yeah," he said simply. "Yeah."

Twenty minutes later, Jake and Deputies Morse and Corbin stood outside Shane Edwards's house on Wyman Road. Mary had never lived there, he knew. It was a modest duplex with a postage-stamp-sized backyard. From the untouched drifts of snow over the driveway, Jake knew nobody had driven in or out since before the storm hit. Still, Shane could be sleeping or passed out inside. But after five minutes of pounding on the door, Jake gave up.

"The hell you doing making all that racket?"

The adjoining neighbor poked her head out of her front door. Her own driveway hadn't been plowed either.

"I'm looking for Shane Edwards," Jake called out. "Have you seen him?"

Shane's neighbor looked to be about seventy. Her face had the texture of a raisin. She scowled at Jake as a dog barked from inside. "He ain't here!" she yelled back. "Haven't seen him since the day before yesterday. He's supposed to shovel this snow and take care of the yard. I give him a break on his rent. So that ought to tell you what he's good for."

"Can you tell me your name?" Jake asked.

"Who's asking?"

Jake flashed his badge. "Detective Jake Cashen."

"Yeah. I know you."

Jake resisted the urge to yell at her why she asked. "Great. And you are?"

"Francine Beadle. And you're standing on my property."

"You have any idea where Shane might be?"

"I told you. He's supposed to maintain this property. It's a condition of his lease. I think you better tell *me* when you find him. Tell him I'm gonna take him to court this time."

"Mrs. Beadle?" Jake said. He was done shouting. He trudged through the foot of snow separating Shane's front door from Francine Beadle's. He pulled his card out of his pocket and handed it to her. "The minute you see Edwards, I need you to call me. Can you do that for me?"

Francine Beadle snatched Jake's card with two grubby fingers and stared at it. "Can't see," she said. "I need my readers."

"Tape it to your fridge," Jake said.

"What's he done?"

"I just need to talk to him. It's important."

"My property is important. Me being able to get in and out of here is important. How am I supposed to do that with a foot of snow out there? Your deputies over there. There's a shovel by the side of the garage. My taxes pay your salary. Why don't you do something to earn it for once?"

Jake felt a flush of heat creeping up his neck. He took a breath to keep his anger from rising. "Mrs. Beadle, do you have a cell phone number for Shane Edwards?"

"For who?"

"Your tenant!" Jake shouted. "Do you have a cell phone number for him?"

She eyed him. "Won't do any good. He ain't answering. I called him three times when the snow started falling. Went straight to voicemail."

"I need that number," Jake said. "Can you please get it for me?"

"Whoa boy," she said. "You're sure hot and bothered. He must of done something bad. What good's that fool gonna do me if he's in jail? Maybe I should just lose this card and tell you to get off my property."

He was losing patience fast. He never moved, but Francine Beadle must have read something in Jake's face. She pursed her lips and slipped his business card in the front pocket of her house coat.

"You just wait there," she said. "Don't need you coming in dripping snow all over my floor."

"Wouldn't dream of it," Jake muttered. Francine slammed her screen door shut and disappeared inside her house. Jake heard her swearing, then the squeal of at least one cat. A moment later, she came back holding a folded piece of paper. She opened her storm door a crack and slid the paper through. Jake took it. In a shaky hand, she'd scrawled the phone number.

"I surely do appreciate it," Jake said.

"You gonna call somebody to shovel my street so I can get out of here?"

"The road commission handles that," Jake said. "The plows are working double time. It's going to be a while until they get out this way. We're under a level three snow emergency now. You shouldn't be driving unless it's an emergency. You got enough food in the house for a day or two?"

"I can take care of myself!" Francine bellowed, contradicting her own arguments.

"Fine," Jake said. "You take care of yourself. Thanks for this." He slipped the number in his coat pocket and headed back down the driveway.

"I called Gansett's Body Shop," Deputy Morse said. "Shane's not scheduled to work today. He's a regular at the Rusty Bucket though. You want us to ask around out there for him?"

"That's helpful, yes," Jake said. The sun was beginning to set. Jake had two incoming texts. He checked the first one. Birdie was at Connie Rathburn's house. The text read simply, "Broke the news. She's holding up, considering. She wants to get to her grandson. Any word on where Shane and the kid are yet?"

"Negative," Jake texted back. "Stay with her. Find out who Mary's family liaison is. I want them at the house 24/7. Whatever Connie needs."

"Copy that," Birdie texted back.

Jake's second text was from Mark Ramirez. "Have initial findings. Meet me out at the scene."

Jake climbed behind the wheel of his cruiser. He headed back to Mary Rathburn's house, wishing he could be anywhere else in the world.

Five

The snowplows had come through. They cut a path just to the entrance of Mary's driveway. Two patrol cars blocked anyone else from getting to it. The BCI crime scene van was parked just inside the perimeter. Jake pulled in behind it. It was eight o'clock in the evening. He'd been on twelve hours with no end in sight.

New snow began to fall. The weatherman predicted another four inches by morning. Jake shoved his hands in his coat pockets as he made his way up Mary's front walk. It hadn't been shoveled, but the snow was packed down from the ins and outs of Mark Ramirez's people throughout the day. As he got to the front door, Ramirez met him there.

"Hey, Jake," he said. "I'm so sorry about this. I didn't realize she was your partner."

"She was working on it," Jake said. Ramirez had two boxes on the porch for gloves and booties. Jake grabbed pairs of each and put them on. Ramirez had three crime scene techs moving through the house still collecting whatever evidence they could. The house already smelled different from this morning from the chemicals and solvents they'd been using. But beneath that, Jake could still smell death, even though Mary's body was long gone.

"Thanks for coming out," Mark said. "I know you've gotta be operating on fumes by this point."

"I'm fine. You have anything for me yet?"

Ramirez guided Jake to a taped-off path to the right of the living room furniture.

"I'll know a lot more after the ME's report and my lab. But yeah. There's quite a bit."

Jake followed Ramirez through the dining room and into Mary's galley kitchen. The room was littered with yellow evidence markers. All over the floor. The counter tops. Leading to the back door off the pantry.

"No sign of forcible entry anywhere," Ramirez started. "Both the front and back doors were unlocked. I understand the victim primarily used this back door here to go in and out rather than the front door."

Jake nodded. "That's what I recall too."

"Based on the blood patterns, it's pretty clear your killer entered through this door as well. She's got a laptop in the bedroom. A free-standing safe in her closet. Some jewelry in a drawer. None of it's been disturbed. There were some valuables in the little kid's room on the second floor as well. Gaming system. A tablet. All still there. As far as I can tell, this was all confined to the downstairs. Killer never even ventured up there."

"So not a burglary," Jake said.

"I don't believe so, no. Best I can tell, it was an ambush. Her hair was still wet from the shower. And how she was dressed, just in a robe, socks, underwear ..."

"He lied in wait," Jake said. "Came through the back door by the pantry. Could probably hear her in the shower."

"It's a solid theory. The initial contact took place here," Ramirez said. He led Jake back through the kitchen and over to the bedroom hallway.

"Hammer said the lights were off in the living room," Ramirez said. "There was just the light on in her bedroom. So the killer would have been in the shadows here. She had two stab wounds to the lower back."

Ramirez turned and pointed to the space on his own back right above his kidneys but below his rib cage. "Two wounds," he said. "Obviously, I can't say for sure until we get the ME's take, but most likely he punctured her lungs. So maybe a basic understanding of anatomy. The guy knew what he was doing. Maybe he was a hunter."

"He *was* a hunter," Jake whispered. He'd hunted last night. Only Mary Rathburn had been his prey.

Jake closed his eyes and tried to imagine the terror Mary must have felt. She survived the first attack, but she would have immediately struggled to breathe. Adrenaline would have fueled her from then on.

"She fought, Jake," Ramirez said. "It got real bloody, real quick. There was a struggle here in the living room."

"She ran," Jake whispered. "She had the strength and presence of mind to run."

He stood over the shattered glass coffee table. Droplets of blood had dried on some of the shards.

“She had an empty wine glass sitting on it,” Ramirez said. He pointed to the glass. It landed on its side on the carpet. Jake could still smell the fermented grapes.

“Moscato,” Ramirez said. He shined a pen light near the base of the couch. Then he pulled out a small tablet and showed Jake a picture of the space taken before Ramirez had bagged and tagged some of the evidence.

“Broken bottle came to rest right here at the base of the couch. I think she might have hit him with it. There was blood all over it.”

Ramirez touched the screen with two fingers, closing in on what was left of the base of the bottle. Blood was smeared all over the white label.

“And here,” Ramirez said. He took Jake back to the kitchen, pointing out three evidence tags on the floor. “We found blood droplets. Obviously, we’ve gotta wait for the lab results to come back. But I’m gonna take an educated guess that blood didn’t come from your victim ... er ... Detective Rathburn. To my eye they were more consistent with someone still on their feet. Your killer might have been bleeding on his or her way out the back door.”

“You’re certain that’s the way he left?”

“Yes.”

Jake walked back into the bedroom hallway. In his mind’s eye, he could still see Mary lying there. Now, there was nothing left but the outline of where her body lay. The wood floor still ran red with Mary’s blood. The largest concentration of it was just outside her bedroom door.

"She ran to the living room," Jake said. "Fought him there. Then she came back this way, trying to get to the bedroom."

"Yes," Ramirez said.

Jake carefully stepped around the evidence markers and stood at the threshold of Mary's bedroom. Her bed was still made. A pair of pink and green flannel pajamas were laid out on the end of it, ready for her to slip into. His gaze went to her nightstand.

"Her service weapon," Jake said. "She kept it there."

It's where he kept his. He turned to Ramirez.

"She was trying to get to it. She was dying and she was trying to get to her gun."

"Probably," Ramirez said, his expression pained.

Jake stepped into the bedroom. *It was just a few more feet*, he thought. She would have known she was dead for sure without her gun. Her strength was already starting to leave her.

"Jake," Ramirez said. "She fought like hell. This is one of the bloodiest crime scenes I've ever processed where there was only one victim."

"She knew," Jake whispered. He walked back into the hallway and stopped just short of where the body lay. There, near the baseboard, he saw the lettering scrawled into the wood in Mary's blood.

Jake took his flashlight out of his pocket and shined it on the spot.

"She tried to write something, we think," Ramirez said. But Jake already knew. He froze. Trying to imagine what Mary would have been thinking. Trying desperately not to.

"Of course, we'll know a lot more after the ME's through. There didn't appear to be any injuries to her ... it didn't look like a sexual assault. But you know I can't say that for sure."

Still frozen, Jake nodded. He kept his light trained on Mary's scrawling.

"She had hairs in her fist," Ramirez said. "The killer had long hair. She got a hold of it. The nail on her middle finger was broken. She looked like she'd had a fresh manicure. So that was odd. It won't shock me if the ME finds skin under her nails."

"She scratched him," Jake said. "She pulled his hair out by the root. Then she tried to describe him."

"What?"

Jake pointed to the scrawling. The blood had dried since he last saw it. It wasn't as prominent against the dark wood as it had been earlier this morning. But Jake could still read it.

"W/M, 5 ... something."

"Does that mean something to you?" Mark asked.

"White male, five foot ... I can't make it out. A one maybe. So five ten. Five eleven."

Mark cocked his head. "You could be right. But that's a pretty big assumption. You know you'll have a hard time getting a jury to hear that."

"All a half-decent prosecutor would have to do is show them any one of Mary's reports on any case she worked on with me. It's her shorthand. It's ... *my* shorthand."

"Jake, I can't imagine what you must be going through. I'm gonna do everything I can to fast-track this one. Top priority. And if you need it ... I don't want to step on your toes. You know that. But if you need me to ..."

"I appreciate that, Mark," Jake said. "But I've already had this conversation with Landry. I'm keeping the case."

Mark nodded. Jake knew he'd never bring it up again.

"Do you have any initial theories on this one?" Mark asked.

Jake remembered the note Francine Beadle had scribbled out for him. He took it out of his pocket and handed it to Mark.

"Shane Edwards," he said. "Mary's ex. They were embroiled in a custody dispute over her son. I've been trying to find him all day. The boy's supposed to be with him. That's his cell. Can you track it?"

"Absolutely," Mark said. "I'll put a rush on it. It would make sense. This whole thing seems so ..."

"Personal," Jake answered for him.

"Right."

"I appreciate it. All of it."

"You know I've got your back, Jake. This one's personal for me too. I didn't know Mary well, but she was a good kid. I know that much. This whole scene. The whole time I've been here. It just feels like she's trying to tell me something. Like she knew what we'd be looking for. What I'd need. How we were gonna catch this monster."

"Yeah," Jake said. He couldn't take his eyes off those letters and figures written in Mary's blood. He walked past them and stood at the threshold of Mary's bedroom. Her nightstand was no more than fifteen feet from where she died. He could see what she saw. What she was after before her body finally gave out. Her badge lay on the nightstand, her gun beside it still in its holster. Beside that, he could see her cuff case.

"Mark, do you need any of that?"

Mark followed his line of sight.

"It's all department issued," Jake said.

"No. Everything's been photographed in place. Her gun was never fired. You can take it back to your property room. Just document it for me."

Jake walked over to the nightstand. He collected Mary's gun, cuffs, and badge. "Thanks," he said to Ramirez.

Ramirez gave Jake a tight-lipped nod. "So when you do start interviewing suspects. Whether it's this ex of hers or somebody else. Jake, look for injuries. She probably would have tried to hit him in the face with that bottle. Or if we do find skin under her nails."

"Give me a few hours," Jake said. "I'll have my people run this cell number. It'll take longer for the full report, but if we can ping it and give you a location ..."

As he said it, Deputy Morse walked in the front door. He stopped just short of the first evidence tag.

"Detective Cashen," he said. "Just got a call. They picked up Shane Edwards at home. That landlady called it in."

Jake's pulse quickened. He turned to Ramirez. "Run the cell anyway. I want to know where this guy's phone has been in the last twenty-four hours."

"You bet," Mark said.

Jake gave Ramirez a solemn handshake, then headed out Mary's front door.

Six

Jake had met Shane Edwards once. He'd come to the station to drop Mary's son off after he took him to lunch. It had been contentious then. The man just decided he was done taking care of their kid and left him with Mary while she was in the middle of a shift.

Today, Edwards sat in a chair in the interview room, tapping his heel against the floor. Agitated. Intoxicated or high, maybe. It was just past midnight.

Jake stood outside the room, looking through the one-way mirror. Meg came in to join him. "Has he said anything?" Jake asked.

Meg shook her head. "The deputies were careful not to say anything, either. The landlady called. Said you'd told her to let us know when he showed up."

"Where's the boy?"

"He was home. Sleeping. He's got a girlfriend staying with him. She's there now. I asked Deputy Stuckey to stay nearby. He's in a patrol car sitting about a block away."

"Good. Depending on how this goes," Jake said, "somebody needs to get a hold of Connie Rathburn. I don't know if Shane's going home tonight."

"It'll be taken care of."

"Hey!" Shane got out of his chair and walked over to the mirror on his side of the glass. He couldn't see Jake or Meg, but the man knew he was being watched. He tapped on the glass.

"Hellooo!" he said. "I asked for a water. Whatever you people want, I'm losing patience."

Jake felt his fists curl.

"Jake," Meg said. He knew she was about to caution him. He didn't want to hear it. Jake grabbed a pen and blank pad of paper off the chair behind him and headed into the room with Shane Edwards.

Shane was busy huffing a circle with his breath in the mirror. He traced a phallic shape into it with his finger. It lingered there for a moment before his breath dissipated. He turned to Jake and smiled.

"Have a seat," Jake said. "I'll try to make this brief. I know it's late."

He expected Shane to flip him off, or worse. Instead, the man took his seat and crossed his leg over the opposite knee.

"You wanna tell me what this is about?"

"I will. Yes. But first, I need you to tell me where you've been for the last twenty-four hours."

"None of your business."

"Shane? My name is Jake Cashen."

"You think I'm messed up in the head or something? I know who you are. I know what you are."

"Yeah? What's that?"

Shane narrowed his eyes. For a moment, Jake tried to imagine what someone like Mary Rathburn ever saw in him. She was ... had been ... pretty. Smart, with a sensible head on her shoulders. So far, Edwards hadn't displayed any amount of charm. Still, he wasn't a bad-looking guy. Trim build. Dark hair. Dark eyes. Jake supposed he was the kind of guy women would describe as having rugged good looks rather than traditionally handsome. He wore a pair of faded jeans and work boots. A plain black t-shirt with the threads coming loose on one sleeve. He had a Carhartt jacket flung over the chair beside him.

Jake couldn't see any scratches or injuries on his face, neck, or arms. His hair was slicked back and shoulder length. Ramirez's words ran through Jake's mind.

Mary had gotten a fistful of her attacker's hair.

She knew Shane though. If she'd seen his face, she wouldn't have needed to write a generic description. W/M, five foot something ... She would have just written his name.

He could have worn a mask though.

"Your whereabouts," Jake said. "Since midnight last night. Can you share that with me?"

"What for?"

"Because I'm asking you nicely."

"You gonna stop being nice if I don't tell you?"

Jake was tired. His brain buzzed from the caffeine he'd mainlined throughout the day. He knew if this guy made a move on him, he'd flatten him. Part of him wished he'd try.

"You had Kevin overnight, right?"

"Why the hell are you asking me that?"

"Shane, look. Give me a break. I'm asking you a simple question. Where have you been for the last day?"

"With. My. Son. You answered your own question."

"You weren't at home though. I came looking. Had a nice little conversation with your landlady. She's a real peach."

This got a laugh from Shane. "Peach? She's something. It ain't that."

"Can't be easy living next to her. She tried to get my deputies to shovel her driveway. You can guess how well that went over."

"I hope they told her where she can stick her shovel."

Jake smiled. "They did."

"Good."

"So where were you, Shane?"

He regarded Jake. Whether it was their small moment of bonding over the delight that was Francine Beadle, or something else, Shane finally answered the question.

"I was in Oakton. My cousin Brad lives there. His kid was having a birthday party. She's four. Same age as Kevin. So I took him. Look. This was all prearranged. Mary said she didn't have a problem with it."

Jake picked up the pad of paper he brought along with the pen and slid it across the table. "You think you could write down your cousin's address?"

Shane frowned, but took the pen. He wrote down an address and started to slide the pad back.

"Hold on," Jake said. "Can you write down your cousin's full name? Tell me who else was at the party who can verify you were there."

"You know, this is bullshit. I don't appreciate you sending two uniformed cops to my front door in the middle of the night, man. This is overkill. Even for Mary."

"What do you mean?"

"She couldn't stand it, could she? She knows how much Kevin's been looking forward to spending time with me. It was a little kid's birthday party. One he's been excited about. She just can't stand it. I could sue you, you know?"

"For what?"

"For harassment. She's using her job to cause me grief. There's gotta be a law against that."

"You think Mary put me up to this?"

Shane leaned forward. "I think Mary will use every chance she can to screw me over."

"So tell me about that. She's new to the detective bureau. You have to know there were a lot of people in line for her job. You saying she maybe doesn't deserve to have it?"

"What is this?"

"I'm just trying to get a clear picture of what's going on with you two. That's all."

"Oh, you want me to think you're on my side or something? I know you. You cops all stick together. Where the hell is she? Is she watching behind that glass? You in there, Mary? Guess what, Kevin doesn't want to come home with you. He's having fun with me. With his *dad*!"

Shane launched himself out of his chair and charged the mirror. He pounded on the glass. "You can knock this crap off. I don't care about your badge. I don't care about some piece of paper you got some judge to sign. You probably slept with him too, just like half the town. She get her hooks into you?" Shane turned to Jake.

"I think you need to sit down and calm down, Shane."

"We're done here. You asked your question. I answered it."

"Names," Jake said. "Tell me who you were with at your cousin's party in Oakton."

Shane grabbed the pad of paper and scribbled down three names. He shoved the pad toward Jake.

"What time did you get to your cousin's?" Jake asked.

"I don't know. I picked Kevin up at Mary's. She wasn't there. Her mom was. She asked me where I was headed and I told her it was none of her business and that I expected Kevin's things to be packed. She handed me his backpack and I took my son and left."

"You went straight to your cousin's from there? What time was that?"

"Noon, maybe. I took Kevin to lunch at McDonald's. He played on the slide. Then some kid puked in it and I got him out. We went to my cousin's after that. His wife Rashelle gave him a bath and fresh clothes. He played with the rest of the kids there. We had the party. When the kids went to bed, the rest of us hung out."

"You were there all day?"

"Yeah. Is that a crime?"

"These people can confirm it?"

"Look, I'm done with the third degree. I had a right to take my kid. The court said I could. No. The court *told* Mary she can't interfere. So here's what's going to happen. I want the names of every deputy that showed up at my house tonight and dragged me here in front of my kid. We'll see how the judge likes all this."

"Shane, when was the last time you spoke to Mary?"

"What?"

"Did you see her? Text her? Call her?"

"Screw you."

"I'm going to find out, so it's better if you tell me the truth now."

Shane reared back. Then hatred filled his eyes.

"Oh, I get it. Man, I gotta be some kind of idiot not to have seen this for what it is. She's boning you. Of course she is. You said it yourself. There were a lot of other people in line for her new job. Now she's pissed because Kevin wants to spend time with me. So she bats her eyes and gets you to do her dirty work. I knew she was screwing somebody at work. She kept denying it but I know how she operates. Let me tell you something, buddy. Consider it a favor. Run away from this chick. She's trouble. She's a black widow. She'll suck you dry and ruin your life."

Jake's anger began to rise.

"Yeah," Shane said, laughing. "Hoo boy. She got her hooks into you good. I'll give her credit. She's good at exactly one thing. You better be careful though. She'll tell you she's on the pill, then the next thing you know, you'll be a daddy too."

"Shane?" Jake said. "Mary doesn't have her hooks in me. She doesn't have her hooks into anyone. She's dead, Shane. She was stabbed to death in her own home last night."

Shane had a smile frozen on his face. Only a tiny flicker in his eyes registered the news. Was it news? Or was this all an act?

Then Shane slowly sank back into his chair. His face turned ashen. "Wait a minute. Wait a minute. Wait a minute! You son of a bitch! This is a setup. You think I did something to her?"

"I think I want to find out what happened."

"No! No, man. No! This wasn't me. You are not pinning this on me. This is a trick. A lie. This is ..."

"Shane, have a seat."

"No way. I'm done talking to you. Are you gonna arrest me?"

"I'd like you to submit to a DNA test."

"Fine. I didn't do this. I wasn't in that house. You won't find anything."

"And your phone," Jake said. "You have a problem with me going through it?"

"No way. I know how you'll try to twist things."

"I'm just trying to get to the truth. If you were at your cousin's like you say, then giving me your cell phone data and a cheek swab is the quickest way for me to clear your name."

"I'll do the cheek swab. Call the cell phone company. I don't care. I'm outta here. I wanna go get my kid."

Jake stood up. "You listen to me. It's not gonna go well for you if you do something stupid. I'm gonna find out who killed Mary. Bet on it. The worst thing you could do for yourself is skip town.

Okay? I'm gonna have more questions for you. I better be able to find you. We clear? Wait here."

Jake stepped out and grabbed the swab kit. Five minutes later, he had Shane's DNA sample in a tube ready for BCI. It would take a few days for Ramirez to call back with the results, but the fact Shane had submitted to it made Jake believe his story.

Shane kept shaking his head. He looked like he was about to be sick.

"Can I go now?"

"I'm not arresting you. But remember what I said. Stay available. I'm gonna have more questions."

"Do whatever you gotta do." Shane grabbed his jacket off the chair and rushed past Jake. He had some choice words for a few of the deputies on his way down the hall.

Jake picked up the pad of paper Shane had written on. Three names. His cousin and two others. It would be easy enough to run down.

"What do you think?" Meg said, poking her head back in. He knew she'd been listening in on the entire interview.

"I don't know," Jake said. "That's the truth."

"A guilty man wouldn't have submitted to DNA that easily."

"No," Jake said. "Probably not. I'll have Ramirez run his cell phone. The tower hits will show if he's lying about where he said he was."

"Go home," she said. "Come at this fresh tomorrow morning. The ME should have a preliminary report by the end of the day. You've been running this as a one-man band. I can't let you do that long term. You know that."

Jake gave her a bitter smile. “I had a partner,” he said.

“I know. Tomorrow we’ll talk about finding you a different one. If only on a temporary basis.”

Jake tore off the top sheet of paper from the pad and put it in his pocket. He wrote another name down on a fresh piece of paper and handed it to Meg.

She looked at it, her brow furrowing. “Are you sure?” she asked. “This is who you want?”

“Yeah.”

“Get some sleep. We’ll talk tomorrow.”

She looked at the name on the paper one more time, then took it with her as she walked back to her office.

Seven

Rain? Jake thought. For a moment in the quiet darkness, he hoped it had all been a nightmare. There had been no snowstorm. Mary Rathburn was alive and well and ready to meet him at the office with her good mood and a cup of coffee. Because it was raining outside and that couldn't be possible in mid-January with sub-freezing temperatures.

Then his stomach growled with hunger as he smelled bacon and knew that the sound was sizzling bacon, not raindrops hitting the roof of his cabin.

Bacon?

Jake threw off the covers, grabbed a pair of drawstring sweatpants off the floor, and slipped into them. His teeth felt fuzzy. Hell, his brain felt fuzzy as he opened his bedroom door and walked out into the kitchen.

His sister Gemma stood over the stove. Two pieces of toast popped up from the toaster beside her. She plated those, then deftly flipped a fried egg in the skillet in front of her.

For a moment, Jake panicked that he'd overslept, but it was still dark outside.

"You look like hell," Gemma said. She found a smile and slid two eggs, sunny-side up, onto the plate with the toast. She took tongs and added four strips of bacon to it and put the plate on the small bistro table Jake kept near the door. His place wasn't big. Just a tiny kitchen off the living room. One bathroom and two bedrooms, the second of which he rarely went in. His grandfather had built this cabin decades ago and lived in it with his grandmother while the Big House was under construction. The clock on the microwave read 6:17 a.m. Jake had grabbed just five hours of sleep. More than he usually got while working a homicide case.

"I didn't hear you come in," he said. "You're lucky I didn't shoot you."

"Oh, you were snoring like a grizzly bear. I didn't have the heart to wake you."

Gemma plated another egg and three more strips of bacon for herself. She put it on the table and grabbed a pot of coffee and two mugs.

"What's all this?" he asked, biting into a piece of bacon. She had a knack for it, always getting it crisped on the outside but somehow tender on the inside. In a way, that was the perfect way to describe Gemma's personality as well.

"I figured you had a bit of a day yesterday. And I'm assuming today might even be worse. So I'm gonna get at least one solid meal into you before you head in. You'd just slam stale coffee and a day-old donut otherwise. If that."

"Thanks," he said, sipping his coffee. She made it strong.

"Are you okay?"

He opened his mouth to answer, but Gemma cut him off. "Never mind. Don't answer. You'll just say you're fine. You'll tell me not to worry. I'll say I won't and we'll both be lying."

"Gemma ..."

"Mary Rathburn," she said. "Jake. I know you. You're going to start blaming yourself for this one. Or you're going to run yourself into the ground while you're working this case."

"Ryan filled you in? He was there when Deputy Tuttle came and got me at practice yesterday morning."

Yesterday morning. Had it only been twenty-four hours since he walked into Mary's house?

"He said he saw it go through you, Jake."

"Saw what?"

"Don't play dumb. I know what he meant. I've seen that look, too. Every time, this stuff chips away at you more and more. Makes you harder."

"Don't worry about me."

She slammed her mug down. "I said don't."

He sighed, then reached across the table and covered her hand with his. "Thank you. I appreciate you coming over. I do."

"I hate your job, you know?"

"Sometimes I do too."

"I know you won't tell me, but ... Jake ... what happened? Do you know who did this? Connie Rathburn's got to be shattered. I can't even imagine it. And that little boy. Jake, was Kevin there when it happened?"

"No to your last question," Jake said.

"Thank God. He's barely more than a baby, but old enough that he'd remember it if he ... if he saw her like that."

If he saw her like that. Of all the people in the world, Gemma knew what it was like to see someone like that. At the tender age of twelve, she had been the one to discover their parents after their father had shot their mother in the chest and then himself. They never talked about it. But Gemma carried it inside of her every day of her life. Jake wished he could take that burden away from her. He wished for a lot of things.

"Gemma, will you check in on Connie? I'm going to go talk to her as soon as I can."

"Of course."

"To your other question, whether I've got any leads. You know I can't talk about that yet."

"I know. It's just ... a lot of people are scared this was some kind of home invasion. They're saying she was ... was she raped, Jake?"

Jake knew the Worthington County rumor mill would start churning hard.

"I don't know yet. Even if I did, that's not something I want out there."

"Neither do I. Plus you know I can keep my mouth shut."

"How well did you know Mary?" he asked.

"Didn't you?"

"We worked together. She was just promoted a couple of months ago. I didn't know her much outside of work. She's a ... was ... a good cop. I think with time she could have been a great detective."

"I knew her a bit," Gemma said. "I know Connie more. You know she was in Mom's circle of friends."

"Birdie said that. I had her break the news to her."

"I'm glad. Connie loves Erica. If it couldn't have been you ... and I'm not trying to give you crap for that, I know what you're up against ... I know Erica took care of her."

"Yeah. Me too. I'll go see her though. I promise. I'm gonna have to. I just wanna be clear. I get that Ryan said something to you about what happened in the gym yesterday. He's not talking to anyone else, though, is he? I need you to make sure."

"Ryan understands your job, Jake. He knows the drill. You can trust him."

Jake cut into his eggs. Though it was in him to tell her not to have gone to all this trouble, he was glad she did. She was right. He probably wouldn't eat again all day. There'd be no time.

"So, Mary," he said. "Anything you know that might help me?"

Gemma raised a brow as she took a sip of coffee. "I'd actually been running into her more lately. Her little guy, Kevin. He's in preschool at Stanley Elementary. His classroom is right across the hall from Aiden's. So I've seen her at different school functions. Talked to her a few times while we were waiting to pick the boys up. She's always friendly. I congratulated her on her promotion. She asked me for tips on how to handle you."

"How to handle me?"

Gemma was smiling behind her mug. She set it down. "Yes. I told her it helps when you've got a plate of bacon in front of you."

Jake was in mid-bite on a fresh strip.

"Funny," he said.

"Jake, have you talked to her ex? I know they were having issues. He showed up a couple of times to pick Kevin up when he wasn't supposed to. I know the teachers got copies of her latest custody order so they'd know what was allowed. I heard some rumblings that he caused trouble for Mary at the parent-teacher conferences a few weeks ago. Showed up drunk or something."

"It doesn't surprise me. Did you ever talk to her about it?"

"You didn't?"

"She kept her personal life away from the office. At least ... she kept it away from me."

"Well, she was completely embarrassed by Shane, I know that. We didn't ... I didn't want to pry. But once, when Shane showed up to take Kevin he made a scene. Mary handled it pretty quickly, but I could tell she was upset. Again ... embarrassed. I went up to her and I just told her I had some experience with what she was going through. I told her if she ever wanted to talk, I had an empathetic ear. That was maybe two months ago. She thanked me, but never took me up on it."

"I'm glad you did that. I'm sure she appreciated it."

He finished his coffee and poured himself a second cup. As he refilled Gemma's mug, a chill of fear went through him.

"Gemma? About your ... uh ... experience. I need you to swear to me, if Dickie Gerald starts causing trouble for you and Aiden again, you let me know."

The moment he said it, fresh rage roiled through him. Dickie Gerald had tried to sue Gemma for custody of his eight-year-old nephew Aiden a while ago. Before Jake moved back to Ohio, he'd gotten physical with Gemma. She'd kept it from him, knowing how he'd react. An image flashed into his mind. A new nightmare. He saw Mary Rathburn as she lay in her own blood. For an instant, her face changed and it was Gemma.

"Jake," Gemma said. She grabbed the coffee pot from him. He realized his hand was shaking. Coffee sloshed down the side of it.

"Sorry," he said. "But I mean it. If Dickie ..."

"I haven't heard from Dickie in months. He hasn't exercised any of his visitation in almost a year. And yes. I promise. If he starts up again, you're my first call."

"I'll end him," Jake muttered.

"He knows that."

Jake couldn't move. His vision went white. He imagined wringing Dickie Gerald's skinny, tattooed neck and shaking him senseless.

"Jake!" Gemma was on her feet. She put a hand on Jake's arm. When he squeezed his eyes shut, he couldn't get the thought of Gemma lying in her own blood out of his head.

"Hey," she said. "I'm not Mary Rathburn, okay? And Dickie's not ... well ... I don't know what he is. But he's not a threat to me or to Aiden."

He hated that she could practically read his mind. He hated that Mary hadn't come to him with whatever was going on between her and Shane Edwards. He just ... hated ...

His phone rang. He had it on the charging dock on the counter behind him. It was a county government number. He answered it as Gemma busied herself cleaning up the dishes. "Cashen," he said.

"Jake, it's Ethan Stone. I'm heading into the office in about an hour. I've got my initial findings on Mary Rathburn's postmortem ..."

"I'll meet you there," Jake said. He clicked off.

Gemma poured the remains of the coffee into an insulated tumbler for him. She went up on her tiptoes and planted a kiss on his cheek. “I won’t bug you with calls or texts today,” she said. “But promise me you’ll at least eat dinner tonight.”

“Yeah,” he said.

“And take a shower before you leave. I love you, little brother, but you reek.”

EIGHT

"They're inside."

Sandra Ketcham had served as Dr. Ethan Stone's administrative assistant for as long as he'd been working for the county. Rumor was she tried to retire about a dozen times but Stone guilted her into staying. She was a formidable woman, standing nearly six feet tall. She kept Stone on schedule and organized. Jake knew whenever the day came that Sandra had enough, Stone would probably follow. It would be a tremendous loss.

"Do you want to go in or do you want to wait in his office?" Sandra asked. "She's in there, honey."

He knew what she meant. Mary was in there. Stone called Mark Ramirez right after he called Jake.

"You don't have to go in there," she said. "Ethan can brief you from his office. He doesn't need to put on a show."

"I've seen her, Sandra."

"Well, once is enough. Have a seat in his office. I'll pry him out of there. You want some coffee or anything, honey? We had some donuts delivered. They're still hot. Did you eat something?"

Jake smiled. Sandra was the second woman trying to take care of him this morning.

"I'm fine. My sister made me eat breakfast."

Sandra laughed. "Gemma's one of my favorites. Only don't let her know. She'll get a big head."

Jake put a finger to his lips. "Your secret's safe."

Sandra unlocked Dr. Stone's door. Jake took a seat on the couch he kept along the wall. Sandra disappeared. A moment later, Stone and Ramirez came to join him.

"Morning," Stone said. "Hope you got yourself a good night's sleep. You've got a long day ahead of you, I imagine."

Ethan Stone was well past the age he could have retired. At seventy-six, he was one of the oldest county MEs in the state. His was a physically demanding job, one that kept him on his feet all day and muscling his way through the human anatomy.

"I appreciate you fast-tracking this one."

"Don't be ridiculous. That girl needed me last night. Now she needs you more."

"How'd your interview with the baby daddy go?" Ramirez asked.

"He provided an alibi that's pretty easy to check. Says he was in Oakton at a cousin's. Gave me four names he says can confirm it."

Ramirez pulled up his phone. He scrolled through something.

"Yeah. That tracks with his cell phone data. I was going to send you what I have so far. But it pinged two towers in Oakton. Marvell County."

"Well, that just means his phone was there," Stone said. "What I've got is gonna be dispositive if you can get this guy's DNA."

Mark put his phone down.

"Walk me through it," Jake said.

Stone pulled out a tablet. On it, he had Mary's autopsy photos stored. In the first one he pulled up, all Jake could see was Mary's back and the two large, now bloodless entry wounds.

"Let me run down the list," Stone started. "Detective Rathburn has a penetrating stab wound through the lower inferior lobe of her right lung. Clean in and out. So this would have been quick. Precise. And made by a stiff blade, extremely sharp. My guess is a hunting type knife. No serration. And in all the wounds I'm gonna describe, I didn't find anything in her as far as metal. That's a pretty common finding with stab wounds when they're made with what I'll call lesser weapons."

"You mean like a kitchen knife," Ramirez said. "She had a knife block in the kitchen. We bagged it all. So far, nothing was missing from the block. Doesn't mean she didn't have something mismatched in a drawer or something. We'll have everything tested for blood, of course, but at the moment, nothing jumped out as suspicious."

"Well, like I said," Stone continued. "I don't think you're dealing with a kitchen-grade weapon. Your guy used something extremely sharp and intended to kill."

Stone flipped to the next picture, a close-up of the second wound to Mary's back.

"Here," he said, "she's got a second stab wound to the left side. It's higher and penetrates the superior lobe. This one's deeper than the other one on the right. It nicked the pulmonary artery."

"Which would explain the initial blood loss," Jake said.

"These wounds in and of themselves would have been fatal. I think even if she had medical attention right away. I found massive internal bleeding."

"She didn't die right away though," Jake said. "The crime scene points to a struggle."

"Oh, she put up a hell of a fight," Stone said. "She has defensive wounds on her hands."

Stone flipped to another photograph with a close-up of Mary's right hand. Her knuckles were scraped and lacerated.

"There's a fresh hairline fracture along the metacarpal of her right index finger."

"She punched something hard," Jake said, leaning in close to get a better look.

"Like a jaw bone," Ramirez surmised.

"Maybe. Or she swung and missed. Hit the wall or something. Hard to say," Stone said. "She's also got lacerations on her right forearm. One of them is an inch deep. My guess is she managed to deflect at least one of his attempts to stab her. Cut her down to the bone."

The scene unfolded in Jake's imagination like a nightmare. A horror movie. She had nothing. No weapon. Not even the thin protection of a coat or a pair of jeans. Mary Rathburn fought for her life with her bare hands.

"Quite a few shards of glass embedded into her back and buttocks as well," Stone continued.

"The glass-topped coffee table was shattered," Jake said.

"A broken wine bottle too," Ramirez added.

"Well, this glass was ground in," Stone said. "I'd say she rolled in it a bit. Probably struggling with this guy. Or woman. I guess I shouldn't assume yet. But whoever it was had to be pretty strong. As far as the fight, Mary would have been losing a lot of blood very fast. She would have been having a tough time breathing as her lungs started to collapse. It really is a hell of a thing that she lived as long as she did."

"The defensive wounds," Ramirez said. "I noticed she had a broken fingernail. We did a nail scrape at the scene. That's going to take a little while to get the labs back, but ..."

"Your people did a good job out there, Mark," Stone said.

"She made my job easy," Mark said, his tone grim.

"Yeah," Stone agreed. "She had a fistful of hair in her left hand, Jake. Dark in color. Could have been dyed but I suppose Mark's lab analysis will get that answered for you. Plenty of the strands had the roots still attached. She yanked the stuff right out of her assailant's head, Jake."

"She knew," Jake whispered. "That's the thing that's killing me about all of this more than anything else. She knew what I was going to need."

The three of them fell silent for a moment. Jake knew they were all haunted by what Mary tried to do in her last seconds on earth.

"This here," Stone said, advancing to the next photo on his tablet. "The wound to her neck. Her external jugular vein was fully severed. Death would have come within a few minutes at most."

"She had time," Jake said. "Just enough to try to write me a message in her blood."

"You said that," Mark said. He pulled his phone out and opened his own camera roll. He pulled up an image of the markings scrawled in Mary's blood. He showed it to Stone.

"I'll be damned," Stone said. "Jake, this is remarkable. I know it probably doesn't make you feel any better. But after all the damage that had been done to this girl, she still had the presence of mind to try to identify her killer. I've never seen anything like it."

"It was very ... Mary," Jake said, his tone bitter. "She was a good detective until the very end."

"You gotta catch this bastard," Stone said. "You know I'm here for anything you need."

"Doc, what about evidence of sexual assault?" Jake asked.

Stone put his tablet down. Jake knew he had more pictures associated with his question, but out of respect for Mary, he didn't pull them up. Jake would have plenty of time to sit with that particular horror later.

"The short answer is no. I couldn't find any evidence that would specifically point to sexual assault. There was no tearing or abrasions to any of the external genitalia."

"There was evidence that she'd had intercourse recently," Stone said. "Probably within twelve to twenty-four hours of her passing. There was semen present. But ... obviously pending the results of any further labs, if you need a quick answer, I'd say it was consensual sex, Jake."

"I appreciate your thoughts."

"Any idea who she was seeing?" Ramirez asked.

Jake shook his head. "We worked together. But not for that long. We were just getting to know each other. But mostly, our conversations were about work. Cases we had. She was private."

"I'm sorry, Jake," Stone said. "This one's god-awful. She didn't deserve this. We can't undo what happened, but we can make sure we do the best we can for her now. As rough as this is on you, I'm glad it's you handling this case. I'll go out on a limb and say it's what Mary Rathburn would want."

"Thanks," Jake said.

"I'll forward my full report to you minus toxicology by the end of the day."

Jake rose. He shook Ethan Stone's hand. Mark said his goodbye and the two of them walked out into the parking lot together. Mark's phone buzzed. He pulled it out of his pocket and read the screen, frowning.

"Anything I'm gonna like?" Jake asked.

"Maybe. I've got more details on the phone data from the ex. Night of the murder the phone pings a tower on the west side of Oakton in Marvell County. It's sitting there from early evening through noon the next day."

"That tracks with what Shane Edwards told me. He said he was at a cousin's house out there. Just because his phone's there doesn't mean he was. He might have been smart enough to leave it there, knowing it's the first thing we'd check. But you've got the sample from his cheek swab. That'll tell us for sure."

"I'll be in touch," Mark said. "We'll get that DNA back just as soon as humanly possible. In the meantime, I'm a text away if you need anything. If you think of anything."

"I appreciate it," Jake said. As he did, a text came through from Meg. She had the team assembled in the war room. It was eight a.m. She wanted a daily briefing at the start of the day shift.

Mark split off to go to his own vehicle. Jake slid behind the wheel of his. It looked like the snow had finally stopped for the day.

Five minutes later, Jake walked into the war room. Meg stood at the front of the room behind a lectern. "I'll be giving the first press conference in about an hour," she said. "Minimal details. Hey, Jake. You're just in time."

Jake thanked her and joined her at the lectern. The team consisted of five deputies handpicked by Jake, including Birdie. Lieutenant Beverly, Meg, and Sergeant Jeff Hammer. If Meg approved his request, he was going to have Birdie partner with him on a temporary basis. It was the name he had written down for her. But that was a conversation for later in the day.

"Just came from the ME," Jake said. He gave the group a rundown of Dr. Stone's findings. He hesitated when he got to the most sensitive one. He hated every part of having to discuss it.

"Look," he said. "There's evidence that Mary had intercourse sometime the day before she died. So if anyone in this room has info about who she was seeing, I need you to bring it to my attention."

"You don't know?" Meg asked.

Jake repeated what he'd just told Stone. "We didn't talk about our personal lives much. Maybe in time we would have. It was still early days for us as partners, Sheriff."

"Understood," she said.

"Stuckey, Morse, Bundy, I need you to continue canvassing with Mary's neighbors. Any strange vehicles they might have seen coming or going. Find out when she last talked to any of them. I'm going to finish buttoning up Shane Edwards's alibi. I'll be heading to Marvell County later in the day to talk to the cousin."

Once Jake was certain the group had their marching orders, he let Meg dismiss them.

"Birdie ... sorry. Deputy Wayne, can you hang back for a second?" Meg said. Birdie looked perplexed, but stood at attention.

As the rest of the group dispersed, Jake started to walk toward Birdie. Before he got there, Sergeant Hammer grabbed Jake's arm.

"Hey, Jake. You got a second? I've got something important I want to discuss with you."

"Is it about the case? Can it wait?" Jake asked. Over Hammer's shoulder, Birdie gave him an expectant look. She had to be wondering if she was in some kind of trouble.

"It'll just take a minute," Hammer said. "I don't think it can wait."

Jake let out an exasperated sigh. If Hammer had something to share about the case, it would have been better if he'd done it while the entire team was still here. This was exactly the kind of crap this meeting was designed to streamline.

"Sheriff," Jake said. "I'll be back in five minutes."

Jake went with Hammer across the hall into Jake's office. When he shut the door and turned to Hammer, the man's expression told him whatever he had to say Jake wasn't going to like.

Nine

Hammer walked into Jake's office and headed straight for the coffee. He poured himself a cup.

"I've got to head over to Connie Rathburn's," Jake said. "I haven't had a chance to speak to her personally yet."

"Oh man," Jeff said. "Please send her my condolences. I heard Amanda Carter is Mary's family liaison. I'm glad Mary picked her. She's got a good head on her shoulders."

"She's been at the house with Connie since yesterday morning."

"Where's the boy?" Hammer asked.

"Still with the dad."

"That would kill her," Jeff said. Then his face fell. "You know what I mean. Mary was trying to make it so Kevin never had to be with that bum at all. Do you think there's anything we can do to help with that?"

"It'll be up to the court," Jake said. "And as much as I wish I could solve her family situation, I'm a little backed up trying to find out who killed her."

"Yeah. Right. Sorry. I know you've got to get back out there. Listen. I don't even know how to get into this. But with what you said. Stone's certain Mary had ... um ... intercourse? She wasn't raped?"

"I can't say one hundred percent until we get the results of the rape kit back. But Stone didn't see anything obvious that would point to forced penetration."

Jeff winced. It seemed an odd reaction. The man had been a cop for twenty years. He didn't exactly use delicate language in casual conversation.

"Listen ... Jake. I know this is going to sound worse than it is. I don't even know where to start. The thing is ... I think I know who Mary might have been sleeping with. Er ... who she was seeing."

Jake picked his notepad up off his desk. He sat in his chair and held his pen poised to write down what Jeff knew.

"Who, Sarge?"

Jeff Hammer's entire posture changed. He went stiff and his face turned a little purple.

"Me."

It took half a beat for his meaning to take shape in Jake's mind. He looked at Hammer.

"Jeff?"

"It was me. Okay? Mary and I were seeing each other. It wasn't ... it wasn't serious. Not yet. She understood my situation. I understood hers. But the night before last, we had … um … relations. If there's evidence …"

"Stop," Jake said, rising to his feet. "Stop talking, Jeff. Not another word. Come with me."

Jake's own heartbeat clamored in his ears. He grabbed Jeff's arm and led him into the interview room across the hall.

"Jake," Jeff said. "If we could just …"

"I meant what I said. Not another word. I need you to sit here until I get back. Don't talk to anyone. We clear?"

Hammer opened his mouth as if he were going to protest. Then he settled into a chair and dropped his chin against his chest.

"Yeah," he said. "Yeah, Jake. I understand."

Jake shut the door and went straight for Sheriff Landry's office.

He knocked once but didn't wait for her to answer. He barged right in. Meg was on the phone. She held up a finger.

"Of course," she said. "The minute I'm in a position to put together another press release, you're my first call."

She put the phone down. "What do you have?" she asked.

"Jeff Hammer's going to need a union rep," Jake said. "And a lawyer. Whatever you've got scheduled for the next couple of hours, cancel it."

Meg rose to her feet. A shudder went through her.

"Jake?"

"Come with me," he said.

Meg knew Jake well enough to understand the look on his face. She didn't ask him any more questions. She grabbed her blazer off the back of her chair and slid her arms into it. Then the two of them went back down to the interview room.

Hammer sat slumped in his chair. His eyes filled with worry as Jake walked in with Meg.

"Sheriff," he started.

"Hammer," Jake said. "Call a lawyer. Sheriff, can you arrange for a union rep to get down here now?"

"No," Hammer said. "I don't need any of that. I don't want any of that. I haven't done anything wrong."

Jake felt like a small explosion went off in his brain.

"You sure about that?" he boomed.

"Jake?" Meg stepped in. "What's going on?"

"Tell her what you told me," Jake said.

Hammer gritted his teeth. "Look, I'm not proud, but I'm not ashamed either. I'm a grown man. Mary was a grown woman. But I told Jake she and I were ... well ... we were intimate. It was new. But if the ME is saying Mary had intercourse the day before she died ... I was with her in that time frame."

Meg's jaw dropped. She looked from Hammer to Jake. Then anger settled into her face.

"Jeff," she said. "Jake's right. You need representation."

"And I'm telling you I decline it. I don't need it. You need me to sign something, I'll sign it."

"Jeff, I don't recommend you talking to Jake without at least your union rep present."

"And I'm telling you, I've got nothing to hide. Nothing."

Jake felt like throwing one of the chairs against the wall. He did a quick five count in his head.

"Jeff," he said. "I don't think you appreciate the seriousness of what's about to happen to you. You're the one who found Mary's body."

"Which I called in immediately ..."

"And for over twenty-four hours, you knew you had material information that was going to impact my murder investigation. You're a witness, Jeff. And a law enforcement officer. And you sat on it. You didn't come to me right off the bat. Are you starting to understand how this is a bigger deal than you're getting?"

"You've sat in on the briefings, Jeff," Meg said. She leaned forward, resting her palms on the table, putting herself right in Jeff Hammer's face.

"I know. I'm sorry. The last thing I'd want to do is get in the way of anything. I was trying to figure out the best way to tell you ..."

"I'm going to be asking the questions now," Jake said. He took a seat across from Hammer. Meg stepped away from the table. She covered her mouth with her hand and started to pace at the other end of the room.

Jake grabbed the empty pad of paper from the center of the table. There was a pen clipped to it.

"Start with telling me everywhere you were in the twenty-four hours before you called in Mary's murder. And I'll need your cell phone."

Jeff shot a helpless look at Meg, then pulled his smart phone out of his pocket and slid it across the table to Jake.

"Password's 193732," Jeff said. Jake wrote it down.

"Day before yesterday," Jake said.

"You can check my time card," Jeff answered. "I worked my regular shift. Clocked out at three. I knew there was a storm coming so I offered to take Mary home. I'd been giving her a ride all week. Jake, you know her car was on the fritz. She told me you took her home earlier in the week for the same reason."

"Then what?" Jake asked.

Hammer sighed. "She invited me in. She knew I couldn't stay long because Sarah was expecting me."

"Your wife, Sarah," Jake asked. He'd met the woman once or twice at various union functions.

"Yes. I texted Sarah and told her I had to work over a couple of hours."

"You lied to her."

"Yes! I lied to my wife. I'm not proud of it, okay? We've been having problems for a while. We'd actually gotten into a pretty bad argument earlier in the week. Sarah was threatening to divorce me. She's done that for years. This time, I was going to tell her to go through with it. It was just so close after Christmas. I was looking for the right time. Anyway, Mary knew I was having a rough week on that front. She was dealing with her ex as well. That's how this whole thing started initially. We got to talking. She confided things in me. I confided in her. Mary was a good listener. She said I was too. One thing led to another and we started being intimate."

"How long has this been going on?" Jake asked.

"Five, six months? Look, we both knew what it was. Mary wasn't looking for another husband. And she didn't take it lightly that I was married. I don't want you to think badly of her. If there's anyone to blame, it's me. She was vulnerable. I knew that."

"Let's get back to the night before last. You said you brought Mary home after day shift. You stayed at her place?"

"Just for a couple of hours. I shoveled her driveway. She offered to make me dinner but I told her I had to get home. We just ... we had sex after work. Talked a little. She was feeling lonely because her kid was with his dad. She was worried about that. We just commiserated. It was simple, you know? Comforting. I stayed for a couple of hours. I was gone by seven. I told Mary I'd pick her up for work in the morning. And that's the last I saw or talked to her. Not until I came over to pick her up. The rest of it you already know. I gave my statement."

"You gave a false statement," Meg said. "Jeff, I think I need to insist you let me call a rep."

Jeff waved his hand. "Do what you have to do. I understand."

"How often did you and Mary get together?" Jake asked.

"It wasn't every day or anything. It started after that K9 fundraiser last summer. She was in the middle of her court case over custody of her kid. She'd just won a temporary order. She was having a rough time because Shane wasn't cooperating. He showed up at the Union Hall yelling at her. A bunch of us stepped in and threw him out. Afterwards, Mary was pretty upset. She was embarrassed. She'd been drinking a little so I offered to drive her home. We got to talking. One thing led to another. That was it. That's how it started. We thought it was just gonna be that one time. I don't know. She was just ... she was easy to talk to. She was calm. Sensible. Not like ... well ... not like Sarah. And for her part, I think Mary appreciated that I wasn't anything like Shane. We were going to end it though. Mary wasn't asking me to leave my wife for her or anything. We were more than casual, but it wasn't serious, you know?"

"You left Mary's house at seven? Did you go straight home?"

Hammer looked like he was about to throw up. “No. I drove around for a while. Sarah kept calling and she was just wound up. I knew she was gonna scream her head off when I came home so I just avoided it. I went to the hall and had a beer. Maybe two. It was probably ten or a little after when I finally got home.”

“And you told your wife you were working over?”

“Yeah.”

Jake rubbed his eyes. “Jeff, you’re telling me your alibi is that you drove around and then had a beer?”

“At the Union Hall, Jake. There were maybe a dozen people there. Beverly was there. So was Morse. You can ask them. I paid my tab with a credit card. I just gave you the passcode to my cell phone.”

Jake resisted the urge to spew the sarcastic comment he had in mind. Hammer’s whole demeanor changed. He buried his face in his hands and started to cry.

“You know I didn’t kill Mary. This has been tearing me apart for the last two days. She’s someone who mattered to me. I’ll do anything I can to help you find out who did this. I just … I don’t know what to do. Jake? Tell me what I’m supposed to do?”

Jake put his pen down. If Jeff Hammer was looking to him for comfort, he was the last person who could give it.

“Jeff, there are a series of things that are going to have to happen now. But I think the first thing you need to do is talk to your wife. Because before the end of the day, I’m going to have to.”

Jeff Hammer looked up. His eyes were swollen and bloodshot.

“And the second thing you’re going to do is submit a DNA sample.”

Hammer looked at Landry. Then his shoulders sagged with resignation.

“Yeah,” he said. “Yeah.”

“Wait here,” Jake said. “Ramirez will send someone over from BCI within the hour.”

Jake got up. He couldn’t stand looking at Jeff Hammer for another second.

Ten

Jake sat in the driveway of Connie Rathburn's house in the Timber Valley subdivision. It was one of the first platted neighborhoods built in Worthington County in the late sixties. Once upon a time, these were coveted luxury homes boasting all the modern conveniences. Now, they were still well maintained, but dated. Connie lived in a bi-level with red brick on the first story and green siding on the second. A flash of memory slammed into him.

She had brought him here, his mother. He'd been maybe five or six years old. At the time, Connie had no children of her own. She offered to babysit Jake while his mother went ... somewhere. Until this moment, Jake had forgotten it all. Part of him wished that were still true.

"We can't sit out here forever."

Birdie sat beside him in the passenger seat. She'd made the initial notification to Mary's mother at Jake's request. But now, he knew what was expected of him. Something he'd done dozens of times. Console. Reassure. But make no promises.

"Yeah," Jake said. "I know." And yet, he didn't want to move.

Birdie took matters into her own hand. She climbed out of the car and started up the driveway.

It had been shoveled for Connie. Jake knew the deputies were taking shifts for things like that.

The front door opened. Deputy Amanda Carter walked out and met Birdie halfway. Jake stepped out of the car and walked up to join them.

"She's been asking for you," Amanda said. "She hasn't slept yet. I'm trying to convince her to call her doctor and get some Xanax or something. She's pretty wired. Maybe you two could try. She might listen better to you."

"How are you holding up, Amanda?" Birdie asked. She stepped closer and pulled Amanda Carter into an embrace.

"I'll feel a lot better once we catch the bastard who did this. If there's anything you need from me. Anything."

"Right now, you sticking close to Mrs. Rathburn is what I need," Jake said. "And what she needs, too."

Amanda nodded. To her credit, she didn't break down. Jake didn't know her well. But she was a good choice for Mary's family liaison. Pleasant, personable, and not prone to gossip, from what Jake knew.

"She's in the kitchen," Amanda said. "I was able to get her to eat something for breakfast. Small victories, you know?"

Jake put a comforting hand on Amanda's shoulder. "It's a major one. Just keep doing what you're doing. And don't be afraid to reach out for help if you need it for yourself. It's going to be a rough couple of days for everyone in the department."

Amanda led Jake and Birdie into the house. It was crowded with people. Friends. Family members. Someone was busy making sandwiches. Connie Rathburn sat alone at her kitchen table, staring out the back window. Jake saw a snowman on the patio. He was listing to the right a bit, his knit cap sliding halfway down his head.

"A couple of deputies finished that for me yesterday evening," Connie said, her tone flat. "Shane was supposed to bring Kevin by this morning. They thought he'd like it. I started it the night before. He was supposed to be here after preschool."

"I'm so sorry for your loss, Mrs. Rathburn," Jake said. Connie whipped her head around. There had been so many people coming in and out. He imagined she hadn't truly appreciated who anyone was. Now, she locked eyes with Jake. She rose from her chair and went to him. Her eyes glistened. She put her hands up and cradled Jake's face.

"Look at you," she whispered. "You look so much like your father. Oh, he was so handsome. You have no idea how many of the girls had crushes on him. He only ever had eyes for Sonya though. He took one look at her and that was it. Did you know I was the one who encouraged her to go out with him?"

"No," Jake said. He took Connie's hands in his. "I didn't know that."

"Jacob was shy. You wouldn't think that. He was so gifted in sports. So smart in school. Your mother though, she was anything but shy. Oh ... she had a way about her. Just drew all the attention in the room. Jacob knew we were friends. He asked me if I thought Sonya would say yes if he asked her on a date. She played it so coy. Pretending like she wasn't totally in love with him like every other girl in the ninth grade. She was though."

"I'm sure she was something to see." Jake smiled.

Tears spilled from Connie's eyes. She wiped them away. She took a step forward and drew Jake to her. She collapsed against him. He held her for a moment. Every other conversation in the room ground to a halt. As if everyone held their breath waiting for Connie Rathburn to find the strength to keep going. For a moment, Jake wondered if he could. He felt as if Mary were here, too. Watching him. Judging him. Waiting for him to do what she was depending on him to do.

The weight of it came to him in a rush. Mary was depending on him. They were all depending on him. He felt his back go straight. The knot in his shoulder became a boulder.

Finally, she sat back down but kept clutching Jake's hand.

"Was it Shane?" she whispered. "Did he do this to my baby?"

"I don't know for sure yet," Jake said, giving her the most honest answer he could. "He has an alibi that's going to be pretty easy to check. My gut feeling is no. I don't think he did this."

Connie blew out a breath. "Kevin's safe with him? Are you sure? He's taking care of him?"

"Yes."

"He won't let me see him," Connie said. "He was supposed to bring him this morning. He texted me a little bit ago and said Kevin just wants to stay with him. I don't believe that. Kevin is used to being with me during the week when he's not in school. It's not his normal routine to be with his dad. Don't you think that little boy should stay with his normal routine? I don't even know what Shane's told him about Mary. I don't know if he's told him anything at all. Can you do something about it? Can you make Shane bring Kevin to see me?"

"I'll do whatever I can," Jake said. "But we'll make sure Kevin is being cared for. You don't have to worry about that."

"I do worry. The court said Shane shouldn't have custody of him. They said Kevin was better off with his mom."

"Mrs. Rathburn, I know Deputy Wayne asked you some questions yesterday. And you know I'm the one investigating what happened to Mary."

"She would want that," Connie said. "You know that. I need you to know that. She wouldn't want anyone but you looking after her now. Jake, she was so happy to be working with you. She knew she would learn so much. All she ever wanted was to be a detective. And she knew how good you are."

"Thank you." Again, he felt Mary there, watching him.

"I'll tell you everything I can remember," she said. "I've been thinking and thinking who might have wanted to hurt Mary like that. It was only Shane who ever gave her trouble. You have to make sure. He lies, Jake. I've watched him lie to the judge. I've heard him say the most awful things to Mary. Every horrible name you can imagine."

"I'm sorry you had to deal with that. That she had to deal with that. Do you remember the last time you spoke to Mary?"

"The evening before last. I always made her call or text me when she got home from work. It's not easy being the parent of a cop, Jake. Mothers worry. I talked to her on the phone. She called me when she got home. Four o'clock or so. We didn't talk for long. Mary was kind of preoccupied. She said she wanted to go to bed early, that she hadn't slept very well the night before. She never slept well when Kevin was with Shane. He was down to two overnights a month with him. She called me again that evening. Seven o'clock. It's the last time I talked to her. I wish I'd known it would be the last time, you know?"

"But it was a normal conversation other than her anxiety about Kevin being with Shane?"

"Yes. I don't even remember all that we talked about. Can you believe that? I didn't know it was going to be my last conversation with her. If I'd have known ..."

"Don't do that to yourself," Jake said. "You were a good mother to her. She knew that. She knew you always had her back. She told me that."

"I just wanted her to be happy. I wanted her to be safe and happy. Oh Jake. Was it painful? Was it quick or was it painful? Nobody will tell me."

Connie still held Jake's hand in a vise grip. He kept her eyes. He could lie to her. But someday, there might be a murder trial. If Connie Rathburn sat in the courtroom, she would hear about her daughter's last agonizing moments in exacting detail.

"I don't believe she was in pain for long, Connie," Jake said. It was the kindest truth he could give her. Jake took the small notepad out of his pocket. He'd written down the three names Shane Edwards had given him. The adults he claimed were at his cousin's kid's birthday party the night Mary died.

Ian Burke. Brad and Rashelle Edwards. Brad and Rashelle had confirmed Shane's story, at least initially. He was still trying to track down Burke.

He handed the note to Connie. "Do you know any of these people?"

Connie picked up her readers from the kitchen table and slipped them on. She took her time reading the note.

"I don't know this one," she said, pointing to Ian's name. "Brad Edwards is Shane's cousin. They have a little girl roughly Kevin's age. They play together. I've met the mother, Rashelle. She's always been very nice. Almost apologetic for all the drama Mary had with Shane. Mary liked her. I can't say whether she liked the cousin, Brad. But this is where Kevin was going that night. The birthday party."

"That's right," Jake said. "I talked to them yesterday. So far, Shane's alibi seems tight."

"You don't think any of them had anything to do with this?"

"No. That's not why I'm asking. I'm just trying to confirm everything he told me."

Connie handed back the note. "I don't know them well, as I said. But that's where Shane told Mary Kevin was going to be."

"Okay. That helps. Thank you." At least Shane Edwards's story was so far consistent with everyone he told about it. Connie frowned. She looked over her shoulder. Her relatives had moved off into another part of the house, giving her and Jake some modicum of privacy. Connie leaned forward and whispered.

"I think she had a boyfriend. Or somebody she was seeing, Jake. I don't know who. And she denied it when I asked her about it. She didn't like to talk to me about dates she went on. I tried not to nag. But Mary never made the best choices when it came to men. She picked ones that didn't treat her right."

It killed Jake that he couldn't tell her what he knew. Yes. Mary was seeing someone. She was seeing a married man. And if Jeff Hammer's story was true, he was there with Mary when she talked to Connie that last afternoon.

"I'm going to find all of that out," Jake said, stopping just short of a promise. It was tempting to do that. But he respected Connie Rathburn and her daughter too much.

"I know you will. I know you're going to make sure whoever did this doesn't get away with it. I hate that you have to. Oh, honey. This can't be easy for you either."

"Of all the things you've got to worry about, I'm not one of them. Okay?"

"I wish she could have seen you grow up. She'd be scared for you. Just like I was for Mary. But she'd be proud. It's something we could have shared. Both of our children becoming cops."

"Deputy Carter's going to stay with you," Jake said. "Are you okay with that?"

Connie nodded. "She's been so sweet. Everyone has been. Two deputies came and shoveled my driveway and sidewalk. They took my garbage out to the curb."

"You're family, Mrs. Rathburn."

"You'll tell me what you can when you can. Can you promise me that?"

"Yes," Jake said, grateful to be able to make a promise he knew he could keep. "Absolutely."

"Good then. Good. Is there something I should be doing? Arrangements I should be making? They don't ... nobody tells you how to do this. Bury your child."

"Mary filled out paperwork," Jake said. "She made her wishes known as far as arrangements. The department is handling everything. There's nothing you need to do."

"All right."

"I'd like it if you got some sleep though. Deputy Carter says you haven't for two days."

Connie started to withdraw then. Her gaze drifted back to the window and the snowman outside. She stared at it for a few moments then turned to look at Jake.

"She's counting on you," she said. "I can feel it. Can you?"

Jake stopped himself from asking her who she meant. Mary? His mother? Then she turned back to the window. Jake hoped she could make it through the next few days. They would be the hardest of all.

Eleven

Sarah Hammer wore a black tracksuit with pink trim. She'd done her hair, curling it around her face with enough spray it didn't move even as she trembled in the chair opposite Jake. She folded and unfolded a handkerchief then pulled at a loose string on the corner of it.

"Mrs. Hammer," Jake started. "Do you understand why I need to talk to you today?"

Her tears fell, but she didn't wipe them away with the handkerchief. She let them fall. One slid down her cheek and dangled from her jaw for a moment before hitting her collar.

"Jeff's in some trouble," she said.

"I know you had a difficult conversation with him last night. It's understandable that you're upset. It's not my intention to add to that, but ..."

"You can save the speech. I've been married to a cop longer than you've been one."

"Yes, you have."

"Just ask me what you need to ask me. I'd like to be finished with this so I can go home. I've got some decisions I need to make."

"Sure," Jake said.

"It's hot in here," she said, unzipping the jacket of her tracksuit. She wore a matching pink tank top underneath it. Jake knew the thermostat in the room was set at sixty-eight. She was in her fifties, he knew. It was possible she was experiencing a hot flash. She took off her jacket and put it on the table.

"Mrs. Hammer?" Jake said. "Is that what you prefer I call you?"

"I'm Sarah," she said. "We've met before, Jake. You don't have to be so formal."

"Okay, Sarah. Like you said, you've been married to a cop for a long time. I respect that. If ..."

"You think Jeff killed Mary Rathburn?" she blurted.

"I didn't say that. But it's my job to gather the facts here. Part of that means I've got to reconstruct what was happening in Mary's life. The last twenty-four hours of her life. Where she went. Who she was with."

"Jeff! She was with Jeff. He told me that. I know he told you that."

"Yes. And again, I'm sorry things have to be this way."

"So am I. But do you really think Jeff would do something like this? He's a cop, Jake. If he was going to kill someone, don't you think he'd do a better job of it?"

"What do you mean?"

"I mean, he wouldn't make a mess of it. He wouldn't leave her like that ... in her own home."

"Jeff's told you about the crime scene?" Jake kept his face neutral.

"Don't do that," Sarah said. "Don't you dare try to do that. Pit us against each other. Listen to me, I'm mad at Jeff. Livid. He's hurt me in ways you can't even imagine. But I won't sit here and let you twist my words."

"I'm really not trying to do that."

"Telling me you're just doing your job. The hell with you. The hell with Jeff. And I know what happened to that woman is awful. And she has a son. I couldn't give Jeff kids. And she's got this sweet little boy who needs a good dad. The whole thing ... I know she's the victim. I *know* it. And yet ..."

"You're angry with Mary Rathburn too. Sarah, I don't think anyone would judge you for that under the circumstances. People are more than just one thing. Mary's death ... the way that she died ... it doesn't absolve her of mistakes she made while she was alive. It doesn't make her a saint."

"You're damn right. And I do feel guilty. I feel horrible."

"But she destroyed your family."

Sarah sobbed. "Yes."

"Okay. Sarah, let's just get through this."

He sat back. Sarah's hand flew to her neck. She wore a gold necklace with a pink pendant. She turned the pendant between her fingers. It was then that Jake noticed some scratches on the left side of her neck.

"Can we focus on Sunday night?" Jake asked. "Why don't you tell me about your day?"

"It was a normal day," she said. "Jeff was working. He promised he was going to help me take the last of the Christmas decorations down when he got home. He was supposed to be home by three thirty but he said he was going to have to work over. I expected that. I knew the flu was going around in the building. You guys were short-staffed. So I took care of things by myself."

She bit out the last word. Jake had a pad of paper in front of him. He picked it up and started to write on it. It was nothing of consequence. Doodles. But Sarah didn't know that. She was rolling now and Jake didn't want to interrupt her flow.

"He called me," she said. "I don't know. Maybe it was six o'clock. You can check my phone. Jeff told me I should hand it over to you. Give you permission to search it. Whatever. I don't care. I don't have anything to hide."

"That would be helpful."

"To rule me out. That's what Jeff said."

"Right."

"Well, you already know he didn't come home by six. He was with her, I guess. He's telling you the truth. Just because he lied to me doesn't mean he lied to you. He'd never do that. Oh no. Not to another cop. There's a code."

She said the word code with vitriol. It was hard not to sympathize with her about that. Right now, Sarah Hammer had to feel like the entire sheriff's department was complicit in her husband's affair.

"What did you do while Jeff was gone?"

"Watched his dinner get cold. Wouldn't be the first time. I ate without him. I cleaned up without him. I went to bed at ten. Jeff came home a little after that."

"Were you still awake?"

"I don't ... I think I had just fallen asleep. But I heard him come in."

"A little after ten. Did you talk to Jeff when he came in?"

"I don't think I said anything. I was angry. No. Not really angry. Just disappointed. But I'm used to that."

"How so?"

"No. No way. That's none of your business what goes on between a husband and a wife."

"Sarah, it became my business when the husband of that wife was the last one to be intimate with a murder victim within a few hours before she was killed. Do you see my point?"

"You asked me what time Jeff came home. I'm telling you he came home a little after ten o'clock at night. No. I didn't talk to him. I believe he apologized for missing dinner, kissed me on the head, and went to sleep on the couch."

"Why the couch?"

"You'll have to ask him."

"All right. Did you go back to sleep after that?"

"Yes. I woke up at my normal time, six thirty. I started making breakfast. The snow had come down pretty heavily overnight, as you know. Jeff woke up early, too. Told me he was going in early and that he was going to pick Mary up because her car was on the fritz again. We had a conversation about that. He knew I was irritated by it."

"Sarah, I have to ask you. Did you suspect Jeff was having an affair?"

She pursed her lips. "Things were off. They've been off for a while. Let me give you some advice, Jake. Don't get married. Not while you're a cop. You all say you're going to put your family first but you never do. You all say you'll try to keep everything at work, but you never do. I didn't like the attention he was giving Mary

Rathburn. He seemed to be at her beck and call and I told him so. I knew what it would look like."

"Which was?"

"People were going to think he was screwing her. That's what I was worried about. I told him that and he blew me off. Told me I was being paranoid. Well, it turns out I wasn't."

"No," Jake said. "You weren't."

"Then he left for work. After that, you already know what happened. So, are we done now?"

"I just have a few more questions." Jake put his pad down, flipping it so she couldn't see what was on it. "Sarah, there are a few things I have to ask you that might make you uncomfortable."

"You mean more uncomfortable?"

"Yes."

"I noticed you have some scratches on your neck. How did you get those?"

Sarah's hand flew to her neck. She covered the scratches with her palm.

"You think Jeff did this? Oh hell, Jake. Jeff's not a violent man. This is nothing."

"So, how did you get them?"

"We have a cat. Well ... we don't *have* a cat. There *is* a cat. He started hanging around in our yard a few months ago when he was just a kitten. I put some milk and food out for him. Jeff's allergic, so I couldn't bring him in the house. But I built a shelter for him now that the weather has turned. Anyway, the other day when I tried to pick him up because I thought I saw a burr in his paw, he got a little feisty and scratched me."

"Do you mind if I take a picture?"

"It was a cat! It has nothing to do with this."

"Sarah, I believe you. But you need to understand I've got a job to do. The more you cooperate, the easier this is gonna be and the less likely I'm going to need to come talk to you again."

"Easier. Sure. Easier. Whatever. Take a picture. Do you want to strip search me too?"

"That's not necessary. Just sit tight for a second."

Jake walked out of the interview room and grabbed a digital camera he kept for things like this on his desk. Landry was further down the hall, pacing, waiting for Jake to finish. He shot her a thumbs up and went back to Sarah Hammer.

She turned to him, the anger on her face plain. As Jake raised the camera, she thrust her neck out and pulled her hair back. Jake snapped a few pictures from different angles.

"Thank you."

"I'm telling you. It was the cat, Jake. Jeff didn't do this."

"I'm sure that's true."

"Now can I go?"

"There's one more thing I have to ask you. Would you be willing to submit to a DNA test?"

"A what?"

"A DNA test. It'll be a simple cheek swab."

"I don't see why that's necessary, but I told you I have nothing to hide. Jeff told me I should do whatever you asked. So fine. Yes. Take a cheek swab."

Jake handed her a clipboard with the consent forms. Sarah jerked them out of his hand, signed the last page almost violently, then shoved the forms back at him.

Jake already had the kit in the room. He grabbed a pair of latex gloves. He opened the kit and pulled out the long cotton swab. Sarah glared at him the whole time. She opened her mouth and stuck her tongue out.

As gently as he could, Jake took the sample and closed up the kit.

"And your phone," he said. "You're willing to hand it over?"

"Yes," she hissed. "I told you. Whatever I have to do so I never have to see anyone in this building again."

"I really do understand how you feel."

"I'm certain you don't. This is humiliating. Never mind my husband's behavior. I'm being treated like a villain in this. Mary Rathburn wasn't the only victim."

"I know that. You didn't deserve any of this either. I'm not your enemy."

"He says as he seals up my DNA and takes pictures of me like I'm some criminal. You're not my friend, Jake. I have no friends in this building. You think I don't know you're all complicit?"

"In what way?"

"You cover for each other. Cover for Jeff. Now I'm just his poor shrew of a wife and Mary Rathburn is a martyred saint. She's going to have her name enshrined on a plaque out in that courtyard."

Jake didn't want to hate Sarah Hammer. She was right about a lot of the things she said. Mary knew Jeff Hammer was married when she decided to get involved with him. He was clear-eyed enough to know she wasn't a saint.

"I think we're done here," Jake said. "Thank you for coming in."

She didn't wait for him to show her out. Sarah flew out of the interview room. She was in tears again by the time she made it to the elevator.

Landry was waiting for him as he walked back to his office.

"How big of a mess was that?" she asked.

"I don't know," Jake said. He was holding the DNA kit with Sarah's sample. "I need Ramirez to run her phone and this as fast as he can."

"You don't think ..."

"I think Sarah Hammer's rage is a tangible thing. And I think it's good enough to give her a motive."

Meg Landry closed her eyes and let out an unsteady breath. "At least the press doesn't have a hold of this yet. But somebody's going to notice when I reassign his stupid ass. I can't have Hammer in command right now."

"You need to do what you need to do, boss."

"Right. But yes. Tell Ramirez to hurry."

Twelve

Four days later, in the bitterest cold Jake could remember, Mary Rathburn was laid to rest. The tiny Methodist church on County Road 17 wasn't big enough to hold the nearly eight hundred mourners who showed up to pay their respects. Those who couldn't fit inside the one-hundred- and fifty-year-old church, built just one year after the founding of Stanley, Ohio, stood outside, huddled together against the elements. Most of them didn't even know Mary. They were representatives from nearly every law enforcement agency in the State of Ohio. Dozens upon dozens of patrol cars lined the streets. They would follow Mary's hearse in a solemn parade through town, snaking their way through the winding streets until they reached the cemetery where Mary would be laid to rest in a plot next to her father. He himself had been an Ohio State Trooper. He'd never gotten to see Mary earn her badge. He died from a massive stroke when she was only seventeen years old.

"He'd be so proud," Connie Rathburn kept saying. For most of the service, she'd wanted Jake nearby. She had family around her, of course. Two brothers. Her sisters-in-law. They closed ranks around her when members of the local media tried to snap pictures. Connie bore it all well. The only time he saw her break down was when her grandson, Kevin Rathburn, finally saw her.

Mary's small son broke through the crowd and ran toward his grandmother, wrapping his arms around her legs before she had a chance to pick him up.

Shane Edwards hung back. He stood with his girlfriend, Marissa Nagy. She wore a tight-fitting purple dress with sequins on the shoulders. *A strange choice for a funeral*, Jake thought.

It was a simple service. Reverend Jonas Flynn had led the Methodist church for as long as Jake could remember. A pleasant man. No fire and brimstone. Just kind words and comfort to Mary's mother and son.

Jake stood rigid, one row behind Connie and Mary's family. Young Kevin stood on the pew so he could see what was going on. From time to time, he squirmed and twisted, turning to look at Jake.

Jake found a smile for the boy. He played with a shiny silver toy badge someone had given to him. His little dress shirt became hopelessly untucked from his tan trousers. Some sort of diaper or pull-up poked out from the waistband. It occurred to Jake the boy might be too old for that. Unless the events of the last week had made the poor kid regress. He would reach out to Connie to make sure she knew what resources were available to her if Kevin needed to talk to someone. Or if she did.

Meg stood on one side of Jake, Birdie on the other. Jake stared at Mary's flag-draped coffin. Her academy picture had been blown up, framed, and propped on an easel beside it. She looked so young. Fresh-faced. Idealistic.

Jake looked out at a sea of cop uniforms in the church pews. One woman sitting among the Ohio State Troopers caught his eye. She wore plain clothes, but the troopers around her clearly knew her. They spoke to her in whispers. She smiled. Whispered back. She was pretty. Thick brown hair and a kind face. She seemed to stare straight through Jake as if she knew him or knew what he was thinking. He turned away.

When the Pipe and Drum Corps began the first haunting strains of Amazing Grace, Jake felt as if a ten-ton weight slammed into his heart. He hated the sound of bagpipes.

Then it was his turn. Connie had mercifully not asked him to speak. But she'd asked him to serve as one of the pallbearers. As the pipers' notes cut through him, Jake took his place at one end of the casket and carried Mary out of the church. He concentrated on each step. He would not falter.

The graveside service was painful. Both Connie and Kevin fell apart as the honor guard handed Connie a folded American flag.

Jake wanted nothing more than to escape to his cabin in the woods. Not see anyone. Not speak to anyone. Just process his grief for his fallen sister-in-arms alone. But there was a reception to follow at the Union Hall. Meg expected him there. So did Connie.

Birdie rode in the car with him. They were silent for a while. Then Jake turned to her. "Did you recognize any of them? The men standing near Shane Edwards? His friends?"

"No," she said. "None of them was the guy I saw harassing Mary at the bar."

"You're sure."

"Positive. We'll see if anyone new shows up at the hall."

"Good. Keep a lookout."

"She's handling things pretty well considering. Connie, I mean."

"I don't think the gravity of this has truly hit her yet. And she's trying to keep it together for the boy."

"I wish we could do something for her. Connie's right. Mary would be horrified to know Kevin's with Shane now. She fought so hard to limit the time he had with him."

"I know. But he's the kid's father. He deserves a chance to step up. And we know he didn't kill Mary. He might have hated her, but he didn't kill her. His alibi checked out."

"So he's not a murderer, just a lousy dad. But I know you're right. People can surprise you. Maybe he'll take this opportunity to prove everybody wrong about him. I'm just worried about what it's gonna do to Kevin. Shane wasn't involved in raising him up until this point. It was Mary and Connie. Right now, it feels like he didn't just lose his mom. He's losing his grandmother, too."

"Have Amanda put Connie in touch with our union legal services. Maybe she can file a motion and request visitation."

Jake parked the car. He and Birdie got out and started toward the Union Hall entrance. Three men stood to the side of it. They were waiting for Jake.

"Go on ahead," he told Birdie. She followed Jake's gaze. When she saw who he'd spotted, she smiled.

"Who invited those wise asses?" she joked.

"Wise Men!" Virgil Adamski shouted, feigning indignation. Virgil Adamski, Chuck Thompson, and Bill Nutter were three retired cops who met every Tuesday at Papa's Diner in town. They referred to themselves as the "Wise Men," though nobody else would.

Jake hadn't thought to reach out to them. Virgil had been out of town for months. He himself hadn't made it into the diner in a while. But now, as the three older men waited for him, he realized there was nobody else he'd rather see.

Virgil came to him first. He hugged Jake.

"This was a rough one, son. How are you holding up?"

"I'm all right. I don't have time not to be. Mary needs me at my best, you know?"

Chuck stepped forward and shook Jake's hand. Nutter followed suit.

"Is there anything you can talk about?" Nutter asked.

"Still early days," Jake answered. He wondered how much they knew. Rumors were already starting to swirl around Jeff Hammer. His secret would never leave Jake's lips, but enough people knew he'd interviewed him at length the other day. And Landry had no choice but to pull him from the daily briefings. One look at Virgil, and Jake realized these men probably already knew.

One by one, people seemed to find Jake as they walked passed him into the hall. Mary's uncles. Friends. Every one of them said some version of the same thing.

"We know you'll do right by Mary."

"We're all counting on you."

"Mary can rest easy knowing you're the one going after whoever did this."

Jake knew they all meant well. But each comment, each pained look, felt like a weight being added to his shoulders. And there was Mary herself. Her smiling face from her academy picture seemed to follow him wherever he went. It got hard to breathe. Another group of cops walked past them into the hall. As the door swung open, Jake spotted Ed Zender, glad-handing a bunch of other cops near the front entrance. It made his skin crawl. That's when he decided he was going to drink today.

"He's something else," Virgil said, looking Zender's way as Jake did. "He's campaigning."

"We miss you down at Papa's," Chuck said, cutting through the din in Jake's mind. "Tessa's been asking about you."

"I know. When things calm down a little, tell her I'll make a point of stopping in."

"That won't satisfy her," Nutter said. "I'm surprised she and Spiros aren't here."

"They don't like funerals," Jake said. "Especially not ones where young women die leaving a parent behind."

Spiros and Tessa Papatonis had lost their own daughter to violence years ago. A day like today would be too much for them to handle. Though Jake predicted they'd pay a visit to Connie Rathburn soon enough. Probably with a whole truckload of Greek meals to feed a hundred people.

Jake heard laughter behind him. He turned. Shane Edwards walked out with another man. Neither of them turned to notice Jake or the others. Jake recognized Shane's companion as one Brad Edwards, Shane's alibi witness. He'd vouched for Shane's whereabouts the night Mary died. Jake watched as Shane lit up a cigarette. His cousin pulled a flask out of his pocket and took a swig. Jake wished he'd thought to do the same right about now.

Jake and the Wise Men watched for a moment. When Shane realized Jake was nearby, he nudged his cousin. The two of them disappeared back into the building.

"He's got some nerve showing up here," Chuck said. "This is for cops and Mary's family. He's neither."

"Let him be for now," Jake said. "Like it or not, I need him to think I'm on his side. He's more likely to cooperate with my investigation that way."

"Connie's saying he won't let Mary's boy come over," Nutter said.

"Do you know her well?" Jake asked.

Nutter shrugged. "I was tight with her old man, Bud Rathburn. We went to the trooper academy together. I was at their wedding. Good guy, Bud. It's a blessing he's not here today. This would have killed him if he weren't already dead. Mary was his angel."

An odd thing to think, but Jake found himself grateful Bud Rathburn wasn't here either. It was one less layer of pressure on him. But Mary was a cop's daughter. That was heavy enough.

"Come on," Jake said. "The three of you are gonna freeze to death out here. I don't need one of you keeling over on me."

He led the three men into the hall. It was packed with cops. Little Kevin Edwards had come completely untucked and shoeless. He ran around the hall giving high fives to various police officers while Connie looked on smiling.

Two uniformed deputies from Muskingum County walked up to him. Jake braced himself for another well-meaning comment about how justice depended on him.

"Hey, Jake," the deputy on the left said. She was tall, at least six feet. She exchanged a look with her colleague. "My name is Bonnie Smalls. I hate bringing this up here of all places, but do you have a second?"

"Sure," Jake said. The Wise Men said hasty goodbyes and headed for the bar.

"We're working a case in Zanesville we wanted to run by you. A home invasion. Our victim was attacked in her shower last night.

Stabbed in the back. I understand you may have a similar MO with your victim?"

"I'm still listening," Jake said quietly. He looked around, hoping nobody else was listening.

"Well, it just struck me. There are a couple of other similarities."

"Such as?"

"My victim was a security officer. Worked at one of the hospitals. I mean, it was private security, but she went to work in a uniform, you know? And your victim is a cop. I was just thinking ..."

"Christ," Jake said. "Yeah. Do you have any suspects?"

"Not yet. My victim hasn't regained consciousness yet. I'm waiting to take her statement."

"She's alive?"

"Miraculously, yes. For now, at least. Listen, I'll send over my crime scene report. Perhaps you can do the same."

"Smalls, I'd appreciate that."

"I hope they're not related. But I wanted to make sure. And again. I'm sorry. I know this isn't really the place, but ..."

"No," Jake said. "But I appreciate it anyway. Thank you. I'll take a look at what you have and get you what I can as soon as I can. I'd like to talk to your victim when she wakes up."

"Sure thing," Smalls said. Then her colleague tugged on her arm, pulling her away.

An hour went by. Then another. Most of Mary's family left, but the cops stayed. It was like this at every law enforcement funeral he'd ever attended. And there had been too damn many. As Jake made his way from group to group, the booze began to flow. A shot of bourbon here. A whiskey there. After his fourth shot, Jake realized how much he'd needed it. It helped drown out the well-meaning comments.

Mary's counting on you, Jake.

War stories were shared in every corner. Jake just listened, sharing none of his own. It wasn't his way.

He meant to leave long before he did. But after his fifth or sixth drink, he found himself not wanting to be alone. He didn't want to listen to his own thoughts. He wanted to drown out the awful sound of those bagpipes.

"What about you?" a female voice seemed to come out of nowhere.

Jake sat at a table against the wall. The brunette who he'd seen with the contingent of state troopers walked up. Dark hair, red lipstick. "What about me?" Jake asked.

She took a seat beside him. His head spun a bit. Her smile radiated warmth. She smelled good. With his buzzed brain, he heard himself say she smelled too good to be a cop? Had he really said that out loud? If so, she didn't react.

"No war stories to share?" she asked. "It's been riveting." She rolled her eyes.

She put a draft beer in front of him, then sipped her own. Jake was about to tell her he'd had enough for one night, but the foam looked just right.

"Not my style," he said.

She had a husky quality to her voice.

"Oh, I think I've heard some about you. You were FBI, right? Chicago Field Office? We all heard you had something to do with taking down the Blood Money Kings. I would have thought they'd have pinned a medal on you for that. Instead, here you are."

"Here I am," he said, raising his cup to her. She raised hers and touched it to Jake's. "I'm surprised that story made it all the way to a trooper like you."

She smiled at him, cocked her head to the side, and took another sip of her beer.

"I hate these things," she said. "Nobody ever knows what to say. It was a lovely service. What does that mean? There's nothing lovely about a thirty-year-old single mother getting lowered into the ground."

Jake took a swig of his beer. In some back corner of his brain, he knew he shouldn't have. He was good and drunk now.

An older man came up to him and slapped him on the back, making Jake nearly spit out a mouthful of suds.

"Glad it's you," the old-timer said. Jake recognized him as the former chief of police in Columbus. "You get this bastard, okay? We can't have this."

Jake raised a glass to him. Mercifully, he staggered back into the crowd.

"I know why I'm here," he said, turning to the woman beside him. "So why are you?"

"Bethany," she said. "Bethany Roman." She extended her hand to him. Jake took it. She had a firm grip. Confident.

"I'm from Dayton," she said. "My boss asked me to come to this. So here I am."

"You drew the short straw?"

"Something like that. I don't mind paying my dues."

Jake took another sip. His head swam in the best of ways. Bethany Roman really did smell good.

"Your dues? Is this your first one of these?" he asked.

Bethany looked around. "Cop funeral? No. I wish it were. It's part of the deal though, right? The code?"

The code. Jake had lost count of how many funerals he'd been to like this.

"Well, welcome to Stanley." He finished his beer. His head spun. Time to stop. Time to figure out a way to get home or sleep in his office. He scanned the room. The Wise Men were in the corner, far worse off than Jake was. Virgil had broken into song. He knew he should probably find Birdie. It would be like her to stay sober while he drank himself sloppy.

Jake got to his feet. The room started to spin. He grabbed the table for support.

"Whoa there, cowboy," Bethany said. She got her arm around him. She felt as good as she smelled. In the back of Jake's mind, he knew that spelled trouble.

"Where do you think you're going?" she asked.

"I've had enough."

"Enough booze?"

"Enough of this day," he answered. "And yes. Enough booze. Enough of all of it."

"Well, you're in no condition to drive and I've just had the one beer. Why don't you let me drive you home?"

Jake looked around the room again. Landry and her husband Phil were in one corner. The Wise Men were in no condition to render assistance and Birdie was AWOL.

"Come on," Bethany said. "I don't bite, and my car's parked right outside the kitchen entrance. Seems to me you have two choices. You can make a clean getaway with me, or you'll be forced into an Irish goodbye situation."

She wasn't wrong. There were at least forty people between Jake and the front doors. Each of them would notice Jake trying to leave and want to stop him. Tell him how sorry they were about losing Mary. Try to blow smoke up his ass by telling him how happy Mary would be to know he was the one in charge of her case. He couldn't stomach it. Not any of it. Not for another second.

"Lead the way," Jake said. Bethany was even prettier when she smiled. She took Jake by the hand and led him to the kitchen, unseen.

Thirteen

"It's beautiful here!"

Bethany turned off her ignition and marveled at the deep woods surrounding Jake's cabin. "How far back does your property go?"

"It belongs to my grandfather. Though, I guess someday it'll belong to me unless my sister gets her way. He owns two hundred acres, including a half of a private lake in the northwest quadrant. But it's hard to get to on account of it's at the bottom of a ravine."

"Your sister? Is she trying to cheat you out of your inheritance or something?"

Jake smiled. "No. She just had dollar signs in her eyes. She's wanted to take ten acres up by the road and build Airbnbs."

"Oh, you'd make a fortune. Maybe you should listen to her."

"Yeah ... you don't know my grandfather."

"Well, it's beautiful, Jake."

"You should see it in daylight."

It was a casual comment, but the words hung there for a moment, becoming more weighted with each second.

Bethany turned to him. Even in the dark, her eyes seemed to shine.

"I'd like to," she said. Then she leaned across the center console and pulled Jake's face closer to hers.

She kissed him. Light. But not unexpected. Still half-drunk as he was, Jake knew what he was doing when he got into her car.

Her hair brushed against his cheek, giving him a whiff of coconut and vanilla.

Before he could think it through, Jake heard himself say to her, "Would you like to come inside?"

Bethany leaned back. She still had a hand against his cheek. It felt good. Warm. Soft. Feminine.

She unlatched her seatbelt. A moment later, he led her inside.

"Sorry for the mess," he said as he flipped the kitchen light switch.

"If this is what you call a mess, you must be some kind of neat freak."

It took a second for Jake's eyes to adjust to the light. When they did, he saw what Bethany meant. This morning, he'd left the half-full coffeepot in the machine. He had two days' worth of dishes in the sink. But now, the countertops were pristine. The chrome sink polished to a shine. Everything was in its place. He could see through to his bedroom. It was made with new sheets and fluffed pillows.

"Gemma," he said under his breath.

Bethany walked in further. She went to the bedroom doorway.

"Gemma?" she repeated. "Look, Jake, if you're, um ... entangled, then ..."

"She's my sister," he said.

Bethany smiled, then peeled her coat off.

"Can I offer you something? I think I might have a bottle of wine ... somewhere."

He didn't want another drink himself. He wasn't sure what he wanted. Every instinct in him told him this was probably a bad idea. He didn't know anything about this woman. After tonight, she'd go back to the Dayton P.D. or wherever.

"Maybe we could just sit and talk for a little while," she said. "All day, it just looked to me like you could use a friend. Was Mary Rathburn your friend?"

Jake took his coat off and put it on the hook by the door. Bethany seated herself on the end of the couch and draped one leg over the other. Her skirt rode up a bit.

He went to her and sat on the opposite end of the couch.

"Mary was working on being my partner."

"How was that going?"

"She was talented. I'd handpicked her to be Ed Zender's replacement."

"Zender," she said. "Where have I heard that name before?"

"He's running to try to replace my boss in this year's election."

"Ah. That's it. He was schmoozing anyone who would listen at your Union Hall. What a creep. How do you feel about that?"

"Right now? It's the last thing I care about. Zender's incompetent. He'd make a terrible sheriff. But that's a problem for another day."

"That's got to be a lot of pressure on you, though. This case, Rathburn's murder, could be a jewel in Meg Landry's crown or an albatross around her neck, depending on how it goes. And she was your friend. I'm just ... I'm sorry."

"It's the job." If his head hadn't been swimming, he might have thought to ask her how she knew anything about Meg Landry, being so far away from her own jurisdiction.

Bethany moved closer to him. She put her hands on Jake's shoulders and started working the knots she found there. A groan escaped his lips, unbidden. God, she felt good. Maybe he did want a glass of wine.

"Poor Jake," she said. "Why do I get the feeling you're everyone's rock around here?"

He didn't answer. He didn't want to talk. He just wanted to be.

"And you're all alone here? You don't have someone special, Jake?"

"It's easier," he said.

"Easier. Sure. But lonely."

He didn't feel lonely. Not until that moment. Later he would tell himself it was the alcohol, the emotions of the day, the pressures of the past week. All of it. But for that instant, he needed a connection. A different kind of vice.

He couldn't remember if he moved first or if she did. But a moment later, Bethany straddled his lap. He reached up and threaded his fingers through her hair. Jake Cashen became a man of intense need. Drunk. Thirsty. Grief-stricken. But alive.

He wrapped his arms around Bethany's waist and slowly rose to his feet with her still straddling him. He carried her into the bedroom and kicked the door shut behind them.

Sunlight stabbed through the window and seared through Jake's pounding head. His stomach roiled and for a moment, he thought he'd lose it.

"That bad, was it?"

Bethany Roman stood in his bedroom doorway wearing one of his faded FBI t-shirts. As he sat up, he realized she was *only* wearing the t-shirt. Her clothes were in a pile against the wall. She carried two mugs of steaming hot coffee and handed him one.

"Bless you," he said.

She sat on the edge of the bed. "I thought you were a goner there for a minute. I had to check to see if you were still breathing."

"Sorry. You didn't have to do this." He raised his coffee mug. She made it strong.

"I don't mind. I know this is maybe going to sound insensitive considering the circumstances, but I had a great time with you last night."

She leaned in and kissed him.

"You're a brave woman," he said. "Can't imagine what my breath smells like right now."

"Oh, you're like a garbage truck sitting out in the August heat. And yet, somehow, still charming."

"Charming? I don't get a lot of charming."

"Then you, my friend, have been hanging with the wrong class of people."

Bethany got up and set her mug on Jake's nightstand. She went to the corner of the room and bent down to pick up her clothes. For a moment, it gave Jake an unfettered view of her backside. In spite of his pounding head and layer of fuzz on his teeth, the sight stirred a different part of his anatomy.

Bethany pulled her skirt on. Wearing that and Jake's t-shirt, she looked sexy as hell. "Well, the rest of this is pretty much wrecked," she said, holding up her tattered underwear and hopelessly wrinkled blouse. "And my bra seems to have gone missing. Damn shame. It was one of my favorites. Keep an eye out for it, will you?"

"It was pink if I recall," he said.

She pointed a finger at him. "You don't miss much."

Jake stood up and became aware of his own state of undress. Bethany watched him as he padded over to the chair in the corner and pulled on a pair of drawstring sweats.

"What time is it?"

"Seven thirty," she said.

Jake rubbed a hand over the scruff of his jaw. "Damn. I'm sorry. I've got to ..."

"You're late," she said. "I left you plenty of hot water for your shower."

Jake realized his other predicament. "My car," he said.

"Is still at the Union Hall," she said. "It's okay. I can drop you off on my way through town."

Jake knew that would raise a whole other set of problems. He'd have to run the gauntlet of gossip and questions at the station if someone saw him get dropped off. And he would for sure be seen by someone.

"Yeah. I'm not sure that's a can of worms I want to open. I work with a bunch of nosey Nellies."

"You ashamed of me already, Detective Cashen?"

"What? No. I didn't mean that. Crap. I'm sorry. I feel like I've bungled this."

Bethany laughed. "Relax. I'm teasing you. Don't worry. I get it. Believe me, I know cops are the worst gossips in any small town."

"Right," Jake said. "You're one of us. I guess you would. And it's okay. I can just walk up the hill and take my grandpa's truck. It needs to be driven anyway. He lost his license a while ago."

"Then I guess you're under control. I had a good time last night. I also know that's all it has to be. The last thing I want to do is be another person to put pressure on you."

Jake felt like a jerk. Since he'd woken up, he'd maybe acted like he was trying to get rid of her.

"Thank you," he said.

Her eyes widened. "Thank me? Was I doing you a favor?"

"What? No. Dammit. I'm sorry. I'm making a mess of this."

Bethany came to him. She went up on her tiptoes and kissed him. "You're not. I'd like it if you called me again. But I'll understand if you don't. Seriously. No pressure."

"Your number," Jake said. He grabbed his cell phone off the charger. Bethany took hers out. They quickly exchanged contacts and she fired off a text to him.

"You have to at least let me make you breakfast," he said. If he'd acted like less than a gentleman last night, he was damn sure going to make up for it this morning. He went to the kitchen, popped bread in the toaster, and set about scrambling some eggs. Gemma had left some cut fruit in the fridge the other day. He put it out. Bethany took a seat at his bistro table, sipping her coffee.

Ten minutes later, he served her a decent, if simple breakfast.

"You're very sweet for doing all of this. I can't remember the last time a man made me breakfast."

"I'm glad you could stay," he said and he meant it.

"But you can't," she said, finishing the last of her coffee. "I know you're late. It's okay, Jake. Really. We both have to go to work."

"This was ... I don't usually ..."

She put a hand up. "Let's not. Not yet. Call me later. When you can. But don't worry if it slips your mind. This case has to take priority for you over everything. I know the drill. Believe me."

"Yeah." He smiled. "I guess you of all people would. Thanks for that. Thanks for all of it. Have a safe drive back to Dayton, okay?" he said.

Bethany started to say something, but settled on a smile instead. She grabbed her coat off the couch and walked out the front door.

Jake was sorry to see her go, but couldn't shake the feeling he'd made a huge mistake. He'd started to tell her he wasn't in the habit of having alcohol-fueled one-night stands. But somehow, saying it could have made it worse. She seemed to understand. He hoped she wouldn't hold it against him. And he really did want to call her again. He watched her drive away.

He texted Landry and told him he'd be about thirty minutes late coming in. She didn't immediately text back. But another call came through from a number he didn't recognize.

Jake answered. "Cashen."

And then a voice he hadn't heard in years and never thought he'd hear again answered back.

FOURTEEN

"Hello, Jake."

It took a moment for Jake's brain to catch up with his ears. It was a voice so familiar to him. His initial reaction was joy. But then something else settled in and darkened his heart.

"Frank."

Frank Borowski. His former mentor, coach, father figure, detective. Now fugitive from justice.

Jake walked out onto the front porch. Snow began to fall. It covered Bethany Roman's tire tracks. By afternoon, there'd be no trace of her here at all.

"I'm sorry," Frank said. "I saw the news. It's not easy when we have to bury our friends."

Jake looked again at the caller ID. No doubt Frank was calling from a burner phone he'd destroy and toss in the trash the second Jake hung up. As his initial anger dissipated, Jake realized Frank

Borowski had been the one person he'd wanted to talk to the moment he knew what happened to Mary Rathburn.

"I'm sorry for your loss," Frank said. "I wish I could help you carry this load."

So did Jake. He squeezed the phone tighter in his hand.

"What do you want, Frank?"

"I've been where you are. More times than I'd like to remember. I swore to myself a long time ago I'd never go to another cop's funeral. I'm sorry I couldn't be at this one."

Jake didn't know what to say. It bothered him that Frank's words comforted him even a little. It would be easier if he could just hate this man. But he didn't. He never would. It changed nothing.

"Where are you, Frank?"

He heard Frank take a breath and knew he was smiling on the other end of the phone.

"Is it the ex?"

"What?"

"Mary's ex. Have you ruled him out?"

"I can't talk about this with you. I can't talk to you at all."

"Sure you can. It's just us, Jake. You and me. I know you've got an instinct with this one already. A gut feeling. What happened to that girl was passionate, wasn't it?"

"What do you mean?"

"It was somebody she knew, wasn't it?"

Jake took his coat off the hook. He had a long walk up the hill to get to his grandfather's truck. The seconds ticked by on the call.

He wanted to keep Frank on the line even though he knew it wouldn't matter.

"Yeah, Frank. I think it was someone she knew. Or someone who hated her for a reason."

"I know what you'll do to yourself over this one. God knows I've done it to myself enough times."

"And look where it got you."

Frank laughed. "Yeah. That's my point, kid. I think. Listen, I know you cared about this woman. Don't let that keep you from seeing who she really was. You knew the family. As hard as it is, she has to be like every other victim. Flawed. Imperfect. Somebody who made bad choices just like you and me."

"What's the point of all of this, Frank?" Jake trudged up the hill. In a few hours, the snow would fill in his footprints. It was good he was taking the truck. The last thing he needed was his grandfather trying to hook up the plow or going out in this mess.

"The pressure to put her on a pedestal is going to come from all sides," Frank continued. "Let her family do that. It'll help them with the loss of her. But you can't. Remember that."

"She didn't deserve to die like that."

"No. She didn't. But you know this had to do with the way she lived. Some piece of it anyway. Don't lose sight of that. I know everybody around you is going to try to put extra pressure on you. Even Landry. She's in an election year. Ed Zender's an idiot, but he's not stupid. He'll take credit for your success if you solve this case. He'll use it to bury Landry if you don't. Don't let their bullshit affect what you know you have to do, Jake."

It was exactly what Jake needed to hear, but Frank's words still cut through him. His betrayal cut through him.

“Frank, I’m clear on what I have to do.”

He let his words settle. Frank didn’t say anything.

“You’re a wanted man, Frank,” Jake said. “You know my next call has to be to the US Marshal.”

Silence. For a moment, Jake wondered if he’d hung up. Then Frank’s haughty laughter filled his ears.

“Yeah, Jake. I know. You do what you gotta do. Just know I’m out here thinking about you, too.”

“You could make it easier on ...”

Jake’s words were cut off by three beeps, letting him know the call had dropped. Frank’s phone was probably at the bottom of some lake by now. Jake stared at the screen of his. Then he tossed his phone inside his grandfather’s truck and climbed behind the wheel.

Jake found Meg alone in the war room. She had the television on the wall turned on. She stood with her arms crossed, a scowl on her face. Ed Zender’s voice filled the room. On the screen, he stood behind a bank of microphones.

“Detective Rathburn’s loss is a tremendous blow to the department and to me personally. I handpicked her to replace me and trained her. She was a good cop. She could have been a great detective.”

“Mr. Zender, are you concerned that Sheriff Landry has kept this investigation into her murder in-house?”

“I’m very concerned. We have a dead cop. That’s not something that we can let stand. If I were sheriff, I would immediately turn this investigation over to the Ohio Bureau of Criminal Investigations."

Meg pointed the remote at the screen and turned the volume down.

"Ignore him," Jake said. "He doesn't know what he's talking about. You and I know Ed had zero to do with Mary's hire and training. And Mary knew to disregard everything that ever came out of Ed's mouth."

"You doing okay?" she asked. "You disappeared on us last night. Phil and I were going to offer to drive you home after the wake."

"I, uh ... found my own way," Jake said.

"I don't want to go to another one of those anytime soon, Jake. And you know it has nothing to do with the election."

"I know," he said. Behind her shoulder, Ed silently droned on.

"I can't believe they're actually giving that fool screen time. Every reporter in town has Ed's number. They know my media liaison made a point of keeping him away from the press for a reason."

"Ed's the master of hanging himself with his own rope. He'll do the same this time."

"I hope you're right. We could use some good news around here."

It was then that Jake noticed what Landry had tucked under her arm. For a moment, he lost his breath. Landry held out Mary's handcuffs in their brand-new leather case. The ones he'd retrieved from her nightstand.

"These weren't her department-issued ones," Landry said. "Connie Rathburn told me she bought them for Mary as a gift when she graduated from the academy. She gave them to me yesterday at the funeral."

"Ouch," Jake said.

"Yeah. Felt like I'd been punched in the stomach. Jake? I want you to have them. If ... *when* you catch this guy. Well ... you'll know what to do with them."

She slapped the cuffs onto Jake's palm. They felt heavier than when he'd held them the other day. Silence fell between them. For a moment, it felt like it could swallow them. Then, Landry took a step back.

"What's your game plan today?" she said.

"I've got to go out and interview the last of Shane Edwards's buddies who were with him the night Mary was killed. Birdie and I are still trying to run down who this guy was who made threats to her at the bar."

No sooner had he said it when Birdie walked in. She carried three Styrofoam mugs in a drink carrier. She handed one to Meg and another to Jake.

"Bless you," Meg said. "The stuff Darcy made this morning could remove the paint from the walls."

"I had 'em make yours extra strong, Jake. Figured you could use it after last night. How's your head?"

"My head's fine," Jake said, though the coffee was a godsend.

"What's that idiot still blathering on about?" Birdie said, pointing her mug to the silent television screen.

"He's a menace," Landry said.

"Well, he's a connected menace. I heard a rumor there's a certain county commissioner backing his candidacy." Birdie leveled a look at Jake.

"Good old Uncle Rob?" Jake said. "That doesn't surprise me. Rob Arden knows he can pull Ed Zender's strings if the people of this county are dumb enough to give him Landry's job."

"Great," Landry said. "Let's hope they're not dumb enough. Though after yesterday, if someone asked me why I wanted to run for sheriff again, I'm not sure I'd have a good answer."

"It was a good service as far as those things go," Birdie said. "It meant a lot to Mary's family."

"You ready to head out to Marvell County with me today?" Jake said. "Let's button up Shane Edwards's alibi once and for all."

"Sure thing," she said.

Behind Meg, the screen changed. Ed Zender was no longer on camera. Instead, it was a wide shot of the building they were standing in. A reporter stood on the steps of the sheriff's department, holding her microphone. Jake nearly spit out his coffee. "Sheriff?" he said. "Can you turn that back up?"

"I can tell you that sources within the department will dispute former Detective Zender's interpretation of events," the reporter said. The shot switched to Hugh Wyndham, one of the morning anchors for Channel 9. He was old as dirt and a one-man institution in local news.

"Can you elaborate on that? Are we expecting Sheriff Landry to put out a statement of her own in response to Detective Zender's allegations?"

"I can't say for sure," the reporter said. "But it's no secret there's no love lost between Sheriff Landry and her opponent. I've spoken to an inside source and many believe Detective Zender was incompetent. At the same time, I'm certain Sheriff Landry's lack of field experience is going to be a recurring theme in Detective Zender's campaign."

"Who's that?" Landry asked. "Is she new?"

Jake felt ash in his mouth. His chest hollowed out. She really was pretty. She'd changed into a crisp blue suit that popped on camera. Her hair was now neatly styled and curled around her face.

"Well, we trust you'll stay on top of this developing story, Bethany," Hugh Wyndham said. He smiled at the camera. "Once again, we're happy to introduce viewers to our newest crime reporter, Bethany Roman. She comes to us from our affiliate in Dayton. Looking forward to her reporting. We're at the top of the hour now. Right after this, we'll have Tom Spencer with traffic and weather."

The station cut to a commercial.

"Son of a bitch," Jake muttered.

"Jake?" Meg said. "What's the matter?"

Fresh anger heated Jake's blood. An inside source? He wanted to hit the wall. Hell, he wanted to disappear through it.

"Birdie," he said. "Do you mind if I have a word with Sheriff Landry alone?"

Birdie gave him a quizzical look, but didn't argue. "Sure thing," she said. "Come find me when you want to head out to Marvell County."

She shut the door as she left. Landry stood with her hands on her hips. She knew Jake well enough to understand whatever he had to say wasn't good news.

"That reporter," he said. "Meg, I swear. I had no idea. She was ..."

Meg looked back at the television. "She was what, Jake?"

"She ... Christ. I thought she was a cop. A trooper or something. I think I said it. She never mentioned ... she didn't ... she let me think ..."

"Jake?"

"Her inside source," he said. He tried to run through all the things he'd said to Bethany Roman last night. He'd talked about Ed. He told her he thought Ed was incompetent. She'd used it. He curled his fist and beat the side of his leg.

"I'll fix this," he said.

"You?" Meg said as Jake's behavior started making sense to her. "You talked to her? You ... oh ..."

Jake wanted the ground to open up and swallow him. Or Bethany Roman.

Meg opened her mouth to say something, then clamped it shut. For that, Jake was grateful.

A moment later, Birdie knocked and opened the door. "I'm sorry to interrupt. But Jake? I just took a call from a Bonnie Smalls from Muskingum County. She said she spoke to you about the home invasion case with a similar MO?"

Jake tore a hand through his hair. "Yeah."

"We'll talk about this later, Jake," Meg said through gritted teeth.

"Yeah."

"Again, sorry," Birdie said. "Smalls says her victim is awake and talking. We can be there in a half an hour. Figured you'd want to question her yourself."

"Yeah," Jake said. "The trip to Marvell County can wait for now." He downed the rest of his coffee and regretted drinking anything stronger last night. He was beginning to regret a lot of things.

Still frowning, Meg Landry brushed past him and left the room.

Fifteen

Her name was Sophia Osterman. Birdie and Jake met Detective Ben Harry and Deputy Bonnie Smalls in the lobby of the Genesis Hospital. Harry had been on the job for almost thirty years. Jake heard he'd already retired once but couldn't stay away and came back one year out.

Jake never wanted to be that guy. Someday, somehow, he wanted a life beyond murder cases and broken victims and dealing with those who hurt people.

"She's fragile," Harry said. "But she bore up pretty well to questioning. She saw your case on the news from her hospital bed. It shook her up as you can imagine. Hate that it happened but she's anxious to talk to you. She's terrified that this creep is still out there somewhere hurting women."

"Thank you for calling me," Jake said. "This is my partner, Erica Wayne."

It was the first time he'd said it. Birdie blanched a bit. She covered quickly and shook Harry's hand.

"You guys are getting younger every day," Harry said as he elbowed Deputy Smalls. "I swear I've got stuff in my fridge older than some of you people with detective shields."

"Well, hopefully I hold up better than curdled cheese, Detective," Birdie said. Bonnie Smalls covered her laugh with her hand.

Harry's face fell. "I didn't mean anything by that. I'm sure you'll do fine. Probably good you brought a woman with you, Cashen. Might put Miss Osterman at ease."

Jake saw Birdie clench her jaw. She was used to backhanded compliments like that from guys like Harry. She shot Jake a knowing smile and let Harry lead them down the hall to Sophia Osterman's room.

She was sitting up in bed eating a cup of applesauce. One of the nurses had just finished checking her vitals. She excused herself as they walked in.

"I'm just down the hall if you need me, Sophia. You know how to hit the call button."

Sophia looked small in the bed. She wore a pink hospital gown that hung off her. Jake could see bruising on her clavicle. Both of her eyes were blackened and she had a split lip. Her right arm was in a cast and Harry had told him she suffered a few broken ribs, multiple cuts, and superficial stab wounds to her legs and abdomen. Those were the external injuries. Jake knew the emotional ones would take even longer to heal.

"Sophia," Harry said. "This is Detective Cashen and Detective, uh ... sorry."

"Wayne," Erica said. "But you can call me Erica."

Sophia Osterman's smile seemed genuine. Having Birdie there appeared to have put her at ease. Birdie sat on the radiator next to the bed, leaving the chair for Jake.

"I was just telling Detective Cashen how you saw something on the television about his case. The woman who was attacked down in Worthington County. It's similar enough. It's good you're willing to talk to Jake, here. You can tell him what you told me."

"Thanks," Jake said. Though he now wished Harry would leave the interview to him. He knew he'd get better information from this witness the less coaching or direction she got from Harry. There was something else. Sophia's entire demeanor changed when Harry spoke. He had a booming voice that bounced off the tile floors. If anything, Sophia tried to make herself smaller in that bed.

"I appreciate that," Jake said. "You mind if I take it from here?"

Harry frowned. "I was just trying to help her focus. That's been an issue."

"I'm sorry," Sophia said. "I'm really trying."

"You're doing fine," Birdie interjected. "You've been through hell. You're alive. Bottom line, that's the only thing that matters."

"Fine," Harry said. "I sure don't like stepping on toes." His tone dripped with sarcasm, but at least he followed through on his comment and left.

Jake waited a moment until he could hear Harry chatting up the nurses on the other end of the hall. He felt bad for them, but relieved for himself. Deputy Smalls took up sentry outside the door. By the knowing glance she gave Jake, he knew she'd be just as useful in keeping Detective Harry out.

"I'm sorry about your friend," Sophia said. "That she died."

"Thank you," Jake said.

"Do you really think what happened to her … that it was the same person like Detective Harry thinks?"

"Is that what he told you?" Jake kept his voice even. He didn't want Sophia to sense any tension from him. Though he'd like to throttle Ben Harry at the moment for putting that kind of suggestion into this woman's mind.

"Sophia, the last thing I want you to do is rehash memories that are painful for you."

"If it was the same guy … then he's not done. I've seen enough true crime shows and listened to podcasts. God. I can't believe I'm sitting here like this. I can't believe this happened to me."

Jake gave her a moment. Sophia didn't cry. She went completely still, staring at the wall. After a full minute, she locked eyes with Jake.

"I didn't see his face very well. I know that's what you want to know."

"It's okay. Tell me what you do remember. If you can. And if at any point you need to stop …"

"No. I don't want to stop. I want you to catch this guy. I want you to make sure he doesn't do this to anybody else. If it's the same guy that murdered your friend, I know what it means. He didn't kill me. So he's escalated."

Birdie stood up. She came around to the side of the bed. "Maybe. But you're not responsible for that."

"Can you start from the beginning?" Jake asked.

Sophia pulled her sheet higher up, bringing it under her chin. Her feet poked out from the opposite end. She wore red slippers with treads and the hospital logo on the side. Birdie grabbed a thin blanket from the end of the bed and covered Sophia's legs.

"I was in the shower," Sophia started. "I'd just let the cat back in. She got into the neighbor's trash the night before so I've been extra careful not to let her roam. I had music playing on my Bluetooth speaker. I play it kind of loud so I can hear it in the shower. When I was done, I wrapped myself in a towel and came out into the bedroom. That's when ... he just came out of nowhere. Grabbed me around the waist. I never saw him. Detective Harry thinks he was hiding in the shadow between the open doorway and the wall. He just was there. He covered my mouth with his hand and threw me face down on the bed. That's when he started cutting me."

"He had a knife?"

"Yes," she said. "It was a fillet knife I keep in a block on the kitchen counter. It's not very sharp. It's a cheap set. My dad's been on me to get a new one."

Sophia described her struggle with her assailant. Much like Mary, she was able to get a hold of a weapon of sorts. A candlestick she kept beside her bed. In Mary's case, it had been a wine bottle. But unlike Mary's case, Sophia's attacker had sexually assaulted her. At a certain point, she blacked out.

"I woke up on the floor," she said. "My head was throbbing. I was sore everywhere. Bleeding. He'd tied my hands behind my back with the sash from my robe. It wasn't very tight though. I was able to get out of it and crawl to the nightstand where my phone was charging. I called 9-1-1."

"Was he still in the house?" Birdie asked.

"No," she said. "There was snow blowing into the hallway. He went out the sliding door and left it wide open. Detective Harry thinks my neighbor might have scared him off. I live in a duplex. We share the garage. She came home from work and Harry thinks when she hit the opener, it scared the guy off and that's why he left so quickly out the back door."

"That's a lucky thing," Jake said.

"Yeah. Lucky," Sophia said, staring off into space again.

"You said you didn't get much of a look at him. But you did see something?" Jake asked. She nodded.

"He had a mask on. Like a ski mask, but that spandex kind. Not knit. Black. It covered his nose and mouth but I could see his eyes. He had bushy eyebrows. Brown eyes. And his hair was long enough it poked out the bottom of the mask."

"Do you have a sense of how tall he was?" Birdie asked.

"Taller than me. I'm not short. I'm five nine. When he grabbed me from behind, my cheek was against his cheek. I think he was at most an inch or two taller than me. At most."

Jake thought of Mary's scrawled note written in blood. White male. Five ten or eleven. He knew from Ramirez's initial evidence collection she was grasping several strands of long dark hair in her right fist.

"I hope that helps," Sophia said.

"Sophia," Jake said. "I understand you work as a hospital security guard."

"Yes. I work here, actually. Do you think that's this guy's MO? Your friend was a cop. I mean, I'm not a cop. Not like you. But Detective Harry said this guy might be targeting women connected with law enforcement. I have a criminal justice degree. I'm waiting to get into the trooper academy. I *was* waiting. Now? I'm not sure."

"That's not something you have to decide now," Birdie said.

"He took all the money I had in my purse. My jewelry box. My laptop. He even found a tin can I keep in the kitchen where I put loose change. There was close to three hundred dollars in quarters in there. He went through the whole house. I don't even know if I can go back there. If I can live there anymore."

"Is there someone you can stay with when you're discharged?" Jake asked.

"My parents live in Columbus. I'm going back home for a while. Until I can figure out what's next for me."

"I appreciate you talking with us," Jake said.

"If there's anything else I can think of, I'll call you. But I just didn't see what he looked like."

"You saw plenty," Jake said. "And you're alive. You did all the right things, Sophia."

"I bet your friend did them, too. I don't know why he didn't kill me. Why do you think he would leave me alive and kill her?"

"Sophia, this may not be the same person. We can't assume that."

"Right. Sure. I know that. I know."

A nurse walked into the room. "Sorry. Time to get you up and moving, Ms. Osterman."

"We're finished," Jake said. "Thank you."

He left a card on Sophia's side table. "You call me if you think of something. If you need something."

"Good luck," she said.

Jake and Birdie quietly left Sophia's hospital room. He thanked Deputy Smalls. Ben Harry had made his way back down the hall. He waited for them by the elevators.

"How was she?" he asked.

"Helpful," Jake said. "Traumatized. Do you know if they've arranged for her to speak to a trauma specialist?"

"They've had a lot of people in and out," Harry answered.

It bothered Jake that Harry didn't seem concerned about Sophia's mental state. And that he carelessly shared facts about Mary's case with her. He had unwittingly spoiled Sophia Osterman's statement. He wondered what else Harry might have spoiled about her case.

"I'll be in touch once I've got DNA back from my crime scene," Jake said. The elevator door fortuitously opened. He and Birdie took the opportunity to leave Detective Ben Harry where he stood. As the doors closed, Birdie turned to him.

"I don't think her guy is our guy."

"Gut reaction, I don't either. Nothing was stolen from Mary's house."

"And she wasn't raped. Those are two totally different MOs."

"The physical description, sparse as it was, was similar."

"But Harry's making a leap that I just don't think is justified by the facts. And what the hell's he doing feeding all of that to his victim?"

"He might have done her more harm than good."

"Good luck telling him that."

"DNA will tell the tale. Ramirez thinks he needs another week before they can build a profile."

"Let's just hope we don't have another victim in the meantime. Where to next, Jake?"

Jake checked his phone. "We're meeting Detective Dave Yun. I sent him the names Shane Edwards gave me of who he was with the night Mary was killed. They backed up his story, but let's finish things up in Marvell County. Talk to some of them in more detail. Are you up for it?"

"You bet."

Jake texted Yun and told him they were thirty minutes out.

Sixteen

The town of Oakton was even smaller than Stanley. Just one county over, Jake had developed a good working relationship with Marvell County's only violent crimes detective, Dave Yun.

Dave met Birdie and Jake in the parking lot of a local business just a quarter mile from Brad Edwards's house. Though Brad had already confirmed his cousin Shane's alibi the night Mary died and Shane's phone records supported his story, Jake wanted to talk to him again. The third name on Shane's list, Ian Burke, was still in the wind somewhere.

Yun climbed into the backseat of Jake's cruiser. He and Birdie made a quick reintroduction. She'd met him a few times in cases when she worked in field ops.

"Thanks for meeting us," Jake said. The snow had stopped, but a bitter wind made it feel like zero degrees outside.

"Thanks for calling."

"What can you tell me about the Edwards family?"

Jake had pulled up Brad's priors. He was hardly a hardened criminal, but no saint either. He had a couple of drunk and disorderlies and had been a witness in a pretty nasty domestic dispute involving yet another cousin last year.

"Brad's a good ole boy," Yun said. "The whole Edwards family is. I've lost count of how many cousins there are. Brad lives in the family house. His grandpa was the patriarch. Mean son of a bitch. Did some hard time for armed robbery."

"Sounds like the Bardos in our neck of the woods," Birdie said.

"Oh, the Bardos are organized. Smart. The Edwardses are just a bunch of idiots. Mainly harmless but troublemakers. On occasion, they're useful idiots though. They're on the periphery of some of the more capable criminals in town. I've knocked on Brad's door plenty of times, looking for information."

"Does he know we're coming?" Jake asked.

"Not when I saw him in town the other day and told him you'd have more questions for him and that it was in his best interests to cooperate."

"Well, let's get this over with before it starts snowing again."

"Brad's house is just at the end of this road. The ugly green one. It's been that color for as long as I can remember. I don't even know where you buy house paint that color."

Yun wasn't exaggerating. The house in question was a two-story, painted lime, almost neon green, with blue shutters. It had a big wraparound porch, but the steps leading up to it looked far from safe.

He let Yun lead the way and he and Birdie followed up to the front door.

Jake could see in the giant bay window in the front. Two men sat on a floral couch watching a big-screen television.

"Hey, Brad," Yun said, knocking on the door. "Come on out and have a word with me."

Birdie stood behind and to the left of Jake. She kept her right hand resting gently on the heel of her service weapon.

"Keep your pants on," a voice called from inside. A moment later, Brad Edwards came to the door and opened it. He was a grimy-looking guy with dark hair and cold gray eyes, and wore a Bengals t-shirt with the collar ripped out.

"What do you want, Yun?" Brad said.

"You know what I want. Come on out here and let's have a proper conversation. You already know Detective Cashen and Deputy Wayne from Worthington County. You know they want to talk to you some more about your cousin, Shane."

"Shane ain't here," Brad said.

"I know that," Jake said.

"I already told you Shane didn't have nothing to do with what happened to his ex. He was done with Mary a long time ago. She was the one who couldn't get over it."

"Come on out here, Brad," Yun said. "Or let us in. It's cold as hell out here."

"Not my problem. And unless you've got a warrant, I'm afraid I lost your invitation."

Birdie took a few steps away from Jake. She had her eyes on the window. While Brad's attention was on Jake and Yun, Birdie peered inside.

"I'd like to know a little more about what was happening out here the night of January 12th," Jake said.

Brad turned to him. "It's like I told you before. My daughter had a birthday party. Shane brought Kevin so he could play with all the kids. The kids had a slumber party down in the basement. I ordered the O'Malley fight on pay-per-view. Me, Shane, and a bunch of the other dads stayed up here and watched it. Shane and Kevin spent the night. End of story. I know Shane's already told you all this. And I know you ran his phone. Nobody here had anything to do with whatever trouble Mary got herself into. If anything, you should be thanking me."

"How's that?" Jake asked.

"Because Kevin was safe here in my house. If he'd been with Mary, he'd probably be dead now, too. Who knows? The kid is busted up. And I'm getting real sick and tired of Shane getting dragged for her bad choices."

"I'll bet you are," Jake said. "But I'm gonna need the names of all the adults who were here with you that night. I asked you for them before and you still haven't answered."

"And I don't think I have to tell you that. Maybe you need a geography lesson. We're thirty miles from Mary's house here. Whoever was here was here, not there, see? So I'd say that's none of your business and I'm tired of letting the cold air into the house. Unless you plan on paying my heating bill for the month, Yun, I'm shutting this door."

"Brad, Mary's dead. Murdered. You get that, right?" Yun said. He stepped forward and put his foot out, keeping Brad from closing the door.

"Jake," Birdie said quietly. She pulled on his sleeve.

He stepped away from the doorway with her.

"What did you see?" Jake whispered.

"That guy on the couch in there. I recognize him. I'd like to get a better look, but I think it's the guy I saw threatening Mary at the bar earlier this month."

Jake turned to the window. Two men sat on the couch. One of them Jake could only see in profile. The other sat in the corner but straight on from where he and Birdie stood. White male. Dark hair that looked shorter than what he'd seen from what Ramirez had collected from Mary's fist. But it was hard to tell. This guy's hair was curly. If you stretched out a strand, it might reach his collar or longer.

Whatever Yun said to Brad made the younger man slam the screen door and go back into the house.

"Yun," Jake said. "Do you know who he's got in the house with him? The one on the left there. We need to talk to him."

Yun peered into the window. Brad Edwards stepped in front of it, flipped a middle finger, then jerked the curtains shut.

Yun went back and pounded on the door. "Brad, get out here. Bring Burke with you!"

"Ian Burke," Yun said. "He runs around with the Edwardses. Another low-level dirtbag."

"Brad!" Yun pounded harder on the door with his fist, shaking the floorboards of the porch.

"We've been looking for him," Jake said.

"Burke?" Yun yelled. "Come out here. We need to talk to you."

"Go to hell, Yun," Brad yelled back. "Told you. No warrant. No cooperation."

"Burke, how about I call your probation officer? You wanna make this tough? Fine. Me too. I'll toss all your phones. Your laptops. Your gaming system ..."

Jake heard swearing coming from inside the house and something crashed to the floor. Birdie moved. She left the porch and watched the side of the house. Jake knew she'd be ready if they had a runner. His fingers played with the butt of his weapon.

The front door swung open. The kid with the curly hair stepped out, scowling at him. He had a lit cigarette in one hand.

"What the hell do you want?"

Birdie came back around.

"For starters, where were you January 12th?" Yun asked.

"Aw, no. No. No. I was here, man. I had nothing to do with whatever trouble Shane's baby mama got herself into. You can piss off."

"You ever been to Wylie's Bar?" Birdie asked. She stood on the last step of the porch, looking up at Burke. He barely acknowledged her.

"What's she talking about?" Burke asked Yun.

"How well did you know Mary Rathburn?" Jake asked.

"Never said I did. I'm friends with Brad and Shane. That's it."

"You want to tell me about a conversation you had with Mary a couple of weeks ago at Wylie's?" Jake asked.

"Somebody's giving you false information," Burke said. "I didn't know Mary. I never talked to Mary."

"Well, that's two lies, Burke. You wanna go for a trifecta? Where were you on the night of January 12th?"

"I told you. Here. Brad'll tell you."

Brad stepped out onto the porch. "Ian was here. He's been staying with me while they fix the plumbing at his place."

"Is your phone going to back that up?" Jake asked. "Because that's gonna be my next warrant."

"You don't have a case," Burke said. "I don't even know you, man."

"We should work on that," Jake said. "Why don't you come down to my office so we can have a proper conversation?"

"This is bullshit," Brad said. "You don't have dick. Not on me. Not on Shane. Now you're just trying to jerk Ian's chain. Whoever told you whatever they told you is lying. I've cooperated. We've been out here twenty minutes. You got nothing."

"And I'm not talking to you anymore," Jake said. He got in Brad Edwards's face. "So why don't you go back inside before I do get interested in you again, Brad?"

Brad looked at Yun. Yun shrugged as if to say he couldn't be responsible for whatever Jake would do next.

Jake took a step toward Ian Burke. "I've got a dead cop, Burke. I don't think that's the kind of trouble you want to mess with if you really weren't involved. Shane Edwards has already given me your name. You're gonna have to deal with me one way or another. And I have a feeling you're the kind of guy who could benefit from having this guy owe you a favor every once in a while."

Jake put a hand on Yun's shoulder.

"Do what he says, Burke," Yun advised him.

"I got plans today," Burke said.

"Fine," Jake said. "Be in my office tomorrow morning. Ten o'clock." He shoved a business card into Burke's hand. Burke took it. Jake figured there was at least a fifty-fifty chance he'd wipe his ass with it before the end of the day. But he agreed to come to the station tomorrow. It was good enough for now.

Jake, Birdie, and Yun left Brad Edwards's house. Jake thanked Yun as he dropped him and Birdie off at Jake's car. Jake brooded as he pulled out and headed back to Worthington County.

"That was good work back there," he said to Birdie.

"If Burke shows up tomorrow."

"I'll get a warrant if he doesn't. And Yun will make sure he doesn't do anything stupid like disappear."

Jake's temper rose out of nowhere. No. Not nowhere. It was Ian Burke's smug attitude. The contempt with which he and the Edwards cousins talked about Mary. He wished he'd known that's what she was dealing with all these months.

Jake smacked his steering wheel as he made the turn and hit the freeway.

"We'll get there," Birdie said. "One of these idiots knows something about something. Whether it's Shane or Burke or somebody else. You're a good interviewer, Jake. You're going to find whoever did this. You've got good instincts. Just trust them."

"Not always," Jake muttered.

He already felt like he'd made a mistake somewhere.

"Don't beat yourself up about Bethany Roman," Birdie said.

Jake jerked his head around to stare at her. "You know about that?"

Birdie shrugged. "I didn't want to say anything. Nobody does. But enough of us saw you leave with her, Jake."

"Am I the only one who didn't know she was a reporter?"

"No," Birdie said quickly. "Most of us assumed she was another cop. It wasn't until she turned up on the news. And trust me, if she thinks she did herself any favors by ..."

"I'd rather not talk about it," Jake said.

"Got it."

That was one thing he liked about Birdie. She understood the value of silence and wouldn't press him on something he didn't want to talk about.

Still, he felt like a jerk. He made a serious mistake with Bethany Roman and no amount of rationalizing would change it.

"Anyway," Jake said. "That was good work back there. I appreciate it."

Birdie smiled but didn't say anything. Jake just hoped he was as good an interviewer tomorrow as Birdie thought he was.

Seventeen

Ian Burke brought his whole attitude the next morning. He plopped down in a chair across from Jake in the interview room, a knit cap pulled low, covering his hair.

"I can give you ten minutes," he said. "I'm working a job in Navan Township."

"What kind of job?"

"Drywall."

"I'll try not to keep you too long. Thanks for coming down."

"I came down because it was on my way."

"Thanks just the same. Can I get you something? Water? We've got a fresh pot of coffee in the other room."

Ian put his hands flat on the table. He was wearing knit gloves. He gave Jake a smug smile.

Sure, kid, Jake thought. Tough guy. Too smart for his own good. He'd leave no fingerprints today. No random DNA. It only made him look that much more guilty in Jake's eyes.

"I want to talk about the night of January 12th first," Jake said.

Ian sat back. He threw a casual arm over the chair next to him. "Told you yesterday," he said. "I was at Brad's. Me. Brad. Shane. Brad's friend Len. The kids were playing downstairs. The rest of us rented the UFC fight. We ordered pizzas. I paid for them with my credit card and had 'em delivered. Delivery girl knows me. Seena Grimes. I dated her older sister Chloe a while ago. Call her. We ordered from Angelo's. You got nothing on me. I had nothing to do with whatever happened to Shane's ex."

"I don't believe I ever said you did, Ian. Why are you getting so defensive?"

"Because I know how this works. I know how Mary operated. Always lording the fact she was a cop over Shane. Over all of us."

"Is that what you think I'm doing?"

"I think you're scared."

"I'm scared?"

Ian leaned forward. "Maybe."

"Of what? Of you?"

"Nah. Not me, man. But it won't look too good if you can't figure out who killed that girl. And you're lazy if you think it was Shane."

"What if I don't think it was Shane?"

"Then that's your business. We done now?"

"Ian, you're a smart guy, that's obvious. I can see I'm not going to be able to put anything over on you." Jake put his pad of paper on the table between them. "So let me get right to what I really want to talk to you about."

Ian smiled. Jake could practically see the kid's ego swell right in front of him.

"You knew about the trouble Mary was giving Shane, right? Listen, I know it got ugly. I can't say I always agreed with the way she handled their divorce, either. A boy needs a father, right? If she was trying to cut him off from having one, well, I'd have had real issues with that too if Kevin were my kid."

Ian said nothing. He turned to stone and glared at Jake.

"There are things only a dad can teach a boy. And if they don't learn it, they can turn out soft. I've got a sister. She's got two boys and their dads aren't in the picture, either. I do what I can. I help coach the older one's wrestling team. But it's not the same as having a real dad. I bet Kevin's a terror when Shane gets him for his visitation."

Still, Ian said nothing.

"Spoiled, right? Probably cries at the drop of a hat."

Ian leaned forward. "What's this got to do with me? You wanna give Shane advice on being a dad? You've got his number."

"Yeah, but I know it bothered you, Ian. I know you tried to tell Mary to quit jerking Shane around."

Ian's smile faded. "The hell you talking about?"

"I'm talking about Wylie's bar. I'm talking about witnesses who saw you approach Mary a few nights before she died."

"What witnesses?"

It was Jake's turn to smile. "You know I can't tell you that. I just want to get your side of it."

"I had nothing to do with what happened to her. I think I told you that and I told you how to check my alibi. Whatever happened to Mary she brought on herself, probably."

"She was stabbed three times, Ian. She had her throat cut. You think she brought that on herself?"

"I don't know who she was hanging around with. Shane's moved on."

"Sure. His new girlfriend."

It was hot in the interview room with the door shut. Ian's forehead glistened with sweat.

"You sure I can't get you a bottle of water?"

Ian sneered. "Yeah. I'm sure."

"So what about that night at the bar? There's surveillance footage, Ian," Jake lied. "The bouncer had to get a little rough with you."

"No crime going to the bar, Detective. And if there was surveillance footage, then you know I never laid a finger on Mary. The bouncer was pissed because the bartender said she over-served me. I walked out of that bar alone and I went home. So whatever witness you think you have is making stuff up. It's a free country and I'm outta here unless you're planning on charging me with something."

"Why are you giving me a hard time, Ian? Huh? Mary's dead. Shane is gonna get what he wants. Unless a court finds him unfit, he'll get to raise Kevin all by himself, however and wherever he wants to. That's gotta be a relief."

"Yeah, I think you can go to hell now, Cashen." Ian rose. Jake rose with him.

"I get Shane's your boy, Ian. Do you really think you're helping him out with this attitude?"

"Shane had nothing to do with hurting Mary. Neither did I. And I'm done talking without a lawyer."

"What do you need a lawyer for if you had nothing to do with it?"

Ian scowled at him.

"You can see where I'd have questions, right, Ian? Smart guy that you are and all."

"I didn't like that bitch," Ian said. "She knew it. But we were nowhere near this. I came down here because your boy Yun wants to make trouble for me if I don't. You got my statement. That's all you're getting."

"If you've got nothing to hide. If you really had nothing to do with hurting Mary, then what would you have against submitting to a DNA test? Every person I've interviewed on this case has provided a sample, including Shane. You do that, then you won't hear from me again."

"I better not hear from you again anyway. You got questions, you can ask 'em through my lawyer."

"Who's your lawyer?"

Ian shoved his chair in. He jerked his chin at Jake, then strutted out into the hall. Jake picked up the pencil off the table and snapped it in half.

A moment later, Birdie came in. Mark Ramirez was with her. Jake knew Birdie had been watching from the observation room next door but Ramirez's presence was unexpected.

"Please tell me you've got news on the crime scene DNA. I feel like I'm spinning my wheels without it, Mark."

"Soon," he said. "Two weeks tops. The lab has made it their first priority. I know you want it rushed, but they're gonna make sure what they give you is unimpeachable."

"I appreciate that."

"He's lying," Birdie said. "Ian Burke got in Mary's face at the bar that night. I'm telling you. If it weren't for me and the bouncer closing in on him, he would have made a move on her."

"He was smart," Mark said. "The gloves. The hat. Declining to drink from a coffee cup. He acted like a guilty man, Jake."

"Seena Grimes," Jake said to Birdie. "Did you catch that part? Can you run that down with the pizza joint in Oakton?"

"It'll be easy enough to check a receipt," she said. "Unless this delivery girl he talked to is covering for him. He admitted they were acquainted. And Ian could have given one of the other guys his credit card information or he could have used it online and not been there when the pizza was actually delivered. His alibi isn't as solid as he thinks it is."

"No," Jake said. "It's not. But I don't have enough for a search warrant. I want his DNA though. You think you can tail him without him seeing you?"

"You know I can," she said.

"He said he's working a drywall job in Navan Township. He smells like cigarettes. He'll throw one out a car window. Or he'll get careless some other way."

"I'll be on him," she said. "Give me a day or two."

"Head out there now," Jake said. "I didn't see what kind of car he drove."

Birdie nodded. She said goodbye to Mark and left him alone with Jake. Ramirez sat down in the seat Ian Burke had just vacated. He frowned.

"You're about to tell me something I'm not going to like, aren't you?"

Mark slapped an accordion file folder on the table. "I've got the phone dumps back from everyone you wanted me to run so far plus the cell tower records from the providers."

Ramirez slid the file folder across the table to him.

"Digital copies are inside on the thumb drive. Mary. Shane Edwards. Jeff and Sarah Hammer. Mary's is pretty clean. She went to work. She came home. There's a text to Shane at two o'clock that afternoon about his plans with Kevin that day. Nothing that raises any red flags. She was only going to and from work for the couple of days before she died. Her last phone call was to her mother at seven o'clock that evening. You already have the preliminaries on Shane's cell. His phone pinged the tower closest to Brad Edwards's house and stayed put until late the next morning. No surprises there. His alibi checks out. The texts he and Mary were exchanging in the weeks before she died weren't friendly, but he wasn't threatening her. You got a cell number for that chucklehead who just left?"

Jake wrote it down on a piece of paper.

"I can get cell tower info on this one. If you get a warrant for the actual phone, I can dump that one too."

"Mark, thanks for bringing all of this. But I know that look on your face. What's in this report that I'm not gonna like?"

Ramirez opened the file folder and turned to a tabbed section. Jake read the name at the top of the page.

Sarah Hammer.

There were three lines highlighted on the report from her cell phone provider.

"She moved around that night," Ramirez said. "Her phone pings the tower closest to her home address at four o'clock. But after eight, she's on the move."

Ramirez turned the page. It was a map of Worthington County with the cell towers marked.

"Eight twenty-eight p.m.," Ramirez said. "She leaves the house. Over the next twenty-seven minutes, she's hitting towers in a direct line to here." He traced a line on the map then drew a big circle on one tower. "She stops here at nine twenty-five p.m. This is the tower a quarter of a mile from Mary Rathburn's."

Jake's heart raced. "Mary's? Sarah Hammer was at Mary Rathburn's?"

"Near there, yeah. Jeff Hammer was already gone by then. We've got his phone pinging the tower near your Union Hall like he said. I've got him leaving Mary's at six p.m. He's at the hall after that for a couple of hours. She makes that last call to her mother an hour after he's on the move."

"She's alive when Jeff leaves. Witnesses and his credit card bill put him at the Union Hall after she makes the call to her mother," Jake said. He believed Jeff. But it was still a relief to see the data.

"She's alive when Jeff leaves," Ramirez agreed. "But this." He turned back to Sarah Hammer's data.

Jake drew in a breath. "She lied to me. Sarah Hammer claimed she never left the house that night."

"Not only did she leave the house, she was near Mary's house well after Jeff left. And within the window of time we think Mary was killed, Jake."

Jake pounded his fist against the table. "She knew. She lied to me about that. She told me she didn't know about Jeff and Mary until Jeff told her after he found Mary dead."

"Looks that way."

"Thanks for this," he said.

"What are you gonna do?"

"I'm gonna have another conversation with Sarah Hammer. Today."

Jake slammed the file folder shut. His phone buzzed with an incoming text. He looked at the caller ID then let it go to voicemail.

Bethany Roman. It was the third time she called.

Eighteen

Four hours later, when Jeff Hammer charged into Jake's office, Jake came perilously close to knocking out the man's front teeth.

"You don't talk to my wife again without me in the room, Jake."

Jake had already gotten the text from Birdie that she had Sarah Hammer set up in the interview room. Now, Jeff stood in the doorway, blocking Jake's exit into the hall. Jake held a file folder with Ramirez's report on both Jeff and Sarah's cell phones. "I know you didn't just try to tell me how to run this investigation. I know you're upset and this has been tough on you. So I'm going to give you one chance to get the hell out of my way, have a seat in the hall, and wait for me to come find you."

"She's a wreck. You have no idea what this thing has done to her. It's my fault. It's on me. One hundred percent. You need to leave Sarah out of this, Jake, I'm warning you."

Hammer took a step closer. Jake squared his shoulders. Part of him wanted Hammer to lay a hand on him. He would have welcomed the release of driving him into the wall.

"Step aside, Jeff. Do yourself a favor and stop talking to me. We can't have any conversation outside the presence of Landry and your union rep, preferably your lawyer."

"And I've told you I don't want any of that. I've got nothing to hide and neither does my wife."

"You sure about that?"

"Go to hell, Jake. I made a mistake with Mary. I know that. I regret it. I wasn't acting with my head. But that's not a crime. Don't you dare stand there and judge me. You're not a saint as far as that stuff goes."

Jeff sneered at him. Jake's blood heated. "You wanna tell me what you mean by that?"

There must have been something in Jake's expression. Hammer blanched. "Nothing, okay. Look, I'm sorry. I was just hoping you could have a little sympathy for my situation in light of ..."

"In light of what, Jeff?"

Jake took a step, forcing Jeff to retreat backwards into the hallway. As Jake feared, they had a small audience. People tried to look away or look casual, but the whole building knew what was up. There were no secrets here and plenty of rumors.

"Out of my way," Jake said. "Do what I told you, Jeff. Sit tight until I come find you. Then we'll talk."

For once, Jeff Hammer had the good sense God gave him. He didn't pursue Jake. Jake went down one flight of stairs and met Birdie in the hallway.

"You good?" she said. "I didn't realize Jeff followed her into the building."

"He's not helping himself or her."

"No. I'll go sit with him. Keep him from trying to interfere."

"I'd appreciate it. How's Sarah's demeanor?"

"She's bawling. I don't think she knows why she's here but she knows enough to be scared."

Meg came down the hall. "What do you need?"

"It's Hammer who needs something," he said. "He's upstairs making a nuisance of himself. Maybe see if you can take another crack at convincing him to hire a lawyer."

After Ramirez left this morning, Jake had just enough time to brief Landry on what Mrs. Hammer's cell phone records revealed. She'd been in damage control mode ever since.

"Him even being in the building is a problem. I can't have it looking like you're giving him special treatment," she said. "Jake, this thing is going to snowball. Zender's just waiting to ..."

Jake put a hand up. "Sheriff, with all due respect, Zender's your problem, not mine. He can't factor into what I'm doing."

"No," Landry said. "I didn't mean that he should. I'm sorry. You just ... do your job."

"I'm trying."

Jake opened the door to the interview room. As Birdie warned, Sarah Hammer had tears streaming down her face. From his peripheral vision, he watched Landry slip into the observation room next door.

Jake walked in, set the file folder on the table, and took the chair opposite Sarah.

"Thanks for coming in," he said. He slid a box of tissues closer to her.

"Is Jeff in trouble?" she asked.

"I can't talk about your husband with you. Not in that regard. We need to focus on you. This is a copy of your statement, Sarah. Why don't you look it over again? If there's anything you want to add to it, now's the time."

He took two sheets of paper out of the folder and handed them to her. She dabbed at her eyes with a tissue and read it over. Her hands were shaking. Two minutes passed and she put the papers down.

"I don't know what you want from me," she said.

"I want the truth. All of it. Good, bad, or ugly. Anything less is only going to hurt you."

"I didn't hurt Mary Rathburn."

Jake pulled the cell phone records out of the folder. "Sarah, it's good that you cooperated and gave me access to your phone data. But do you understand what that data can show?"

She looked at the report in front of her but her eyes glazed over.

Jake turned the pages of the report then showed her the sheet with the cell tower map.

"Sarah, when we spoke the last time, you told me you were home all evening the night Mary was killed. Do you remember telling me that?"

Her face went white except for giant purple blotches in her cheeks.

"But that wasn't true, was it?" Jake asked.

"I didn't hurt Mary."

Jake tapped the section of the map showing the tower nearest to Mary's house. "Sarah, your phone pinged here at nine twenty-five that evening. You didn't stay home that night, did you?"

Trembling, she shook her head no.

"Tell me what happened. All of it. From the beginning."

"I just went for a drive. That's all. Jeff said he was going to come home. Then he didn't. He said he was working overtime."

"But you knew he wasn't."

"I knew he wasn't," she hiccupped. "He didn't kill her either. I know you believe that, Jake."

"I'd like the two of you to start telling me the truth and not what you want me to believe."

"Yes. I knew he was lying. I was angry. Livid. I always know when he's lying. I can hear it in his voice."

"Did you have an argument that night?"

"No. But I was tired of his lies. So I went for a drive. Just a drive. I didn't see anyone. I didn't talk to anyone. I went for a drive."

"You went to Mary's house."

She nodded. "Yes. But not to see her. I didn't want to see her. I didn't want her to see me. I just wanted to see if Jeff's truck was there. That's it. So I drove down the street to look for him."

"Sarah, last time I asked you if you knew Jeff was in a relationship with Mary. You told me you didn't. But that wasn't true either, was it?"

She blew her nose into a tissue. "No. I mean, yes. I mean ... I didn't know for sure. So technically, what I said was true."

"You haven't done you or Jeff any good by twisting the truth like that. You understand what I'm saying? I've got a dead woman, Sarah. Mary was brutally murdered. So you need to tell me what you know about it. No more lies or half-truths or technical truths based on whatever definition you want to create. The truth. Now."

"I didn't know for sure. But I know Jeff. Mary Rathburn isn't the first woman he's had an affair with, okay? I know how he gets. Distant. Short. He finds reasons to not be home. And I heard him talking to her on the phone a few times. Just the way he laughs. His tone of voice. You all think you're getting away with something. But we know. Wives always know."

"So you went to spy on him?"

"I went to see if he was there. It was snowing hard that night. You remember that. Jeff's truck wasn't in her driveway and it wasn't parked on the street. I didn't see any tire tracks. He wasn't there."

"What time was this?"

"Like it says here. Close to nine thirty. It was dark. It was snowing so hard. I saw a light on in Mary's house, but not Jeff. I turned around in her driveway as quickly as I could. I didn't even want to do that, but her street dead-ends. I didn't realize that or I probably wouldn't even have gone down there."

"Nine twenty-five. That's when your phone pings this tower. Sarah, you need to tell me exactly what you saw at Mary's. What do you remember?"

"That's all of it. I swear. I was looking for signs Jeff had been there. When I didn't see his truck or any tracks that could have been from his truck, I turned around and got out of there. I felt stupid. Thought maybe I was paranoid or wrong about all of it. I turned around in her driveway and got out of there as fast as I could. I swear to God, that's the truth, Jake."

"Did you see anyone in the house?"

"No. There was a light on, but further in the house. It was dark near her front window. So maybe a hall light or kitchen light was on or something. I didn't see any people. I didn't see Mary."

"And you're sure you didn't see tire tracks in the snow other than your own?"

"No. Nothing. But the snow was coming down pretty hard by then. If somebody was there earlier, the tire tracks would have been filled in maybe. I didn't see anybody. I just left."

"And went where?" Jake already had a rough idea from the rest of her cell phone data. But he wanted to hear her say it. He wanted to give her a chance to tell the truth for once.

"I drove by the Union Hall. It was on my way home. I pulled into the parking lot and saw Jeff's truck parked near the front door. I was so angry by then. I mean, I was relieved I didn't find him at Mary's, but he was still lying to me. He told me he had to work over but he was at the hall, avoiding me. It felt almost as bad. Jake, I'm sorry. I'm so sorry. I should have told you all of this before. I just didn't think it mattered. I never saw Mary that night. I never saw Jeff until he came home late. I just didn't want to be involved in this."

"Did Jeff tell you to lie to me?"

"What? No. He doesn't know I went to Mary's house. He's going to be so angry with me when he finds out. But I didn't do anything wrong. He's the one who hurt me, Jake. He's a lousy husband. But he's not a murderer. Neither am I. You have to believe me. Are you going to arrest me? You can't!"

Jake closed the folder.

"Jake?"

"You can go home. But you need to stay available in case I have more questions."

"Are you going to tell Jeff about this?"

"I'll leave that to you."

"I'm sorry, Jake. I really am. And I'm sorry for what happened to Mary. I've just been so upset. I wasn't thinking straight. I didn't think any of this would matter because I know I didn't have anything to do with what happened to her."

She didn't see it. She still didn't see it. Sarah Hammer might be the closest thing Jake had to an eyewitness. There was a good chance that Sarah was at Mary's house at the same time as her killer was. Was she lying still?

"Go home, Sarah," he said. "But like I said, stay available."

"Of course. Gosh. Of course. I really am sorry."

Jake couldn't take any more of her tears. He left Sarah in the interview room and started walking back to his office, hoping he didn't run into Jeff Hammer again. It was past five. He hadn't eaten all day.

Landry caught up with him. From the expression on her face, he knew she'd heard everything Sarah Hammer had to say.

"Do you think she's still lying?"

Jake tossed the file folder on his desk. "No. I don't. But she better hope none of her DNA shows up in my crime scene."

Jake grabbed his jacket. He shut the office door and started walking toward the exit and to the parking lot. Landry kept up with him.

"I need to get out of here for a while," he said. "Get a shower. Throw some food down my head."

He opened the door to the parking lot. Landry looked outside before he did. Her face fell. “I’ll give you a minute,” she said. “And I trust you’ll do the right thing.”

Puzzled, Jake was about to ask her what she meant. Then she stepped aside. Bethany Roman was leaning against the driver’s side door of his car.

NINETEEN

Jake hit the unlock button on his key fob. Bethany didn't move.

"I don't have time for this," he said. "If you have questions, you can submit them through the sheriff's media liaison like everyone else."

"Jake, can we please talk?"

"Here? Like this? You ambush me in the parking lot?"

He lowered his voice at the end. The lot was already filling fast as day shift started punching out. There were plenty of people milling around in the public lot across the street. A few of the cops coming out of the building spotted Jake and immediately looked away, which made them even more conspicuous somehow. Jake knew within five minutes, the whole building would know he was talking with "that reporter."

"You haven't left me with much choice. I've been trying to call you for days. I thought we had a good time. Or are you just one of *those* guys?"

"Don't."

"Don't what?"

"Don't stand there and pretend this is that. You knew what you were doing. I didn't."

Bethany laughed. "You think I took advantage of you? That's the story you're going with?"

"You knew I thought you were a cop. I told you things based on that assumption. Things that you turned around and reported."

"You're a grown-up, Jake. And no. I didn't know you thought I was a cop. Not really."

"You didn't tell me you were a reporter. And not just any reporter. They've assigned you to the crime beat. You knew exactly who I was. You want to stand there and tell me you weren't trying to leverage that? That it didn't occur to you when I invited you into my house it was an opportunity for you to get some kind of scoop?"

"Exactly what are you accusing me of?" she asked. Bethany pushed herself off Jake's car and took a step closer to him.

"What you did was unethical," he said. "And if you thought it was some shortcut to a story, then ..."

"Then what?" she said, scowling. He wouldn't let her bait him.

"Are you going to move? Are you going to let me get by you so I can leave?"

"Jake, just give me five minutes. You think the worst of me. That doesn't make me feel good. I didn't have some grand plan to seduce you that night. The things I said to you were genuine. I wasn't trying to work you. I wasn't angling for some in or leverage."

"What was it you said on camera?" Jake said. "Your inside source told you about friction between Sheriff Landry and Ed Zender? That Ed's incompetent? You got that from me, Bethany. Something I told you in confidence."

"You didn't tell me it was in confidence."

"That's the hill you're dying on?"

"Jake ... please."

"We're done," he said.

"Mary Rathburn's murder is news. I have the right to ask questions."

"Not of me, you don't. You call Landry's media liaison like everyone else."

"This is how you're going to play it? I know what you're doing. You've blackballed me with Landry. Nobody will talk to me. Do you want that to be the story? I'm just trying to do my job. You take me back to your place and now not a single cop in this town will talk to me. I know where that's coming from."

"I've never told anyone not to talk to you," Jake said. "I don't respond well to threats of blackmail. You say whatever you want to whomever you want."

She moved. Jake opened his car door and tossed his backpack inside. Bethany grabbed his other arm. He went rigid.

"Please don't be like this. I like you, Jake. What happened the other night wasn't me trying to play you. I swear."

He eyed her. Her expression withered. "Okay. Okay," she said. "I'll admit it. When I sat down next to you at the bar that night, I knew who and what you are to this case. So yes. I was hoping you'd at least give me a quote. But everything else was real. I wouldn't have gone home with you just to try to get a story. And I was going to tell you. It just ... it didn't come up."

"Didn't come up," he repeated. "You knew I thought you were a cop."

She took a breath as if she were about to launch into a rant. Then, she dropped her shoulders in resignation. "Okay. Yes. I knew you thought I was a cop. But I didn't lie to you. I didn't pretend to be anything I wasn't. I just ... I didn't correct your assumption. That was wrong. I'm sorry."

"You knew I told you things based on that assumption."

"All right. Yes."

"See you around, Bethany."

"You have to stop," she said. "Call off your dogs."

"My dogs?"

"Tell the people in that building that I'm not their enemy. I'm not yours either. You're making it so I can't do my job, Jake. And I need this job."

"You think I'm the reason you're not getting cooperation inside that building? Bethany, let me give you some career advice. If you want a good working relationship with the sheriff's department, you have to earn it. You have to build trust. There are no shortcuts. Anybody who doesn't learn that doesn't last very long around here."

"And you'd like that, wouldn't you? Get me fired. Get me out of your way. Use me for what you want, then toss me aside."

Jake clenched his jaw. He took a breath. "You know that's not what happened. As for the rest of it, I have no comment. You can coordinate your interview requests through the media liaison."

He slipped into the driver's seat and slammed the door shut. Bethany took a step back, allowing him to back out and drive away.

"I don't want to talk about it."

In fairness, Gemma had yet to ask Jake a single question. But she stood in the kitchen, giving him that knowing, big-sisterly glare. He knew it meant somebody had called her the second they saw Jake talking to Bethany Roman in that damn parking lot.

He went to the sink and washed his hands. Grandpa Max stood at the stove, stirring a pot of venison stew. Ryan and Aiden stayed in the living room, sensing the tension among the adults.

"I didn't ask," Gemma finally said. "Though I will say your taste in women continues to suck."

"This isn't about my taste," he said. "And what do you mean, women? The last disastrous date I went on, you pushed me into."

"I thought you didn't want to talk about it?" she said.

"I don't."

"Fine. Then just listen. That woman is trouble. I've done some asking around."

"To whom?" Jake said. "And I don't need you poking around. It'll just make things worse."

"Oh, I don't think I could make things worse. But she can."

"Let the man be," Grandpa said. "Where he sticks his ..."

"Grandpa!" Gemma and Jake shouted it together. Aiden and Ryan were still within earshot.

Grandpa grumbled. "How are those two ever going to learn anything if you keep 'em in bubble wrap their whole lives?"

"Asking you to be sensitive about how you talk about things isn't bubble wrap, Gramps. I may not like the woman, but you don't have to speak with disrespect."

"I wasn't. I was about to agree with you if you'd have let me finish."

"Really? Then, by all means, agree with me."

Grandpa turned to Jake. "Your sister's right. This woman sounds like trouble. She ruffled some feathers down at the lodge the other day asking questions about you. Not very nice ones either."

"She what?"

"Things that are none of her damn business, that's what," Grandpa continued. "I don't like her."

"Noted," Jake said. "Now, can we drop the subject?"

"Have you talked to Connie Rathburn this week?" Gemma said as she put the rolls on the table. "She's beside herself. She hasn't seen her grandson since the funeral. It's been almost two weeks. No calls. Nothing. Mary's ex has frozen her out."

Jake put the spoons on the table, then took his seat. "I'm sorry about that."

"Is there anything you can do about it? Talk to Shane or something?" Gemma asked.

"He's the boy's father, isn't he?" Grandpa said. "Which isn't to say he's not also a dirtbag. But does Connie even have a legal leg to stand on for visitation?"

"Probably not," Jake said. "Not unless she could prove he was unfit."

"I've seen him at school," Aiden said, walking in from the living room.

"Who?" Gemma asked.

"Kevin Rathburn. He rides the bus now. His grandma used to pick him up and wait in the hallway. My class walks the younger kids out to the parking lot and helps them line up for when the buses come. I'm Kevin's class's line leader. He cries a lot."

Worry lines creased Gemma's face. "I'm sure he does. That poor kid. Keep an eye out for him, okay, Aiden? Let him know you're his friend if he needs one."

"He's four," Aiden said. "I'm almost eight."

"Do it anyway," Gemma said.

Grandpa came over carrying the big stew pot. He set it down on one end of the table and started filling bowls. Gemma took them and passed them down.

Ryan took his seat. Grandpa poured half a bowl for him. He had to make weight this weekend for sectionals.

"How many pounds are you off?" Jake asked.

"Just three," Ryan said. Jake took a closer look and knew his nephew was fibbing. He was probably closer to six pounds over. Easy to overcome if he was careful.

"Sorry I've been AWOL at practice this week. I'll be there Thursday."

"It's okay," Ryan said. "Coach Purcell and I have things under control. But you'll be there for the tournament, won't you?"

"As long as nothing else comes up," he said. Stanley would host the sectional tourney this weekend. It would be a good distraction for Jake. As long as he made weight, Ryan should have an easy time making it on to Districts the following week. That's when things would start to get hard.

The boys ate their stew in relative silence. But Jake could tell there was still something on Gemma's mind. Something she was holding back until her sons were out of earshot and plugged in to their screens. It happened soon enough.

After Grandpa finished his second helping of stew, he went out to the living room to hassle the boys. Jake helped Gemma clear the plates and load the dishwasher.

"You want to tell me what's on your mind or should I guess?" Jake finally said.

"Nothing that isn't always there," she said, wiping a dish. She turned to him. "You sure you're okay?"

"Yes. Why?"

"Because I know how you get. Broody. Withdrawn. And I have a feeling tonight was the first decent meal you've eaten since I made you breakfast the other morning."

She reached out and poked Jake in the stomach. "You're losing weight, little brother. You're letting this case eat you from the inside out. You're making bad decisions."

"What are you talking about?"

"Bethany Roman? Come on, Jake. That wasn't like you. And bringing her here?" she whispered the last part, looking out into the living room to see where their grandfather was.

"I don't want to talk about it. And I'm handling it."

"You sure about that?"

"I'm done talking about this. Especially with my sister."

She hit him with a towel. "Fine. But I'm dropping off a lasagna for you tomorrow. I expect you to eat it. And I expect you to get at least six hours of sleep tonight."

Rolling his eyes, Jake gave his sister a salute. Then he went to join the boys in the other room. Ryan was busy watching the tape of his last match with Blake McManus from St. Iz. Jake sat down to go over it with him.

It was good, the distraction. Two hours went by before he knew it. Grandpa started snoring from his recliner. Gemma finally came out after cleaning Grandpa's entire kitchen. Had the old man been awake, he would have tried to stop her, claiming he didn't need the help.

When she rounded her sons up to leave, she came to Jake and gave him a hug.

"I love you," she said.

"I love you too. And thank you. Pain in my ass though you are. I appreciate you."

"You better," she said, kissing his cheek.

"Make sure he winds up in his actual bed," Gemma said, pointing to Grandpa. He didn't wake up when she kissed the top of his head. "His sciatica flares up when he sleeps too long in that chair."

"I'll take care of it," Jake said. It was late. "I'll probably stay here tonight anyway so I can plow his driveway when this snow stops. We're supposed to get two inches overnight. Be careful driving home."

He said goodbye to his nephews. Later, Grandpa only protested a little as Jake helped him up to his own bed. Jake took the guest room across the hall. It used to be his father's room. His baseball trophies were still on the shelves. Jake used to take them down when he was a kid. There was a picture of his mother and father in a frame on the shelf. Their wedding day. They'd eloped. His mother wore a powder-blue suit and had gardenias in her hair. His father looked handsome and scared in a black jacket and corduroy pants.

Just before Jake nodded off, his cell phone buzzed. He picked it up. It was a text from Mark Ramirez.

"Meet you at eight," the text read. "Will have DNA back from crime scene."

Jake let out a breath. Finally. He just hoped it would be the thing to wrap up Mary's case for good.

Twenty

"You didn't have to come all the way down here," Jake said, sipping a piping-hot cup of crappy coffee. Mark Ramirez was already in the war room. Jake got a late start this morning. More snow fell than predicted and Grandpa Max's plow took a dive halfway down the driveway. Jake cleared the rest of it with an ancient snow blower. He got to work sweaty and tired.

"I don't mind," Ramirez said. "I'm on my way over to McArthur. Double homicide."

"Never a dull moment." Jake offered Ramirez his own cup of crappy coffee, then the two men sat at the table. Ramirez had a red file folder in one hand.

"Thumb drive's inside," Ramirez said. Still holding his coffee in one hand, Jake flipped the file open with the other.

"You wanna just give me the rundown?"

The door opened. Sheriff Landry walked in with a drink carrier and four more Styrofoam cups of coffee with Tessa's Diner logo stamped on the sides. She put a cup in front of Jake.

"Tessa and Spiros gave me an earful about how you never stop by anymore."

"Thanks for this," he said. "Mark's got the DNA back on Mary's crime scene. We're just about to go over the highlights."

"Perfect," Landry said. She took a coffee and sat next to Jake.

"We identified three distinct DNA profiles at the scene and on the body. One belonged to her kid. Came from hair in the bathtub. Another matched to Jeff Hammer. Semen in the victim."

Landry winced. "He admitted to that."

"Yes," Jake said.

Ramirez took the file and flipped to a page in the report that was highlighted in blue. "Looking at the blood droplets found in the kitchen, on the broken wine bottle, concentrated in the living room, and the skin tissue found under Mary's nails, they match. They came from the same person. Not Hammer. His DNA was found in Mary and then some on one of her sheets."

"Consistent with Hammer's story," Jake said. "He claims they were intimate in the bedroom late that afternoon."

"Makes sense," Ramirez said. "And he's alibied?"

"It's solid," Jake answered. "Witnesses saw him at the Union Hall later that evening. His wife saw his car there. We know Mary called her mother well after Hammer had already left and was seen at the hall."

"Sounds like he's clean, then. At least for this murder. That's got to be a relief in its own way."

"Nothing about Jeff Hammer's conduct is a relief," Landry said.

"Right." Ramirez looked uncomfortable. "Sure. Well, I don't know if you consider this good or bad news, but we're also able to exclude Shane Edwards from any of the samples taken at the crime scene."

"He's telling the truth?" Landry asked.

Jake looked at the reports. The columns of numbers and data points swam in front of his eyes. "Insofar as he wasn't there the night Mary died," Jake said.

"None of the other samples you sent turned up at the house," Ramirez said. "Sarah Hammer. Edwards. We didn't find any of their DNA on scene."

"What about what you did find?" Jake asked.

"As I said, DNA from under Mary's nails, on the wine bottle, from the blood droplets in the kitchen and living room ... all came from the same individual. Profile shows a male, Caucasian, eastern-European descent."

"CODIS?" Jake asked.

Ramirez shook his head. "Doesn't match any of the profiles in the database. So if he's got a felony criminal record, it's nothing that would have triggered him submitting a sample. I sent our data off to a volunteer group we work with affiliated with Tree of Life."

"The ancestry website?" Landry asked.

"Yes. Sometimes we get lucky and somebody's brother or aunt or close relative has submitted a sample to trace their genealogy. If anything pops up, I'll let you know. But for now ..."

"We've got a ghost," Jake said.

"You have any other viable suspects?" Ramirez asked.

"One," Jake said. "Possibly. Guy by the name of Ian Burke. Friend of Mary's ex. Birdie's got him on record, threatening Mary a few days before she was killed. So far, he's been uncooperative. Wouldn't submit a sample when I interviewed him. And I don't have enough for a warrant. His alibi checks out so far."

"Well, if you can get his DNA by some other means, let me know. I'll do what I can to fast track it through the lab."

"Deputy Wayne's tailing him. She'll get what we need."

"By the book, Jake," Landry said. "Does Deputy Wayne know that?"

"Absolutely."

"Good. And good work on this, Mark," she said. "I appreciate your people bringing this case to the front of the line."

"You bet," he said. "Anything I can do. I just wish I had more for you. I wish I had a smoking gun."

"All right," Landry said, rising. "I'll leave you to do your work, Jake. Check in with me later today."

She excused herself. Ramirez did the same a few seconds later, leaving the DNA report with him. Jake stared at the rows of numbers and realized he was nowhere.

He drank the last of Tessa Papatonis's coffee. It was then he noticed something she'd written on the side of it with a black marker.

"First Tuesday of the Month."

He checked the clock on the wall. It was just before nine. The first Tuesday of the month. Tessa's note was an invitation and a reminder. He suspected she'd been put up to writing it.

Jake walked across the hall, tossed the red folder on his desk, and headed out of the building.

Twenty-One

On the first Tuesday of every month, Bill Nutter, Virgil Adamski, and Chuck Thompson held court in the back room of Papa's Diner for their monthly meeting of the Wise Men. On this particular Tuesday, for whatever reason, Tessa wanted Jake to be there. When he walked into the diner, she was behind the counter drying glassware with a checkered red and white towel. Her smile warmed him. She let out a stream of words in Greek he couldn't follow, but got the general gist.

She was glad to see him. She gave him crap for not coming into the diner more often.

"It's a sorry bunch back there," she said, switching to English.

"You gonna tell me why they put you up to this?" Jake asked, holding up his empty Styrofoam mug with Tessa's note scrawled on the side.

She gave him a knowing look, but not an answer. Jake heard raucous laughter. Tessa poured him a fresh cup of coffee, then gestured for him to head into the back room. Virgil Adamski was regaling the others with some story. He looked good. Still tan from his extended stay in Florida. The three men fell silent as they laid eyes on Jake.

Bill got up first and pulled out the chair next to him, patting the seat.

"What are you bunch of ghouls up to back here?" Jake asked.

"You're a sight for sore eyes," Virgil said. "We get tired of seeing people at funerals. Good to have you here in the light of day."

"It's a workday," Jake said. He put his empty foam mug on the table, turning it so the others could see Tessa's note. "You wanna tell me why I've been summoned?"

"It's nothing as dramatic as all that," Chuck said.

"We're just bored," Virgil said. "And tired of hearing bits and pieces on the news. Tessa didn't have to go through all this trouble."

"Say what you want to say," Jake asked.

"Where are you on this case, Jake?" Bill said.

"Who's asking? You three?"

Bill, Virgil, and Chuck exchanged a look. It was an answer.

"Ah," Jake said. "So you've been appointed."

"Not appointed," Virgil said. "But everybody knows we still keep in touch with you."

"Everybody. You mean every ex-cop in the county who thinks they can run this investigation better than I can?"

"Nobody's saying that," Chuck said. "Hell, they know each and every one of us would knock their teeth out if they did. It's more ..."

"They're worried about you," Tessa said. Jake hadn't even heard her walk back into the room. "I'm worried about you. You're too skinny." She reached for Jake and pulled one of his arms up. Then she tousled his hair, earning her laughter from the men. She waved them off and went back into the kitchen.

"We just wanted to check in," Chuck said. "That's all. See if you need anything. A sounding board. Moral support. A beer after work."

Jake exhaled. "I appreciate that. But I don't need a dad, much less three of them."

"This isn't just any old murder case," Virgil said. "We've all been there. We know this is the kind that'll stick with you. That's all we're saying."

"And we all heard what people were saying at that poor kid's funeral," Bill said. "Every well-meaning asshole in town telling you how they're counting on you."

"What else did you hear at the funeral?" Jake asked. The next exchange of looks told him volumes. They knew about Bethany Roman. *Everyone* knew about Bethany Roman.

"You should come out to the lake," Virgil said. "I put up a shanty. Ice fishing's been good this week. It can do wonders for your head, just sitting out there in the cold and the quiet."

"What cold," Bill said. "Guy's got a heated shanty. He rolled a damn Barcalounger onto the ice. He's got Wi-Fi out there and a TV."

Jake smiled. It sounded just like something Virgil would do. Damn if Tessa wasn't right. It did him good to spend a little time with these old farts. They'd seen everything. Knew everyone. But they were the worst busybodies in town. There was something else looming over the conversation. An empty chair on the other side of the table. Jake realized he couldn't let it rest.

"I've been meaning to talk to you guys about something," he said. The group fell silent again.

"Have you heard from him?" Jake gestured to the empty chair. Frank Borowski's seat. It wasn't lost on Jake that in the years Frank went on the lam, the rest of the Wise Men refused to sit in that chair and Tessa kept putting a place setting in front of it.

"No, Jake," Chuck said. "We haven't heard from him."

"He called me," Jake said.

None of them seemed surprised. It didn't mean they were lying.

"What'd he say?" Virgil asked.

"Pretty much the same thing you three have been saying. Cautioned me that this case could leave a mark."

"How'd he sound?" Bill asked.

"Like Frank."

"You gonna call it in?" Chuck asked.

"I already did. You know I had no choice. He knows I had no choice. But Frank's too smart to do anything that'll make it easy to find him."

"That's tough, kid," Bill said. "But you did the right thing. You always do the right thing, don't you?"

Jake wouldn't answer. Or couldn't. The right thing. Sometimes it got harder to know what that was.

He finished his coffee in silence.

"There's a reason that blue line is thin, Jake," Virgil said.

Jake put a hand up in a stopping gesture. He wasn't in the mood for a lecture in morality, if that's what Virgil was trying to do.

"Thanks for the coffee," he said. "But I'm still on duty."

"Thanks for humoring a bunch of old men," Chuck said. "Just don't forget we've got your back."

"Are you anywhere?" Bill asked.

"The truth?"

"Always," Bill answered.

"No," Jake said. "I'm nowhere. This thing is going to take me being more lucky than smart and that's what's killing me."

Virgil smiled. "They're all like that. We just don't like to admit it."

Jake rose from the table. It was starting to snow again. He promised the Wise Men that he'd stay in touch. That he'd try to come out to Echo Lake and check out Virgil's tricked-out shanty. Then he said his goodbyes.

Jake got halfway down the sidewalk to his car when Birdie pulled up in a patrol car. She screeched to a halt, parking at an odd angle.

Jake froze. She burst out of the driver's side, breathless.

"What is it?" he asked, bracing for impact.

Birdie had a huge smile on her face. She held up a gallon-sized freezer bag. It had garbage inside of it. A crushed plastic drink container and straw, a wadded-up hamburger wrapper from a fast-food joint.

"I brought you a present," she said, beaming. "Get in. We can pick your car up later."

"You brought me garbage?"

He knew better than to argue with Birdie when she was on a tear. He climbed into the passenger seat of her patrol car. She practically dove back behind the wheel and peeled away from the curb.

Twenty-Two

"I couldn't believe it," Birdie said, breathless. She took a sharp turn and headed north out of town. "He just threw it out of his car window like the douchenozzle he is."

"I'm sorry," Jake said. "What douchenozzle are we talking about?" He braced himself against the passenger side window as Birdie took the next turn while barely touching the brake.

"Burke!" she shouted. Keeping one hand on the wheel, she held up the bag of discarded fast-food wrappers and drink.

"You sure this is from him?"

"I followed him. He was out in Navan Township on a drywall job. You know that older neighborhood off of Melbourne Road? Proud Acres or whatever it's called. The one with the painted tree stump with the faded letters somebody flipped over so it looks like it says Ser Carp?"

"Yeah."

"I got out there early. Parked in the driveway across the street with the homeowner's permission. Sweet old lady. She told me she had her eye on the people coming and going over there because she's convinced they're trying to steal cars. She's a nutbag really. But like I said, sweet. Anyway, Burke shows up. Works for an hour and a half. He walked in with his fast-food breakfast, then walks out carrying the bag. Drives off. I followed him. Right when he gets to the entrance to the neighborhood, the pig throws his garbage right out the window. It landed next to the overturned tree stump. I took pictures of everything."

"You're sure it was his? He drank from the cup?"

"He was the only one there. And like I said. I watched him walk in with the same bag. It's his. There's got to be saliva on some of this."

Jake's pulse skipped. "Ramirez was here this morning. DNA came back. Shane, the Hammers are cleared."

"And now we've got a potential sample to submit. Jake, this could be it. This could be the break we need."

"That son of a bitch."

"Exactly."

"We've got to get a hold of Ramirez. See if we can catch him. He said he was on his way to a job in McArthur."

"I texted him already," Birdie said. "He's meeting us at the gas station near Exit 42."

She stepped on the accelerator. The roads were slick, but the crews had already been out once with the salt trucks.

"This is good work," he said. "You sure Burke didn't see you?"

"He didn't. He had his radio blaring pretty loud. I don't even think he knew there was a car behind him. I kept my distance. I know how to tail somebody without them knowing it."

"I suppose it doesn't matter anyway. He gave up his right to privacy the second he threw this crap out the window."

Up ahead, Jake saw the giant sign for the Exit 42 gas station. Birdie turned in at her usual breakneck speed. Ramirez's car was parked in the first spot, still running. Birdie pulled in alongside him.

Breathless, she got out of the car before Jake, holding Ian Burke's garbage in the air like a trophy. Jake supposed it was.

She relayed her story to Ramirez. His eyes widened.

"Impressive," he said. He reached into his car and took out an evidence bag. He handed Birdie a clipboard with his chain of custody form and gave her a property receipt.

"How fast can you get this back?" Jake asked.

"I'll tell the lab to clear the decks and get this processed. I can't promise, but five days, maybe?"

"I appreciate it," Jake said. "I owe you one."

"Nah. You owe me about twelve. But I'm not counting. This is a murdered cop, Jake. One of our own. I'm glad to do it. The AG said this takes priority and he means it."

Ramirez took the evidence and climbed back into his car. For the first time in days, Jake felt like they might actually have a chance of breaking this case.

"It's him, Jake," Birdie said as she climbed back behind the wheel. "From the second that scumbag walked into the station, I've just had a feeling. Haven't you?"

Jake looked out the window. It was starting to snow again.

He didn't want to answer. He didn't want to jinx it. Mary Rathburn's last message to him felt seared into his retina.

White male, five ten or eleven …

It was vague. Broad. It fit Ian Burke's description perfectly. *But why,* Jake thought? Why kill Mary in such a brutal fashion when Shane Edwards was the one who stood to gain from her death?

And yet, everything Ian Burke had done so far was the act of a guilty man.

Twenty-Three

The last practice before Stanley High School hosted the sectional championship and the team looked good. Coach Purcell planned a light workout, mostly cardio. Jake ran takedown drills, escapes and pinning combos. Just enough to sweat off the last few pounds.

Jake worked one-on-one with Ryan. He was ready. Jake could feel it. He knew the best thing he could do was help him stay out of his head. He took him aside. "How are you feeling?"

Winded, Ryan rested his hands on his knees. "Good, Uncle Jake."

"You and Trav are the captains. The leaders. The younger members of the team look up to the two of you. They'll be nervous tonight and Saturday. Talk to them. Warm up with them. You know how you felt *your* first sectional."

Ryan nodded. "We've got this. I know it."

"I know it too."

"Let's go again," Ryan said. Sweat poured down his face. He was lean. Strong. Just shy of his eighteenth birthday.

Jake's shoulder hurt. His knees ached. But adrenaline coursed through him. He hadn't been able to get a full-on workout like this with the team since before Mary's murder.

There were a million things on his mind. Had he missed something? Would the DNA match truly be the smoking gun he needed? Would Birdie's testimony hold up if there was a match? He trusted her, but he'd never seen her on the witness stand before.

"Shoot!" Coach Purcell shouted from the corner of the gym. Murphy, the 120-pounder, looked shaky on his feet. He had shoulder surgery over the summer and wasn't all the way back yet. But the kid had heart and grit. It would make all the difference.

Jake snaked his hand around Ryan's right wrist. Ryan twisted out and popped Jake on his forehead. Ryan hit a perfect blast double, putting Jake on his back.

"Two!" the team erupted.

Jake smiled. "Jordan Burroughs would be proud of that one."

His heart thundered. The air in the gym was thick and smelled like sweat. It was horrible and wonderful all at once.

Coach Purcell blew his whistle.

"Good job. Get a shower. Get a good night's sleep!"

Ryan got to his feet before Jake did. He reached down and gave his uncle a hand getting up. Jake must have made a noise when he stood. It earned him some ribbing from the boys. He was the old man now.

Jake had words of encouragement for each member of the team as they filed past him, heading for the locker room.

"He's a beast," Brian Purcell said to him after the last kid went by. "Ryan's got a real shot. He's peaking at just the right time."

"Don't jinx it," Jake said. "This weekend should be a cakewalk for him. It's Districts that will be the real test."

"Travis looks good, too. If the brackets break his way, he's gonna end up on the podium at states too."

Travis had gone up a weight class this year. He filled out. Gone was the gawky little boy Jake had first met a couple of years ago. He was becoming a man right in front of Jake's eyes. He got the same sad twinge every time he looked at him. Travis looked so much like his dad. It killed Jake, knowing Ben Wayne would never get to see his son wrestle again.

"See you this weekend," Jake said.

"Thanks for everything," Purcell said. "I hope I'm not gonna lose you after this year when Ryan graduates."

Jake looked out as the last member of the team walked into the locker room. They were young. Ryan was one of only two seniors on Varsity this year. He thought of the rest of them as his kids, too. "Nah," he said. "I think I might stick around to see how the rest of 'em turn out."

Purcell slapped him on the back. "Good. I'm counting on you."

Counting on you ... Mary's face swam in front of him. Smiling. Laughing. Then the vision changed, becoming the gruesome way he'd last seen her as she lay dead on her hallway floor.

Jake grabbed his gym bag and headed out into the parking lot. He was thinking about Ben. About Birdie and what she'd done this week. And about Mary. One of their last conversations had been about her son, Kevin. At four, he was too young for wrestling, but she'd asked Jake about when he could start. She wanted to have something. A coach if not a dad. A mentor.

Jake walked across the parking lot. There was something going on at the elementary school across the way. Little kids started streaming out of the side.

Jake put his bag in his truck. He was about to climb into the cab when he heard someone shout.

"You whine like that again, I'll give you something to cry about!"

He recognized the voice. Shane Edwards. He was standing about twenty yards away, leaning down. Jake closed the cab and stepped around his truck so he could get a better look.

Shane had Kevin by the shoulder. He shook him. Hard. Tears streamed down Kevin's face. Jake scanned the parking lot. Several other parents were getting into their vehicles with their kids but nobody was close to Shane and Kevin. Shane was parked closer to the high school than the elementary school.

"I wanna go!" Kevin cried. "I wanna see Grandma. She said she was coming."

"Knock it off," Shane yelled. "Get in the car. She's not coming."

Kevin stomped his foot. He tried to shrug off his father's grip. Shane straightened and that's when Jake saw him sway on his feet. He took a stagger step backwards.

"You gotta be kidding me," Jake said. He stepped forward.

"Everything okay?" Jake asked.

Shane whipped around. He had to grip the hood of his car to keep from falling over.

"How are you doing there, Kevin? Don't know if you remember me. I'm Jake."

Tears streamed down Kevin's face.

"Fuck off," Shane said. "Mind your own business."

Jake was close enough to smell the alcohol on Shane Edwards's breath. He had his keys out. He was about to climb behind the wheel.

"Why don't you let me drive you home?" Jake said.

"Why don't you stick it up your ass?"

"Look," Jake said. He stepped around Shane's car. "You're not in any shape to drive. You know I can't let you get behind the wheel."

"Can't let me? I told you to mind your own damn business. I'll report you for harassment."

"Edwards, give me your keys."

Shane held up both middle fingers.

"Nice," Jake said. "We can do this the hard way or the easy way. But I'm not letting you drive your boy in the state you're in."

"Oh yeah?" Shane said. "How you gonna stop me?"

"You serious, man?"

"Yeah," Shane said. "You've been a pain in my ass for weeks."

"Daddy!" Kevin shouted. "I wanna go home. I wanna see Grandma!"

"That's a good idea," Jake said. "Connie lives about five minutes away. Why don't you let her come pick up Kevin and I'll make sure you get home safe."

"The hell I will."

Shane turned his back on Jake. He opened his driver's side door. "Get in the car, kid," he said. "Now!"

"Edwards, don't," Jake said.

Jake held out a hand to Kevin. The boy stepped forward, ready to take it. Shane Edwards whirled around and charged Jake, knocking Kevin backward. The little boy slipped and landed hard on his rear end. It seemed to happen in slow motion. But Shane cocked his right fist and took a swing.

It never landed. Jake dropped low and drove his shoulder into Shane's chest, shoving him back hard against the car. Jake got an arm up and pinned Shane against the car door.

"You better check yourself," Jake said through gritted teeth. "I'm doing you a favor and you're too stupid to even realize it."

Shane Edwards's eyes went black. He sputtered, still trying to break Jake's hold. Shane was taller than Jake and outweighed him by at least twenty pounds. But even on a good day and with a normal blood alcohol level, Jake knew he'd never be able to land a punch on him he knew was coming.

Shane seemed to know it, too. He reared back and spit right in Jake's face.

Red rage clouded Jake's vision. He shoved Shane even harder against the car, his arm up under his chin. He knew Shane would have trouble breathing. He lifted him off his feet like that. Shane kicked out but his feet caught nothing but air.

Jake wanted to kill him. He envisioned it in his mind's eye. Shane was lying on the ground covered in his own blood. Face down. Then it was Mary he saw. She was screaming. She was calling Jake's name.

"Jake! Uncle Jake!"

Suddenly, there were hands on him, pulling him backward. Jake's instinct was to swing. To defend himself. He looked to his left and saw his nephew, Ryan. Ryan had a hold of his arm. Travis and Chris Murphy held his right. They pulled him off Shane Edwards. Edwards slumped to his knees on the side of his car.

Jake reached up and wiped the spit off his cheek.

Coach Purcell ran up. He looked from Jake to Shane Edwards. Ashley Polhemus got to Kevin Edwards. She hoisted the little boy up and put him on her shoulders. Kevin instantly smiled.

"You okay, Uncle Jake?" Ryan asked, concern filling his nephew's eyes.

"Yeah," Jake said. He looked around. A few of the other elementary parents had come closer. One of them went to Kevin perched on Ashley's shoulders. Jake recognized her as Ashley's aunt.

"Hey, Kevin," she said. "Why don't you ride home with us? We were going to stop for shakes at Blizzard Cafe."

Jake glared at Shane Edwards. He'd recovered enough to get to his feet.

"Come on, Shane." Another dad stepped forward. "How about you let me drive you home?"

Shane Edwards finally had the good sense God gave him. He let Ashley and her aunt leave with Kevin. He put his keys in his pocket. Then he walked off with the other dad.

"You okay?" Ryan asked Jake again.

"Yeah," Jake said. "I'm good. Let's go home."

Twenty-Four

Jake stood in front of Shane Edwards's picture on the war room whiteboard. He held a red dry erase marker in his hand. His right hand twitched as he thought about how good it would have felt to have driven it straight into Edwards's nose, breaking it. Watching the blood flow. Seeing him double over from the blinding pain.

But then, in addition to losing his mother, Kevin Edwards would have had a formative memory of his father having the crap kicked out of him ten feet away. Jake shook out his fist and drew a circle around Shane's face then put a line through it.

"You okay?"

Birdie came in behind him.

"I wish people would stop asking me that."

"Fair enough. Only I'm not people."

Jake turned to her. Birdie stood in a ready stance as she tended to do. Hands on her hips, legs slightly apart. She'd proven how well she could handle herself in a fight if it ever came to it.

Jake turned back to the board. He put another red line through Jeff Hammer's face. Another through Sarah's. At the bottom of the board was Sophia Osterman's name, the victim he'd questioned in the Muskingum County home invasion. Jake put a red line through it as well.

"Ramirez called this morning," he said. "Not unexpected, the MOs didn't quite line up. But the DNA in the Osterman case doesn't match ours either. They caught the guy who attacked her. Detective Harry was way luckier than smart. Assailant tried to break into a house a few blocks over from Sophia Osterman's and go after another young woman. Only this one had pepper spray on her night table. She managed to get to it and gave him a face full of it. She ran next door and got help from her neighbor who happens to be a state trooper. He apprehended the guy within minutes."

"It doesn't help us, but that's good news. Good for her," Birdie said. She took a seat at the table and studied the board along with Jake. There was one suspect remaining without a red line through his face.

Ian Burke.

"What's next?" Birdie asked.

Jake turned to her. "You tell me."

He was testing her. She knew it.

"If the DNA comes back, that could be the ballgame."

"Could be," he repeated. "Unless some dazzling defense lawyer manages to either get it all thrown out ..."

"Unlikely," she said.

"Or a jury zones out and ignores it."

"He's on record threatening to hurt Mary," she said.

"With you," he said. "You're a cop. Mary was a cop. If I'm that dazzling defense attorney, I'm going to run with the theory that we all just take care of our own."

"The bouncer at Wylie's knows what happened too, Jake."

"He didn't hear what Burke said. Only you did."

She frowned. "You really think a jury would believe I'm lying? If Burke's skin ends up underneath Mary's fingernails? And she tries to write a physical description that matches Burke in her own blood as she draws her last breath?"

"I want to be able to account for all of it. Have an answer to everything. We don't have a burglary. We don't have any signs of sexual assault. Every piece of evidence in this points to an assailant who wanted to hurt Mary because she was Mary."

"So, where does that leave us?"

"Burke's story," Jake said. "We shore it up."

"He says he was at Brad Edwards's. The other guys at the house vouch for him."

"And maybe they all have a reason to lie. A bunch of good ole boys looking out for each other."

"So let's find out if Burke left a paper trail. He said he ordered pizza from Angelo's," she said. "Identifies the delivery girl who brings it. Jake, of everybody at the house that night, his defense lawyer would try to argue Burke's the one with the best independent evidence backing up his story."

"Let's make sure," Jake said. He grabbed his coat off the hook by the door.

"So we're going to Oakton," she said.

"We're going to Oakton. Only I'm driving. You're a maniac behind the wheel, woman."

Birdie glared at him and grabbed her coat.

Angelo's Pizza Place was a little mom-and-pop hole-in-the-wall establishment. There were only two small tables near the window. You could eat there if you wanted, but it wasn't encouraged. An acne-riddled teenage boy came out when Jake and Birdie walked up to the counter. He wore his baseball cap down low. His badge read "Chase."

"Hey, buddy," Jake said. "Do you have a manager back there?"

"Who's asking?"

Jake took out his identification. The boy read it and rolled his eyes. It gave Jake the impression cops showing up asking for the manager might have been a regular occurrence.

"Just a sec," he said, then disappeared. Thirty seconds later, a middle-aged man with slicked-back black hair and a grease-stained apron came out. Jake identified himself again.

"You're the manager?" Jake asked.

"I'm Paul," he answered, as if that settled the question.

"Paul. I'm interested in a delivery that was made on the night of January 12th."

"Was there a problem?"

"Not with the order," Jake said. "I'm looking for a girl named Seena Grimes. Might she have been working that night?"

"Seena works every Sunday night," Chase volunteered. It earned him a stern look from Paul.

"What's she done now?" Paul asked.

"She hasn't done anything. I'd just like to talk to her if she's here. And if she's not, do you have a home address or a phone number?"

"Seena!" Chase called out.

"Boy," Paul said. "I've had about enough of you today."

Chase looked unfazed. He opened the door to the kitchen and yelled for Seena again.

"This is what comes from hiring family," Paul said.

"I appreciate your cooperation," Jake said. "I really just need to ask Seena a few simple questions. Nobody's in trouble, if that's what you're worried about."

A moment later, the kitchen door swung open and a pretty blonde girl walked out looking annoyed. She was about to say something to Paul when she noticed Jake and Birdie standing there. The fact that Birdie was wearing a sheriff's deputy uniform made Seena freeze.

"They wanna talk to you," Paul said. "We're about to start the lunch rush. You gonna keep her tied up long?"

"Not planning on it," Jake said.

"You can talk in the back," Paul said. "I don't want you two standing at the counter. It's bad for business."

"There's nobody here," Birdie pointed out.

Paul charged back into the kitchen.

As soon as Paul was gone, Seena leaned her elbows on the counter. "What do you want to ask me?"

"I'm just trying to confirm whether you delivered some pizzas to this address on January 12th. The customer was Ian Burke." Jake had written down Brad Edwards's address. He showed it to her.

Seena took it and read it. She frowned. "Ian Burke. I know who that is. He's a real prick. Total creep."

"I won't disagree. Do you remember going out there to that house?"

Seena turned. There was a calendar hanging on the wall. She traced the dates back with her finger.

"It was a Sunday night," Jake offered.

Seena went over to a tablet on the counter. She fired it up and scrolled through it.

"Yes," she said. "That's the last time I was out there. They ordered four large one-topping pizzas and some cheese sticks. There was a party or something going on. I didn't want to go. That's the night of the last big storm. I got stuck on the way back to the store and my uncle was all over my ass about how long it took me to get back. We got into a fight about it. I told him I'm not going back out there again. He can have Chase deliver for them."

"Why's that?"

"I told you. Ian Burke's a creep. There've been nights where he'll have me deliver to him two or three times just to hassle me. Sometimes at this house, sometimes at the apartment where he stays. He asked me out a while back and I turned him down. He's been a dick about it ever since. He dated my stepsister a couple of years ago. Didn't treat her well at all."

"Was he that night? A creep?" Birdie asked.

"No. He wasn't there."

Birdie and Jake exchanged a look.

"What do you mean, he wasn't there? He said he paid for the pizza," Jake asked.

Seena turned the tablet so Jake could see it. She pointed to the sales transaction.

"This was an online order," she explained. "Prepaid. I didn't swipe the card when I got out there. The dickhead didn't even tip me."

"Not even in cash when you got there?" Birdie asked.

"Nope. That's one of the reasons I was so pissed. I refused to do any more deliveries that night after that one. Told Uncle Paul he'd have to drive 'em out himself if there were any more. We closed for the night right after I got back cuz I knew he wasn't going to be bothered hauling his butt out in the snow."

"Let me get this straight," Jake said. "You're saying Ian Burke wasn't at this address when you delivered the pizzas? He didn't come to the door."

"Nope. I was relieved. I was sure he was going to start hassling me again like he always did. He didn't come to the door though."

"Didn't he have to sign your slip if it was charged to his credit card?"

"He was supposed to," she said. "Brad answered and gave me plenty of attitude himself. Complaining it took me longer than normal. The snow was falling like two inches an hour or some crazy amount. He said he wasn't gonna pay for the pizzas and that I should leave them for free. They were all drunk in there. But Ian's card already went through. They were already paid for. I couldn't have cared less who signed the stupid slip. Brad's cousin did it. Shane. He's another piece of work."

"Is it possible Burke might have just been inside the house somewhere?"

"Not that I saw. He drives this crappy rust-orange car. It wasn't in the driveway."

"That doesn't mean he wasn't there," Birdie said.

"Yeah, beats me. But I didn't see him. I remember because I was relieved. That whole crew. Shane, Ian, Brad. They're trash. But Ian's the worst of them. I told you my stepsister dated him. It wasn't a good experience. Lied to her. Cheated on her. And she won't admit it, but I think he knocked her around a couple of times. And one time he hit on me right in front of her. So what's he done now that you're here asking questions about him?"

"Can you make a printout of that transaction?" Jake asked, pointing to the tablet.

"Sure." Seena took the tablet and punched a few screens. A moment later, paper spit out the top of a small printer on a table near the wall. She grabbed the paper and brought it to Jake.

"Have you seen Ian Burke since that night?" he asked.

"No."

"He hasn't tried to get a hold of you?"

She shook her head. "I wouldn't answer a call from him if he did. I'm fine if he drops off the face of the earth, honestly."

Jake reached into his breast pocket and pulled out his business card. He handed it to Seena.

"Can you do me a favor?" he asked. "If Burke does try to get in touch with you, give me a call."

"Sure thing."

"Seena!" her Uncle Paul bellowed from the back room. "We've got orders coming in!"

Seena flared her nostrils. "Don't work for family," she said. "It's not worth it."

Seena pocketed Jake's card and headed for the kitchen.

Jake and Birdie walked out of the restaurant. Once they were in the car, she turned to him.

"He lied. Burke lied. You said he was specific that Seena delivered that pizza and that she'd vouch for him. He wasn't there, Jake."

"We don't know that for sure," Jake said. "We only know Seena didn't see him there. But yeah. The son of a bitch lied to me."

"Now what?" Birdie asked.

"I don't know. I want to talk to Shane Edwards again."

Birdie raised a brow. "He won't talk to you. You know that, right? Jake ... you might want to stay away from him for a little while. I heard about what happened at the school. Travis said he thought you were going to kill the guy before they pulled you off of him."

"He took a swing at me," Jake said. "He spit in my face. He was drunk and about to get behind the wheel with his little kid in tow. I wasn't going to let that happen. And I didn't lay a finger on him. Not really."

"Still. Maybe you should let me try to talk to him for you."

Jake pulled out of the parking lot and headed back toward Stanley. It was a twenty-minute drive. They spent it in relative silence.

Ian Burke lied. It meant he didn't have an alibi for the night Mary Rathburn was murdered. Birdie and Jake walked into the war room. He picked up his red marker and drew four big fat circles around Ian Burke's picture, making it look like a bullseye.

"Talk to Shane," Jake said. "Get him to ..."

Birdie put up a hand. "I know what to say. Trust me, Jake. I've got your back on this."

He put the marker down. Not long ago, he'd had a similar conversation with Mary Rathburn. She'd said the exact same thing.

Twenty-Five

This time, Ian Burke was easy to find. Jake got a tip that he and the rest of his drywall crew were taking lunch at a fast-food place near the Proud Acres neighborhood.

Jake pulled in behind Burke's crappy orange car and waited for him to come out. When he did, he didn't seem surprised to see Jake. He motioned to the two men with him. They climbed into a different truck and drove away. Burke sauntered over to Jake, sipping his soft drink from a straw.

Jake got out and walked up to him. Burke pulled his car door open but didn't climb in.

"Why don't we go back inside," Jake said, "so we can have a civilized conversation."

Burke took a last slurping drink from his straw then threw the cup toward the garbage can on the sidewalk. He made the shot.

"I don't think I will," Burke said. "I think I told you the next conversation we had would be with my lawyer next to me. Since I don't see him here, I think you'll be leaving now."

Burke started to open his car door wider. Jake hit it with the palm of his hand and slammed it shut.

"Let me explain to you what's happening, Burke. I know you lied to me. You weren't at Brad Edwards's the night Mary Rathburn was attacked."

"The hell I wasn't! I told you, Seena Grimes delivered my pizza."

"You're half right. Only Seena says you weren't there. She's got proof. I've got a witness who can put you at the scene at Mary's that night," Jake bluffed. "I've got a credible witness who heard you threatening Mary the week before she got stabbed to death, Burke. You know what that means?"

"Lawyer," Burke said.

"It means I'm gonna get a search warrant. And when I do, I'm gonna get your DNA."

The color drained from Burke's face. Jake turned and walked over to the garbage can. He pulled Burke's discarded drink out of it.

"Or maybe I don't need that warrant," Jake said, looking at the cup. He touched the straw at its center and pulled it out. He threw the cup back in the garbage can.

"You can't do that," Burke said.

"It's a garbage can," Jake said. "I can take anything I want out of it. What's the matter? Something on this straw you're afraid of?"

"You got nothing," Burke said. "If you had, you'd have arrested me already."

"Not exactly the words of an innocent man."

"Go to hell."

"You're bad at this, Burke. And your window of opportunity to do yourself some good is closing."

Burke puffed out his chest. "Loy-er," he said, drawing the word out.

"You know this will be a death penalty case. And the appellate courts in this state love upholding that sentence. The time to do yourself a favor is now."

Burke reopened his car door. "You must be thick in the head. Typical dumb cop. Next time you get anywhere near me I'll file a complaint for harassment. You think I don't know about you? You think I'm just some dumb hick? I bet if I made a couple of phone calls, say to the county commissioner's office, I might find somebody who'd take an interest in what I had to say."

"Ah," said Jake. "So you're the smart one in all this. That's what I figured. Did Shane put you up to it? He was too much of a coward to take care of his own business so you did it for him. Is that it?"

"Man, you got nothing. I told you before. If you had something on me, you'd have arrested me by now."

He leaned over, then spit on the ground, forcing Jake to take a quick step back to avoid being splashed.

"Better not see you around me again," Burke said. "Don't suppose a restraining order against you will look too good, would it? I heard what that other cop said on the news."

Zender. He had to be talking about Zender.

"Maybe I'll give him a call too," Burke said. "Seems to me he said you boys should have had somebody else in charge of this case. Seems to me he's got a point."

"By all means," Jake said. "Please give Ed Zender a call, if that's who you mean. Tell him I said hello."

Burke scowled. He turned the ignition and revved his engine, drowning out anything else Jake would have said.

"You don't move, I'm gonna ram right into you," Burke yelled.

Jake took his time and walked back to his car. Burke held a middle finger out his window until Jake drove forward and out of Burke's way. Burke floored it and whipped around in reverse. His tires squealed as he drove away. Just as he pulled out onto the main road, Jake's phone rang.

"Hey, Birdie," he answered.

"Any luck with Burke?" she asked.

"Well, I'd say I pissed him off pretty good. I don't know if you'd call that luck. But I think we keep a close eye on him over the next couple of days while we're waiting to hear from Ramirez on the DNA testing."

A second call came through. Gemma.

"Sounds good. Shane Edwards didn't show up at work today. Pete Gansett said he didn't bother calling off. Not sure what's going on there."

"Maybe something. Maybe nothing."

"I'm about to clock out for the day. Is there anything else you need from me?"

The phone kept buzzing with Gemma's call.

"No," Jake said. "I'll catch you in the morning. We'll head over to Shane's together. I wanna hear what he has to say about Burke's alibi falling apart. Maybe it'll shake something loose if the two of them are in cahoots."

"Sounds good." Birdie clicked off. Jake pressed the second call and the speaker button. He put his phone on the seat beside him and turned his car around, pointing it toward Cooper Street.

"Hey, Gemma," he said.

"You off work yet?" his sister asked.

"Just heading to the office to handle a few loose ends. I'll be done in about an hour."

"Perfect," she said. "Can you meet me out at the End Zone bar?"

"It's closed down," he said.

"I know. Meet me there anyway. I've got something I need to show you."

It sounded ominous. Especially since Gemma seemed excited about something.

Jake sighed. "All right. Give me an hour. I'll be there."

She clicked off without saying goodbye.

Twenty-Six

The End Zone was right on the border of Lublin and Blackhand Hills Townships. Previously owned by the Weingard family, it had been vacant for the past six months. Jake knew a potential buyer had fallen through at the end of last summer. Since then, there'd been a dozen different rumors about what business might take it over. There was concern it would turn into a pot dispensary.

Gemma's car was parked in the handicap spot of the otherwise vacant parking lot. He saw lights on inside the bar itself. The large for sale sign in front hung crooked as one of the chains had snapped loose.

Jake walked up to the front door and found it unlocked. Gemma was already inside.

"Hellooo!" Jake called out. Chairs were stacked on top of the empty tables. The bar itself had been cleaned out. Only an old St. Pauli Girl sign stood propped against a dusty mirror.

Jake heard a clang from behind the bar, then Gemma stepped out of the kitchen. She was still dressed for work. A low-cut brown-

and-white-polka-dot blouse with frilly sleeves tucked into a tight black skirt and a wide leather belt. She wore brown suede boots with four-inch heels.

"Well," she said, smiling. She spread her hands out wide. "What do you think?"

Jake looked around.

"About what?"

"I think it would be smart to keep it sports-themed. There really isn't any competition on this side of town. I mean, there's the 19th Hole over in Logan, but they haven't been able to keep a chef on staff for years now because the owner is such a tyrant to work for. And that could be a bonus, actually. There's an experienced staff out there just begging for someplace new and exciting to go. I mean, I'm not talking about directly poaching anybody. But if word got out ..."

Jake put a hand up. "Back the truck up, Gemma. What are you talking about?"

"I bought it," she said, gushing.

Jake looked around. "You what?"

"I bought it," she said. "Well, I went in on it. You remember Grace Horak from my office? You know her dad finally passed away this summer. Awful. Pancreatic cancer. Took him quick. I mean, can you imagine? He'd been caring for Grace's mother with Alzheimer's for years and years. She finally passes on and wham ... two months later he's diagnosed with stage IV. Grace thought he'd be cleaned out. Her mother spent so many years in a nursing home. I mean, she just assumed all their savings had gone to that."

"Gemma," Jake said, approaching her slowly. "What are you talking about? You sold the place to Grace Horak?"

"No," she said. "We went in on it. Don't get me wrong. I wouldn't have had the capital myself. I thought about seeing if Grandpa could loan me some. But that would have just opened up a whole other can of worms. But Grace and I have been wanting to go into business together for a really long time. And since I've got some experience in the restaurant business and she had the money to buy the place, well ... we decided this was it. So we're partners."

Jake's head started to pound. He'd been down this road with his sister more times than he could count. Every few years, she got bored and decided to switch careers. She'd been a cosmetologist, a bartender, a medical transcriptionist, and about five other things. Her venture as a real estate agent had been the longest she'd stuck to any one thing. It hadn't made her rich, but she was good at it.

"Gemma, how much did you sink into this?" Jake asked.

"Not much."

"How much?"

"Listen, little brother," she said, her expression turning from joy to anger in two seconds flat. "I know how to manage my money."

"I didn't say you didn't. It's just ... Ryan's about to graduate from high school. I thought you were saving for college."

"I am. But I'm telling you. I can see it. I can feel it. Ryan's excited too. He wants to work here this summer. A bunch of his buddies, too."

Jake took one of the bar stools off the bar, turned it right side up, then sat on it. He wanted to share Gemma's enthusiasm. But all he saw were potential problems. The first of them was directly above his head. He saw a giant brown stain from water damage.

"The roof leaks," he said.

"Jake ... I'm not a fool. It's superficial damage. A couple of ceiling tiles and she's good as new. And this is all pending inspection. And transfer of the liquor license isn't a guarantee either. Everything's contingent."

"But you already signed an offer. And partnering with Grace Horak. Have you talked to a lawyer at least? If things don't work out, what if you're stuck holding the bag?"

"Yes," she said. "I'm talking to a lawyer. Mitch Reynolds who handled my divorce from Dickie. He's drawing up paperwork as we speak."

"Mitch is a family law lawyer and you used to date him. Don't you think you need somebody who specializes in business law?"

Gemma smiled. She came around the bar and put her arms around Jake, planting a fat, wet kiss on his cheek.

"I love you for being protective of me. But I haven't been this excited since ... well ... since I sold my first house. It's going to be great. A family bar. You know it was always a dream of Grandma Ava's and Grandpa Max's."

She wasn't wrong. In the 1930s, Jake's great-grandfather had owned Cashen's Bar in downtown Stanley. It occupied the building right next to Papa's Diner. Grandpa Max still had the front sign down in his basement. It hung behind his home bar.

"And he can hang out here too," Gemma said. "I was thinking that booth in the corner could be where he holds court, you know? Can't you see it? All his old fart friends can come sit over there with him. It'll get him out of the house. Get him doing something social again. And maybe you could start bringing cops here. I'd love it if we could make it a hangout."

"They're pretty partial to Wylie's," he said.

"Screw Wylie's, they serve flat draft beer and soggy French fries."

She wasn't wrong. The declining quality of Wylie's offerings had long been a point of discussion at the Union Hall.

"So what do you think?" she asked.

He didn't want to be the thing that made her smile falter. At the same time, Jake could think of a hundred reasons why this was a terrible idea. Gemma had a tendency to shoot first and ask questions later on all aspects of her life from work to romance. At the same time, whatever made her happy, he wanted for her.

"Oh, never mind," she said before he could answer. "You'll see. It's gonna be great."

"Okay," he said. "Then I'm happy for you."

She threw her arms around him and hugged him.

"Come on," she said. "Help me lock up. If you're lucky, I'll let you pick your own stool when you come in. You can sit there and pass judgment."

"I'm not judging you," he sighed.

Gemma was practically dancing as she walked with Jake out the front door. She had a jangle of keys in her hand. She turned off the lights and locked the door.

Jake's phone rang. It was a number he didn't recognize. He answered it.

"Detective Cashen?" a breathless female voice said.

Gemma walked up to him. She gestured something but Jake put a finger up, silencing her. Gemma waved him off, then mouthed. "I'll see you later."

He nodded. "Yes," he said. "This is Cashen. Who is this?"

"See-Seena Grimes," she said, full-on crying now.

"Hey, Seena. Are you okay? What's going on?"

"You told me to call you. You gave me your card. You said if I could think of anything else to call you."

"That's right."

"He came back."

"Who did?"

"Ian Burke. He just left. He stormed into the restaurant all red-faced. I think he might have even been half-drunk. Ranting and raving. He shoved Chase out of the way and came into the back to find me."

Jake went rigid. "Seena? Are you all right? Did he hurt you?"

"No," she sniffed. "Not physically. But just barely. He was enraged. He backed me into the wall and asked me what I said to you. He said I had no idea the kind of trouble I'd just caused him. He said ... he said ... he said I didn't know how to keep my mouth shut and he'd be happy to show me."

"Where is he now?"

"He left. Broke the towel holder off the wall and stormed out. Uncle Paul wasn't here. It was just Chase and me. I locked up right after he left."

"You did the right thing calling me, Seena."

"If he finds out though ... I don't know. I just didn't know what else to do. He's crazy, Detective Cashen. I mean, Ian's always been a real prick. And I knew he had a temper. But this ... I don't know. This was bad. Chase is terrified to go outside."

"Okay. Seena, I'm going to need you to file a report on this. But you're in Marvell County so I'm going to arrange to have one of their deputies come out. You think you can tell them what you told me?"

"Yeah."

"Okay. Just sit tight. I'll have somebody out there just as soon as I can. It's gonna be okay. We're gonna make sure Ian Burke doesn't come anywhere near you again."

"Okay," she said.

Jake's own temper started to rise. He envisioned wrapping his fingers around Ian Burke's neck and squeezing the life out of him. It would feel good. Too good. Jake broke into a cold sweat and took a breath to steady himself.

"You did the right thing," he repeated to Seena.

He just wasn't sure anymore if *he* could.

Twenty-Seven

That Sunday capped the first weekend Jake had taken off since Mary's murder. Saturday's sectional wrestling tournament provided a welcome distraction. Ryan wrestled smart, ending the day at the top of the podium. If he could stay healthy over the next couple of weeks, his nephew had a real shot at earning his state champion ring later in the month.

For now, though, Jake sat in a corner booth at Papa's Diner. Tessa put out a Sunday brunch that Grandpa Max loved. The old man sat across from him. He had an earbud in one ear listening to the Bengals game. They'd made the playoffs this year. When the Chiefs' Travis Kelce made the game-winning catch, Grandpa threw the earbud on the table and scowled.

Tessa came to the table with a pot of coffee. She didn't have to ask whether Grandpa wanted a refill. He always did. Jake, on the other hand, waved a hand over his cup. His kidneys couldn't take another sip.

"He looks good," Tessa said, patting Jake on the back. "I was worried he was getting too skinny. He always gets too skinny when he's working a case, don't you think?"

The hint of a smile played at the corner of Grandpa Max's mouth. "You sound like his grandmother."

Tessa leaned down and planted a wet kiss on Jake's cheek. "He needs one. But I'm not old like you." She wagged a finger at Max. He laughed at her joke. She was one of the few people in town Grandpa Max truly liked.

"You gonna talk about it?" Max asked when Tessa was finally out of earshot.

"Talk about what?"

"This new cockamamie scheme of your sister's. She thinks I don't know."

"The bar," Jake said.

"She's crazy. She doesn't have the first clue about running a restaurant."

"Gramps, she worked as a bartender for years at the Red Lantern. Rick Sheldon couldn't have run that place without her. He probably should have brought her in as a partner. If he had, he might not have closed down when he got too old to handle the day-to-day."

"So you're on her side?"

"I don't know. She seemed excited about it."

"Hmph. You gonna sit there and tell me you're not worried?"

Jake reached into his wallet and pulled out two twenties. Grandpa had eaten all the scrambled eggs and bacon he was going to for the day. Jake made a show of filling his plate, but didn't have much of an appetite.

"I'm always worried," Jake said. "But she seems like she's got her mind made up. You know how well it goes when we try talking her out of something."

"Stubborn as shit, that one. She's just like her mother. Just like her grandmother."

"Just like you," Jake said. "Come on. Let me get you home. It's going to start snowing again. I don't want you out in it."

"You think I'm gonna wilt?"

"No," Jake said. "I think you're gonna slip and fall on your ass. I'd rather you didn't."

Grandpa swore under his breath, but more or less came with Jake without too much trouble. Jake shouted a goodbye back to Spiros and Tessa in the kitchen. Then he helped Grandpa into the cab of his truck. Jake had taken to driving the beat-up old F-350 exclusively. It could get through any kind of weather and he hated to think about it sitting idle in Grandpa's garage for weeks at a time.

Jake pulled away from the curb and started the ten-minute drive back up Blackhand Hills.

Seena Grimes was on his mind. He'd gone out to Angelo's to talk to her in person after her phone call Friday night. Burke hadn't been back, but she'd seen him driving around town. The girl was scared. Terrified, actually. When Jake thought about Burke bullying her the way he did, his blood curdled. She was just a kid. Barely more than a little girl. He'd put a call in to Dave Yun and asked him if one of his deputies could keep a closer eye on Angelo's for the next few days.

"Earth to Jake," Grandpa shouted right in his ear as Jake made the next turn.

"What?"

"I asked you if you're coming up the hill for chili tonight. It's Sunday."

"What? Oh. Yeah. Probably. If I don't ..."

A car blew through the stop sign. Jake slammed on his brakes. If he hadn't been paying attention, he'd have been T-boned on Grandpa's side.

"Crazy son of a bitch!" Grandpa shouted. He pounded his fist on the dash. "Go after him."

Jake froze. It wasn't a random son of a bitch in the rusted 2005 Orange Nissan Sentra that had just gone west on County Road Twelve. It was Ian Burke, driving like a bat out of hell.

Jake turned the wheel sharply to the left. Grandpa braced himself against the dash to keep from sliding.

"The hell you doing?"

"Where are you going?" Jake muttered through clenched teeth.

He kept his distance, making sure Burke couldn't see him, but he followed.

"Jake!" Grandpa said. "It ain't worth it. It's these crazy kids who don't know how to drive anymore."

"Just a minute," Jake said. "I wanna see where he's going."

"He? Who he?" Grandpa asked.

Burke turned down the next street. He didn't know what made him do it. Burke didn't seem to realize who it was he'd just nearly plowed into. He pulled into the Valero station at the corner of County Road 12 and Barnum.

Jake parked in the bank lot across the street.

"Jake," Grandpa said. "The hell are you doing, boy?"

"I don't know." Jake gave his grandfather an honest answer.

"Is he somebody?" Grandpa leaned forward, peering out of his window. His eyesight was shot. Legally blind, the old man could basically just see shapes and colors these days.

"Yeah," Jake said. "He's somebody."

Jake waited. A few minutes later, Burke emerged from the gas station carry-out with a case of beer. He tossed it in the back of his Nissan Sentra and climbed back behind the wheel.

"He's the one, isn't he?" Grandpa asked.

"What do you mean?"

"The one you think took out Mary Rathburn."

"Maybe."

"Only you can't prove it."

"Not yet," Jake said.

Burke started his car and pulled out of the parking lot, still oblivious to the fact Jake was watching him. Jake put the truck in gear and pulled out.

"Where's he going?" Grandpa asked.

Burke turned down Bailey street, then Wyman. That's when Jake realized where he was headed. Shane Edwards's duplex was a half a mile down the road.

"I should drop you off," Jake said.

"The hell you should. You wanna follow that SOB, don't you?"

Jake took another side street. One that wound around the opposite end of the Edwards's neighborhood. He'd be able to see Burke come back out, but Burke wouldn't be able to see him. He parked in front of a tan two-story house. Through the trees, he had a clear view of Shane Edwards's driveway. Burke pulled in, then blared on his horn. Francine Beadle peered out through her window. Jake opened the center console. Grandpa kept a small pair of binoculars there. He took them out.

Mrs. Beadle scowled as Burke laid on his horn again. A moment later, Shane Edwards came out. He looked like a mess. Disheveled. Shirt untucked. Hair sticking out in peaks and cones. From the doorway he'd just exited, Shane's girlfriend, Marissa, called out to him. She had Kevin Edwards on her hip. Shane jerked a dismissive hand behind him, ignoring whatever Marissa yelled out. He climbed into the passenger side of Burke's car. Burke peeled out and headed north on Wyman.

He probably should have just turned in the other direction. Taken Grandpa home. Gone home himself. But something nagged at Jake. He wanted to know where these two shitbirds were going.

"You mind riding shotgun for a little while, Gramps?"

Grandpa Max's face split into a mischievous smile. "You planning on doing something you shouldn't?"

"Probably."

Jake pulled out onto Wyman. Burke and Edwards made a turn on Hoover heading west. They picked up speed, going seventy in a forty-five through Durris Township.

Jake kept a cautious distance. The two men kept on going. A few minutes later, they crossed the county line into Oakton.

"How far you gonna take this?" Grandpa asked.

Jake had no answer. He hadn't really thought it through. Burke took a turn on Spellman Street. If he kept going, it would take him right past Angelo's. Jake tensed. If Burke were planning on paying another visit to Seena, he'd get a hell of a surprise.

They passed Angelo's. Paul kept it open on Sundays and Jake saw Seena's car in the parking lot. Burke slowed but didn't turn in. It looked like he was casing the place for sure though. But he finally sped up, slamming on the gas hard enough to squeal his tires. Jake wondered if that was intentional, too. Another attempt to intimidate Seena.

Burke drove two more miles, then turned down a side street. It led to an older neighborhood. Jake let Burke get way ahead of him so there was no chance of him being seen. Then Burke pulled into the driveway of a small white house with black shutters. One side of it was covered in old, tattered Tyvek wrap. Jake hung back. He watched Burke and Edwards get out and go inside.

Jake drove down the street, stopping two houses away. Burke had carried the case of beer inside.

He waited.

"So now what, Butch?" Grandpa Max asked.

"I'll let ya know, Sundance," Jake answered. The truth was, Jake was making this up as he went along.

"Foreman Street," Jake whispered. He picked up the binoculars and read the numbers on the house. "Can you write this down, Gramps?" Jake asked.

Grandpa reached back into the center console and fished around for a pad of paper and a pencil.

"1478 Foreman," Jake said. "Oakton."

There was another car parked right in front of the house. It could be a neighbor's. There were parked cars all up and down the street.

"Blue Suburban," Grandpa said. "I'm not gonna be able to read the plate."

"J42-132, Ohio plates," Jake read. Grandpa wrote the numbers down with a shaky hand.

They waited. Ten minutes went by. Twenty.

"You think he did it?" Grandpa finally said. "You think this putz carved up that girl, don't you?"

"Yeah," Jake said. "I do."

"Why? You think she had something going with him on the side?"

"I don't know."

"Kid," Grandpa said. "You think maybe you're hanging on too tight to this one?"

Jake squinted through the binoculars. He could see through the front window of the house. Just shadows though. Two men. Ian and Shane. If there was somebody else in the house, the light was too dim to make them out.

"Jake," Grandpa said. He put a hand on Jake's arm, pushing the binoculars away from his face. "How long do you wanna stay out here? The storm's coming. They might be hunkered down for the night."

"I don't know," Jake said.

"Well I do. Let's go on home. You can't solve this case tonight. And you're certainly not gonna solve it sitting out here like this. I'm worried about you."

Jake looked at his grandfather. It wasn't something the old man said very often. In fact, Jake wasn't sure if he'd ever said it. He probably felt it over the years. But his grandfather wasn't one to talk about feelings.

"You're wound up," Grandpa said. "That can make for bad business."

"I'm fine."

"Yeah? Son, I know you. I know that look you get."

"What look?"

"That one," Grandpa said. "Like you're ready to explode. Man, that used to scare the hell outta your grandma. You used it though. God have mercy on anybody who crosses you. That's why I got you into wrestling. It gave you an outlet for some of that. Now? You don't have one. You just have this."

"You don't have to worry about me," Jake said. "I just wanted to see where he was going. That's all."

"And now you have. Come on now. It's the weekend. Nobody's in trouble. Nobody's in danger. Nobody needs anything. It's just you and me, son."

Jake looked at his grandfather. His cloudy eyes tried to search Jake's face. Jake knew there was no way he could really see any *look* on Jake's face. Not the details. He was sensing something else though. And whether Jake liked it or not, Grandpa knew him just about as well as anyone.

Grandpa put a hand on Jake's arm, feeling him go rigid. "Like I said," Grandpa repeated. "You're wound up tight as a drum. Boy, your dad used to get that way too."

It was a casual comment. Harmless. But a silence settled between them. Grandpa Max rarely talked about his own son anymore. The memories caused too much pain.

Your dad used to get that way.

No, Jake thought. He was nothing like his father. Nothing. Jake took a breath, letting his anger ebb. Grandpa was right. There was nothing else Jake could do out here today. The storm was indeed coming.

Jake put the truck in gear. As he started to pull out, Ian and Shane finally emerged from the house. He couldn't hear what they were saying. Their body language seemed off though. Ian's usual swagger was long gone. He hurried back to his car. Shane followed close behind.

He was carrying something. A plastic grocery bag wrapped around something. He held it close to his body.

"Let's go," Grandpa said. "You don't want those boys to see you, do you?"

"No," Jake said. He backed into the closest driveway and pulled out, going in the opposite direction from Shane Edwards and Ian Burke.

By the time he reached the next intersection, the snow had started to fall. Grandpa was right. There was a hell of a storm coming tonight.

Twenty-Eight

Monday morning, Bethany Roman waited at the service entrance to the sheriff's department. Jake didn't see her at first. He realized later that was her plan.

"Jake," she said, stepping out of the shadows. Lieutenant Beverly and Deputies Tuttle and Stuckey were right behind Jake, coming in to start the day shift. Beverly pursed his lips and had the decency to look uncomfortable as Bethany walked up to Jake.

"This isn't a good time," Jake said.

Bethany waited for the three other men to move past them and into the building.

"You have to talk to me sooner or later," she said.

"Wanna bet?"

"Mary Rathburn's murder is news. The public has the right to know how the investigation is progressing."

"The public can tune in to any number of regular press conferences Sheriff Landry has given on this matter. I have no comment."

"No comment to anyone? Or just no comment to me."

"Anyone."

Jake reached for the door handle. Bethany stepped in his way. She put a hand on his chest.

"You can't do this to me," she said.

"Don't take it personally."

"Look, I'm sorry. I came at this all wrong and I realize that now. I just didn't think anyone was hurt by it. We had fun, Jake. Didn't we?"

Another deputy came up the walk. He sidestepped Jake and Bethany on his way in.

"I can't keep having this conversation," he said. "You lied to me about who you were. Then you used our off-the-record conversation that you got under false pretenses in a story. As far as I'm concerned, we're done."

He moved around her. If she wanted to block him from entering the building, she was gonna have to throw herself at him. Bethany took a step and for a second, Jake thought that was exactly what she intended to do.

"Are you aware of the allegations Shane Edwards has been making this morning?"

Jake stopped. "What?"

"Shane Edwards. Have you seen him lately?"

Jake had one hand on the door. She was baiting him, obviously. He knew he should just slam the door in her face and freeze her out.

His cell phone buzzed in his pocket.

"I'm giving you a chance to make your statement, Jake. Get ahead of this."

It was in him to ask her what she was talking about. He checked his phone. The text was from Landry. It read simply. "My office. The second you get in."

Jake stared at Bethany. She had her own phone out. She was recording him.

Jake clenched his jaw and entered the building. Though he didn't let the door slam, the sound of it locking behind him was satisfying.

"On my way," he texted back to Meg. Something was up. Bethany's words started to sink in.

Shane Edwards. Serious allegations. What in the ever-loving hell was going on now?

When he got to Meg's office, Birdie stood outside the door.

"She wants to see both of us," Birdie said.

"Any idea why?"

"I didn't get the impression it was to pat us on the back. Any word from Ramirez on that DNA I got from Burke?"

"Not yet. Any day now though."

Landry's door opened. Her new assistant, Zoe, stepped out.

"Good," Zoe said. "She was just asking. She's ready for both of you now."

Jake and Birdie traded a glance. Jake held the door open and let Birdie go in first. Landry was standing behind her desk, arms crossed in front of her. She didn't look happy.

"Sit down," she said. "Both of you."

"Something wrong?" Jake asked.

"That depends on what you tell me in the next five minutes."

"Okay?"

Jake and Birdie each took a chair across from Landry's desk. Landry leaned forward, resting her weight on her palms.

"Tell me," she started, "you haven't been anywhere near Shane Edwards in the last twenty-four hours."

Birdie turned to Jake, eyes wide.

"Define near," Jake said.

"Don't make jokes," Landry said. "I need you to account for your time."

"My time? Sheriff, I was off in the last twenty-four hours. Am I being accused of something?"

Landry pulled her chair out and sank into it with a thud. "Shane Edwards showed up in town a couple of hours ago looking pretty rough. Someone's beat the tar out of him. Black eye. Split lip. He's been worked over, Jake."

"He's saying I did it?" Jake asked, thinking about Bethany's cryptic warning about serious allegations.

"You're saying you didn't?" Landry asked.

"Categorically," Jake answered. "I haven't laid a finger on him."

"People saw you," she said. "The other night out at the high school. You didn't think I knew about that, did you?"

"Hold on," Jake said. "Yes. Last week I had a run-in with the guy off the clock. He was drunk off his ass, Landry. Staggered his way out of a school function. I wasn't out there looking for him. I was heading to my truck after wrestling practice. He had Mary's kid with him. He was about to drive off with him. So I stopped him. And there were maybe twenty witnesses there who'll tell you I didn't hurt the guy."

"And that's all? Swear to me that's all?"

"That's all," Jake said.

"So you haven't been anywhere near him since?"

Jake sighed. "Near him, yes. But I haven't touched him."

Landry rubbed her temples. "Explain."

"I was gonna catch you up to speed in this morning's case briefing. Ian Burke's alibi fell apart. The delivery girl he swears brought him his pizza the night Mary died says she never saw him. And that would be one thing all by itself, but the girl called me. Scared to death. Burke went back out there and threatened her. She's terrified now. She's just a kid, Sheriff. Nineteen, I think."

"Well, that's Burke, what about Edwards?"

"The girl said Burke's been driving by the pizza place where she works ever since. She's afraid to go to work. Well, yesterday, I was just out driving. I saw Burke and Edwards in Burke's car together. So I followed them for a little while. That's all. Never talked to them. Never got near them. Just followed them to a house out in Oakton. They went in together. They came out together. That was maybe four o'clock yesterday. And I swear, Edwards was in one piece. So whatever happened to him happened well after I saw him."

"Did they see you? Burke and Edwards?" Birdie asked.

"No."

"You're sure? You're absolutely sure?" Landry asked.

"I'm sure. I know how to tail somebody without being seen. I wanted to make sure they weren't heading back to the pizza place. If they had, maybe I'd have made contact, but I didn't."

"You were alone?" Landry asked. "Is there anybody who can back up your story?"

"What the hell is Edwards saying happened?"

"He's out there implying he had an encounter with the cops."

"Implying it to whom?" Jake asked.

"I got a call from one of the teachers at Stanley Elementary where his son goes. My daughter Paige was reading to his preschool class as part of her service requirement for the honor society. Edwards showed up with his face bashed in and people started asking him about it."

"And he's saying I did it?"

"Not you specifically. But someone from this department."

"And you automatically assume it was me?"

"I automatically decided to ask you directly, Jake," Landry said. "And now you're telling me you were out there following him around last night? Were you alone?"

"No," Jake said. "My grandpa was in the car with me."

Landry threw her hands up. "And I'm sure Max will vouch for you."

"Do you think I'm lying to you?"

"No," Landry said quickly. "I don't. It's just ... Jake, we can't afford any more scandals as far as this case goes. The county commissioners are breathing down my neck as it is. Zender's got them all stirred up. The Jeff Hammer situation is going to break. I'm being accused of a cover-up."

"It's bullshit," Jake said. "It'll blow over. We've handled this case by the book. Nobody touched Shane Edwards on our end. He's lying."

"All right," she said. "I believe you. But Jake ..."

"I'll find out," he said. "And I'll make sure whatever rumor he's spreading gets shut down. Don't worry about it. These fools are just trying to use this case to rattle your cage."

"They're doing a good job," she said. "Consider me rattled."

"You should know," Jake said. "Bethany Roman has this. She engineered a run-in with me as I was coming in. You're gonna get asked about it at the next press conference. I didn't give her the chance to tell me what she was sniffing around about, but I'm sure it's this."

"Thanks," Landry said, though her tone was anything but relieved. "You can go. Just keep me up to speed on anything that happens in this case today. I'll deal with Bethany Roman."

Jake rose. Birdie came with him. They walked down the hall and into the war room together. Once there, Birdie shut the door and turned on him.

"Jake," she said. "If there's something you wanna tell me. Something you want kept just between us. You need to know I've got your back. But if I get blindsided by something you *didn't* tell me ..."

"Hold up," he said. "You think I was lying to Landry just now? You think I thumped Shane Edwards just for the hell of it then lied about it?"

"No."

"Good. Just so we're clear."

"All I'm saying is I've got your back."

"And I've got yours. I didn't beat the crap out of Shane Edwards. But I'm really curious about who did. Like I said in there. The last time I saw Edwards was yesterday afternoon. There wasn't a scratch on him."

"So who did it? Where'd he go last night?"

"I'd like to find out." Jake reached into his pocket and pulled out the note he'd written with the address of the house he followed Edwards and Burke to yesterday.

"They went here," he said, putting the piece of paper on the table. Birdie peered over his shoulder and read the note.

"They stayed inside for about twenty minutes and Edwards came out holding a package. I would have kept following them but like I told Landry, I had Grandpa Max with me and the roads were starting to get dicey. It was going to make it hard for me to keep tailing them without them figuring it out."

"You want me to pick up where you left off?"

"I think we stay away from Shane Edwards for the time being. We know he's not the one who killed Mary."

"So Burke then," Birdie said. "I can keep an eye on him. That's easy. He's supposed to still be working out at Proud Acres on that drywalling job."

"It's a good idea," Jake said. "I wanna try to talk to some of the other guys who were at Brad Edwards's house that night. See if I can get one or two of them alone. I'd bet my next paycheck Burke's asked one or more of them to lie for him."

"You think it was Burke who beat Shane up?"

"Probably. That's who I saw him with yesterday and he wasn't beat up then."

"So Shane knows something. Or he's one of the people Burke's asked to lie for him and maybe he's getting antsy about it. So Burke's trying to intimidate him like that pizza girl."

"Yeah," Jake said. He stood in front of the whiteboard looking at Shane Edwards's crossed-out face.

"Jake," Birdie said. "You're hatching a plot. I can feel it. You heard what Landry said. I heard what you promised her. You can't go talk to Shane by yourself. You shouldn't even go near him today. If he's running around saying a cop did this to him ..."

"I just wanna see him," Jake said. "Lay eyes on him. Maybe make sure he knows I'm watching."

"Be careful," she said. "That's the last time I wanna get called out on the carpet in Landry's office for something I had nothing to do with."

"Point taken," Jake said. But his wheels were spinning. Who had Shane Edwards crossed in the last twelve hours?

Burke. He knew Burke was the key. He could feel it in his gut.

Twenty-Nine

At nine o'clock the next morning, Birdie texted Jake a grainy, blown-up picture of Shane Edwards. She called two seconds later.

"He's a mess, Jake," Birdie said. "The whole left side of his face is swollen."

"I can see that," Jake said. He enlarged the picture even more. Shane's cheekbone had tripled in size. His eye was nearly swollen shut and he had a deep gash through his lower lip that looked like it could have used stitches.

"Doesn't look like he went to a doctor," Jake said.

"I'd say no. With that amount of swelling, I'm honestly worried he might have a concussion. He drove to work. I'm sitting across the street at the gas station. He hasn't spotted me. You want me to try talking to him?"

"Not yet. But keep an eye on him. If he leaves early or does anything unusual, let me know. In the meantime, see what you can find out about that address in Oakton. Like who owns it, for starters."

"Do you want to head out there and maybe talk to the neighbors? Knock on some doors?"

"Not yet," Jake said. "If Edwards is at work, I'm hoping I might have some luck talking to his girlfriend, Marissa. She works as a waitress over at Barnum Bagels. I'm gonna see if I can catch her. Kevin's at school until one. Connie Rathburn says the girlfriend's been picking him up. I've got a small window where maybe I can get her alone."

"She's got to be worried about him," Birdie said. "He looks awful, Jake. When he walked into the body shop, it got noticed. I wish I were close enough to hear whatever excuse he gave those guys."

"Maybe find out after the fact. If he leaves for lunch or something."

"Was thinking the same."

"Good deal. I'll meet you at the office later this afternoon and we can compare notes."

Birdie clicked off. Jake was already halfway to his car. Barnum Bagels was just a three-minute drive. Jake knew the owner, Leslie Barnum, pretty well. If they weren't busy, he didn't figure she'd care if Jake wanted to talk to Marissa Nagy for a few minutes.

The sun was shining. After weeks of intermittent snow, it was a rare, February warm front. It made for a slushy mess all over town.

Jake spotted Marissa's car right away. She drove a little red Honda with a Cleveland Browns bumper sticker that was partially scraped off. He pulled into the spot beside hers.

He'd gauged it right. Just before ten and the breakfast crowd had thinned out to just two customers. There would be a lunch rush in about an hour, but Jake wouldn't need that long.

Leslie Barnum stood behind the cash register. Her face brightened when she saw Jake. Leslie had been married to a cop for a while. It didn't work out, but she was still a friend of the sheriff's office.

"Hey, Leslie," Jake said. "I got a favor to ask. Is Marissa working today?"

"She sure is. I've got her baking for me. Do you need to talk to her?"

"For a few minutes, if that's okay."

"Marissa!" Leslie shouted over her shoulder. She turned to Jake. "I'll tell you what. Why don't you head around the corner through the double doors? Break room's just on your right. You can have some privacy there."

"I really appreciate it."

Leslie lowered her head and whispered. "Is this about that idiot she dates? It is, isn't it? I know he was married to Detective Rathburn, poor thing. I'll make sure Marissa cooperates. If she doesn't, she can start finding another job."

"You don't have to get that involved. I'm not looking to cause issues for Marissa. And I hope you can understand. I can't really discuss aspects of an investigation."

Leslie waved her hand. "Oh I know. I wasn't fishing. Not on purpose anyway. You just head on back to the break room and I'll get Marissa over there. She's due for her fifteen-minute break anyhow."

"This shouldn't take more than that. I appreciate it."

"Come find me when you're done. I'll throw some bagels and cream cheese in a bag. You take it back to the office with you. Set it out at the day sergeant's desk. But tell Hammer they're not all for him. He's getting thick enough in the middle. Sarah was in here complaining about it the other day."

Jake smiled. News of Jeff Hammer's involvement with Mary hadn't hit the Worthington County rumor mill just yet. That was a good thing. It would though. Jake had a feeling this bag of bagels might be the last Jeff would get for free.

He did as Leslie instructed and headed through the swinging double doors and into the break room. Thirty seconds later, Marissa Nagy walked in, dusting her hands off on her red apron.

He had no way of knowing what Leslie told her, but Marissa didn't seem at all surprised to see him.

"I don't have much time," she said. "We've got a big catering order due this afternoon."

"Thanks for coming back to talk to me. This won't take long. Marissa, I'm worried about Shane."

"He didn't kill Mary. You know that."

"I do," he said. "But he got into a fight last night. Is he okay?"

Marissa's eyes flickered. She closed the break room door and sank into one of the chairs at the small table. Jake joined her.

"Marissa," Jake said. "Is Shane in trouble?"

"I don't know why you'd say that." But she wouldn't meet his eyes. "He just ... he slipped on the ice. Mrs. Beadle was supposed to hire a plow service. She can't keep expecting Shane to do it. He's not gonna get up at four in the morning during these storms. And it's not part of his rental agreement. He's only supposed to keep our own walkway clear. Not the common areas."

"You're saying his face got bashed in because he fell on it? Come on, Marissa. You can't expect me to buy that. He's been going around town telling people cops did that to him. You and I both know that's not true."

Marissa's face changed. She began to chew her bottom lip.

"I can't help you," she said. "I don't know what to tell you. Talk to Shane."

"I have. Listen. I know he didn't kill Mary. But he knows something. Or at least somebody thinks he knows something."

"Why would you say that?" She jerked her head back. Tears began to form in the corners of Marissa's eyes.

"Marissa, Shane's in some kind of trouble, isn't he?"

"I wouldn't know anything about that."

"You know someone bashed his face in. He's walking around town, lying about it. And you just made up some thin story about him falling down on the ice."

"That's what happened," she said quickly. "Whoever's telling you Shane said the cops did it, they were misinformed."

"Fine," Jake said. "But you know he's been hanging around Ian Burke a lot, don't you? They were together most of the weekend. Did you know that?"

It was a gamble. But Marissa Nagy seemed scared of something or someone. If Jake's instincts were right, Burke was at the root of it.

"He left you taking care of Kevin while he went off with Burke. That doesn't seem fair to you."

She didn't respond, but her neck turned red. Jake took another gamble.

"Those are some pretty thin walls in that duplex. Mrs. Beadle isn't a big fan of Shane's. You and Shane have been arguing. You don't think she's heard every word?"

"What did she say?" Marissa snapped. "That old bat doesn't know how to mind her own business. We pay the rent on time. Shane does all kinds of stuff for her. Carries in her packages. Mows her lawn even though she never gives him credit against the rent like she promises. He even went over there and fed her disgusting cats when she went down to Florida to visit her sister."

"You don't like Shane hanging around Burke, do you? That's what you argued about. And then he goes off with him and comes back with his face bashed in. Marissa, whatever Shane's mixed up in, he's gonna get hurt. And I mean really hurt. His smashed face was only a warning, if I'm right."

"I have to get back to work," she said. "Leslie's going to dock my pay."

"She won't. I'll make sure of it."

"I'll get behind. I can't get behind. I don't have anything else to say to you."

"All right," Jake said. "So just listen. I don't want Shane getting hurt again, either. I told you. I know he didn't kill Mary. They had their differences, but he didn't hurt her. But whatever he knows. Whatever he's hiding. He's in over his head. The only way out of it is by him cooperating with me. If he doesn't ... Marissa ... I'll be honest. I'm worried about you too. Mary Rathburn was a seasoned cop. She knew how to take care of herself against some pretty rough characters. She had guns in the house and training in how to use them. But none of it mattered. They killed her slow. Painfully. I don't want that to happen to anybody else. Not Shane. Not you."

Marissa bolted out of her chair.

"I want you to go. I have nothing else to say to you. You said you know Shane didn't kill Mary. So do I. I can't talk to you anymore."

She took a staggering step backward, tripping over the leg of her chair. Then she turned and disappeared back into the kitchen.

Jake took out a business card. He tacked it to the corkboard in the break room just above the time clock. She might call. She might not. But Marissa Nagy was terrified. Was it Burke? Or was he just the tip of some iceberg?

Birdie called as he said goodbye to Leslie, picked up his bag of bagels, and headed out into the parking lot.

"Shane's on the move," Birdie said. "He got into one of the tow trucks with another guy. Do you want me to follow?"

"No," Jake said. "I'm done talking to the girlfriend."

Jake climbed behind the wheel.

"She have anything enlightening to say?" Birdie asked. Before he could answer, a second call came through.

"Birdie," Jake said. "I'm gonna put you on hold for a second."

He clicked the hold button and answered the second call. One he'd been expecting for days.

"Hey, Jake," Mark Ramirez said. He sounded breathless. "I got some news. I'll send the report, but figured you'd want the rundown just as fast as I had it."

"Whatcha got?" Jake asked. His car was running, but he stayed put. Through the window, he could see Marissa Nagy running trays of bagels into the front display case. She spotted Jake and frowned.

"Your suspect," Ramirez said. "Ian Burke. The DNA's come back."

Ramirez paused. Jake squeezed his eyes shut and took a breath.

"I'm sorry, Jake," Ramirez said. "I don't have a match."

Jake paused. "Say that again?"

"There's no match. The samples we took at Mary's, the tissue under her nails. None of it belonged to Ian Burke. It's not his DNA. I'm sorry. I know you were hoping this would put your case to bed."

Jake squeezed his phone so hard he thought he might crush it. Ramirez's words echoed through his skull.

There's no match. Burke wasn't the guy.

No, Jake thought. A moment ago, he felt as if he had the threads of this case in his hands, ready for him to tie up. Now, it all slipped away.

Shane Edwards wasn't at the crime scene. Ian Burke wasn't at the crime scene.

So who the hell was?

Thirty

The next morning, Jake stood at the whiteboard after everyone else left. He'd spent twenty minutes briefing Landry, Lieutenant Beverly, and the deputies on the case progress. Rage simmered through him. He held up his red dry erase marker and slowly drew a line through Ian Burke's face. He tossed the marker onto the table behind him.

Birdie came back in. She'd gotten good at navigating Jake's moods. She held a folded scrap of paper in her hand and laid it on the table, spreading it out.

"Rodney and Penelope Whitney," she said. "There's a P.O. Box where the tax bills get sent. It's current through last summer, but the clerk won't give me any info on how it was paid without a warrant or a subpoena."

Jake walked over to the table and picked up the paper. It was the address he'd had Birdie check out over in Oakton. The house he'd seen Burke and Edwards walking out of when he followed them that day.

"What are you planning?" she asked.

Jake crumpled the note and held it in his fist.

"I was sure," he said. "Burke's acted like a guilty man since the beginning. He lied about his alibi. He threatened that girl at the pizza place. Why would he go to all that trouble knowing he wasn't at Mary's house?"

"Maybe he just figured that was the conclusion everybody would jump to. Once he realized there were witnesses the night he threatened Mary."

"It's dumb," Jake said. "Why not just cooperate with me?"

"He doesn't trust cops." Birdie shrugged. "So if you can't get answers from him directly, maybe there's another way in? If Burke's acting guilty, maybe it's because he's guilty of something else?"

Jake pocketed the note. "Maybe."

"You still think that matters?" Birdie pointed to the pocket Jake had just shoved her note into.

"I don't know. But I'm out of ideas. Out of leads. It can't hurt to turn over another stone."

"That's where I'm at too."

"What are you thinking?" Jake asked.

"I don't know. I thought maybe I'd take another pass at Mary's phone records. Maybe there's something we missed."

"Good. It can't hurt." He and Birdie agreed to check back in with each other at the end of the shift. Jake walked down to his office and grabbed his coat off the hook. They were calling for temps near zero degrees.

An hour later, Jake sat in Detective Dave Yun's cruiser outside 1478 Foreman. There was nobody home at the moment, but tire tracks in the snow indicated someone had been there last night.

"You know anything about a Rodney or Penelope Whitney?" Jake asked. He spread out Birdie's crumpled note on the console between them.

"Not off the top of my head, no," Yun said. "This neighborhood's been sketchy for at least a decade. We've done raids at the two at the end of the block. There've been a couple of drive-by shootings one block over. If your boys were hanging out down here, I can guarantee it wasn't for any good reason."

Two houses down from 1478 Foreman, a beat-up, ancient Lincoln Town Car pulled in. An older gentleman got out. He spotted Dave and Jake right away, scowled, then grabbed his mail from a box screwed into the side of the house.

"Let's go have a conversation," Jake said.

Yun unclipped his seatbelt and followed Jake across the street.

"Excuse me," Jake called out. The old man had his key in the door. He shoved his mail under his arm and turned toward Dave and Jake.

"You want something? You selling something? Not interested in either," he said.

His face scrunched up like a raisin. He poked a gnarled finger in the air in front of Jake's chest. Jake took out his badge and showed it to him. The man's expression instantly changed to relief.

"About time you showed up."

"How's that?" Yun asked.

"Tired of all the riff-raff running wild around here. Can't even walk down the street without some kind of trouble."

"I'm Detective Jake Cashen. This is Detective Dave Yun. Would you mind if we asked you a couple of questions about your neighbor two doors down?"

The man twisted sideways, looking at the house. He shook his head. "Nothing but dirtbags over there. I don't associate."

"What's your name, sir?" Yun asked.

"Ralph," he said. "Ralph Bernecki."

"Good to meet you, Mr. Bernecki," Jake said. "I understand the house over there is owned by a Rodney Whitney. Do you know him?"

Bernecki shook his head. The man's ears had turned red from the cold but he hadn't invited them inside. "Whitneys moved out probably fifteen years ago. Don't even know if they're still alive. I heard he went into a nursing home or some such. He had old timer's disease. Used to catch him wandering outside in his underwear. He walked into Mrs. Pomphrey's house by mistake one night. Scared the hell out of her. She almost shot him. I think that might have been the last straw. Didn't see him again after that. They probably locked him up. She was never friendly to begin with, the wife. Didn't even know they still owned it."

"Well," Jake said. "Their names are still on the tax rolls."

"Yeah, I don't know about that. Couple of years ago I talked to the guy who said he was renting it. Big fella. Black guy. Said his name was Cortez. Which I thought was kinda odd. Andre Cortez. Told him I didn't want any trouble in this neighborhood."

"Yeah?" Jake asked, gritting his teeth. "How'd he take to that?"

"Got real defensive."

Yun and Jake exchanged a look. "Sure," Jake said. "I imagine he would."

"Slammed the door in my face," Bernecki continued. "That was maybe three or four years ago. Since then, I bet there's been a dozen different idiots in and out of that place. Each one rougher than the one before. Cars coming and going constantly. Nobody's taking care of the lawn. That Tyvek siding's been up like that, exposed, for two years now. They don't shovel their walk. They're supposed to shovel their walk. It's the law. I've called the Township so many times I've got 'em on speed dial. They don't do anything."

Bernecki abruptly turned and walked into his house. He left the main door open but let the screen door shut in Dave and Jake's faces. A few seconds later, he reemerged, holding a steno pad. He tore off the top two sheets and handed them to Jake.

"I write 'em down every time."

"You write what down?" Jake looked at the pages. Bernecki had scribbled row after row of letters and numbers.

"License plates," he said. "Maybe you can do something about it."

"License plates," Yun said, doing a poor job of hiding his exasperation. "You mean people who've parked in the driveway?"

"The street mostly," Bernecki said.

"In front of the house?" Jake asked.

"Some," Bernecki answered. "Some of 'em parked up and down this street."

"It's a public street, Mr. Bernecki," Yun said. "It's legal to park here."

"Riff-raff," Bernecki said. "Maybe if you lot would do your jobs, we wouldn't have so much of it around here."

"Mr. Bernecki," Jake tried again. "Do you know who's living in the house right now?"

"Some skulky fella. Tried to say hello to him a few weeks back when I was out walking Sasha. He just gave me a dirty look and kept on walking. Rude."

"What did he look like?" Yun asked.

"Told you. Big fella. Had a hat on. White guy."

"What about these two?" Jake asked. He pulled up photographs he had of Burke and Edwards on his phone. Bernecki squinted as he looked at them.

"Maybe I saw 'em. Maybe I didn't. I told you. It's like a revolving door over there. You need to do something about it."

"We'll look into it," Yun said. He reached into his jacket and pulled out a business card. "Maybe if you see either of those two gentlemen again, you give me a call."

Bernecki took the card and stuffed it in his shirt pocket.

"Appreciate your time," Jake said. As he and Yun climbed back into the car, Yun swore under his breath.

"I'm probably gonna regret giving that guy my card."

Jake smiled. "Oh, you're in for a barrage of voicemails rattling off license plate numbers."

Yun pulled out. It was a short drive back to the Marvell County Sheriff's Department building where Jake's car was parked.

"You really think whatever they were doing at that house has anything to do with your murder case?" Yun asked.

"I don't know. I'm grasping at straws at this point."

"It only takes one."

"Yeah. Dave, whatever you can think of ... any known associates of Edwards or Burke's out this way. I keep running into dead ends, but their behavior over the last few weeks has been pretty suspicious."

"They're peons," Yun said. "Low-level scum. We've been over their records. They find themselves in plenty of trouble but it's piddly stuff. A hit on a cop?"

"Would take a hell of a lot of money or clout," Jake said.

"These guys have neither. The only gang nearby that would remotely have the means or methods to carry out something like this would be the Hilltop Boys in your neck of the woods."

Jake shook his head. "And they don't go after cops. If they *did* go after cops, it wouldn't be like this."

"Too messy," Yun said. "Too big of a trail of breadcrumbs at the crime scene."

"Exactly."

"Jake," Yun said. He'd just pulled into the lot and parked in the spot beside Jake's car. "I hate even suggesting this. But is there any chance Rathburn was dirty?"

He turned off the ignition and twisted in his seat so he faced Jake.

"No chance," he said.

Yun nodded, but didn't look convinced.

"Dave, I'm telling you. This woman was straight. A good cop. A good mom. She had lousy judgment in men, is all."

Yun smiled. "Can't throw stones from my glass house on that one. Two divorces for me."

Jake smiled. "Not saying my track record's all that great, either."

Yun laughed softly. "Yeah. I heard about the last one. A reporter?"

Jake groaned. "I'd rather not talk about it."

"Is it gonna cause problems for you?"

"Not so far." Then, "I don't know. Hopefully not."

"Well, I'm sorry to even suggest the dirty cop angle."

"It's okay. Of course I thought about it. But there's just nothing there."

"Good. Listen. Let me sniff around a little more. Reach out to a CI or two. See who Edwards and Burke were running with lately. If they got mixed up in something they couldn't handle. You never know."

"I appreciate it," Jake said. He shook Yun's hand and slid out of the passenger seat. It had gotten so cold, his teeth ached. He slid behind the wheel of his car and started the engine. Reaching into his pocket, he searched for his gloves. He found Birdie's note again with the Whitneys' names written on it.

Another dead end. He looked up. Dave Yun had already walked into the building. Jake slammed a fist into the seatback beside him, then put his car in reverse.

Thirty-One

"I think the fact that no arrests have been made in this case speaks for itself."

Ed Zender stood outside the county courthouse flanked by Tim Brouchard, his campaign manager, and county commissioner Rob Arden.

"Good old Uncle Rob," Jake muttered. "Never misses a chance to get his face in front of a camera."

"Detective Zender, you've made no secret of the fact you thought BCI should have taken over the Rathburn murder investigation from the beginning. Do you think that's what should happen now?"

Ed smiled right into the camera. He had a new haircut. New suit. The bastard looked like he'd gotten a spray tan.

"I've said all I can really say on that. But if I were sheriff, you can be certain the cronyism would end. And you have to wonder, who is Sheriff Landry protecting? And who wanted to keep Mary Rathburn quiet?"

Jake practically choked on his bagel. Birdie walked in front of him and switched off the television.

"He couldn't investigate his way out of a paper bag when he was here, Jake. Don't waste brain space on him now."

"People are actually starting to listen to him. Did you see the op-ed piece in the *Bugler* today? A year ago, nobody at that paper would return Ed's calls. They know what an incompetent blowhard he is. Now they're salivating every time he gets near a microphone."

"Let Landry worry about the politics. We're doing everything we can."

"He's all but accusing Mary of being on the take."

"From whom?" Birdie said. "For what? One week, Ed's taking credit for handpicking her and training her. This week he's implying she was dirty? He can't have it both ways. This is just about him getting his name out there. Before he announced, the people in the county barely knew who he was."

Birdie had the printouts from Mary's phone records spread out on the table. After a full day of going over them again, she found no new leads.

"He's planting a seed," Jake said. "This is a chess game Zender's too dumb to play. Brouchard's putting him up to this. Even intimating that Mary was involved in something corrupt ... he's gonna try to force an internal investigation."

"Over what?"

"Yun asked me the same thing yesterday," Jake said. "People are thinking it."

"Out of thin air," Birdie said. "Jake, there's no there there. Mary was clean. We both know it. We've combed through her financial statements. There's nothing unusual. No big purchases. We've searched the house. She didn't have some mystery bag of cash lying around. There's absolutely no shred of evidence that Mary was involved in any sort of criminal activity. None. This will blow over."

"Yeah," Jake said, but he wasn't convinced. People loved scandal and gossip. Ed just might be successful at inventing something that wasn't there. An investigation, even if bogus, would hurt Landry most of all. But it would hurt Connie Rathburn too. If people heard Mary's name in connection with an investigation, they would assume the worst and ignore the results.

There was a knock on the office door. Darcy poked her head in. "Hey, sorry to bother you. There's a lady out here insisting she needs to meet with you. Says you gave her your card."

"Did she leave a name?" Jake asked. He grabbed his jacket off the chair and put it on.

"Francine Beadle," Darcy said.

Jake looked at Birdie. "That's Shane Edwards's landlady. She lives in the other half of his duplex."

"She's driving Sergeant Nix crazy. Came in pounding on his desk, demanding to be seen," Darcy said.

"She's a trip," Jake said. "Can we set her up in the interview room?"

"You wanna see her? She seems like a kook."

"I'll see her," Jake said. Then to Birdie, "Sit in on this with me. Odds are she's here to complain about her driveway not being shoveled again."

Jake and Birdie waited a few minutes. Darcy buzzed the desk phone when she had Francine Beadle deposited in the interview room. Then Jake and Birdie went down.

Francine wasn't sitting when they arrived. She was pacing at the other end of the room. When she saw Jake, she turned and slammed her palm against the table.

"About time," she said. "I've got a doctor's appointment in twenty minutes. I don't have time to screw around."

"Mrs. Beadle," Jake said. "This is my partner on the Rathburn case, Deputy Erica Wayne."

"Nice to meet you," Francine said. "Maybe between the two of you, you can tell me what's going on?"

"You first, Mrs. Beadle," Jake said. "What did you want to talk to me about?"

"I put up with a lot," she said. "The odd hours. The friends in and out. I even let that boy have a party a few months ago. They parked on my side of the driveway and I didn't raise a stink. And you showing up too. My sister's been telling me for over a year that I needed to throw him out. Serve eviction papers. But I've been nice. The holidays were coming. I was gonna wait until after the first of the year. Well, it's February now. I've waited long enough."

"Mrs. Beadle," Jake said. "If you're here looking for landlord/tenant advice, I ..."

"Something's going on over there," she shouted. She finally took a seat. Jake and Birdie sat opposite her. Birdie grabbed a pen and a pad of paper.

"What's going on?" Jake asked.

"Last night, the girlfriend packed her things into the back of her little Honda and she drove off. And this was after a lot of screaming. I try real hard to mind my own business. Those walls are thin, though. And it's not like they tried to keep their voices down."

"You heard something?" Jake asked.

"Lot of foul language. That's what I heard."

"Were you able to understand the context of their argument?" Birdie asked.

Francine pursed her lips. "I don't like to gossip. I don't like to get involved."

"You're here, Mrs. Beadle," Jake said. "So obviously you think there's something I should know."

"He kept telling her she needed to quit nagging him. I don't know about what. But he kept saying he's got everything under control. She asked him to look in the mirror. That's the thing. He tried to hide it from me, too. But I saw his face. Somebody beat on that man. I told him when I saw him at the mailbox that he better keep whatever trouble he was in away from my property. He flipped me the bird."

"Have you seen anything else unusual at the house? Anyone coming or going that's new?"

"No," she said. "Just that little creep he hangs around with."

Birdie pulled out her phone. She opened her camera roll and showed Mrs. Beadle a picture of Ian Burke. "Was it him?"

"Yes," Francine said. "That little creep. You know? He's even ruder than Mr. Edwards. I was just coming out of my house when he walked up. Getting my paper. I know you younger folks don't even know what a real newspaper is anymore, but I like holding it in my hands. That's real news. Not this online crap."

"Sure," Jake said. "When was Mr. Burke at the apartment?"

"Day before yesterday," she said. "That's what I'm telling you. That's when all the trouble started. That little creep came over.

Parked on my side of the driveway, blocking me in. I went over there to tell him to move it. He was rude. Just plain rude. Told me I wasn't going anywhere so what's the difference? The difference is it's my property. Doesn't matter if I had plans to leave or not. Well, he called me a name I won't repeat. Uncalled for. And I told him that. I went back to my place and had to listen to the two of them yelling at each other for about a half an hour."

"Did you happen to hear what they were yelling about?" Birdie asked. "I mean, I know you weren't eavesdropping. But as you said, the walls are thin and they obviously knew you were home. It's not like they would have had a real expectation of privacy."

"I wouldn't think so," she said. "But it was just more of the same. Lots of foul language. But that little creep? I heard him threaten Mr. Edwards. Said what happened to his face was just gonna be the beginning if they didn't hold up their end."

"Hold up their end of what?" Jake asked.

"Didn't hear that part."

"But you're sure that's what Burke said? You're not paraphrasing?"

"That's what he said. Said your face is gonna just be the beginning. That they had a job to finish and Shane needed to hold up his end."

"What did Shane say?" Jake asked.

"Got kind of muffled. And it's not like I don't have a life of my own. I couldn't really hear what Shane said. I thought about calling the police. They were disturbing the peace. They were disturbing *my* peace. But the little creep left right after that and things got quiet. That is, until later in the evening when the girlfriend showed up and the shouting started all over again. And like I told you, she packed up her things and drove off. Haven't seen her since."

"Mrs. Beadle," Jake said. "Was Shane's son home? Where was he during all of this?"

"I wondered that. When the creep came over, the boy was in school. I saw him get on the bus. I open my part of the garage for him. Did I tell you that? He's too little to be waiting at the end of the driveway alone. I've told Mr. Edwards that plenty of times. It was snowing pretty hard the other morning and he just shoved him out the door. So I've been opening my garage and letting him wait inside."

"That's really nice of you," Birdie said.

"And that's the other thing I'm worried about. I don't know where that boy is."

"What do you mean?" Jake asked.

"He was home when the girlfriend came over and they had their drama. I could hear him crying. I saw her hug him in the doorway before she took off. But since then, nothing."

"Nothing. There've been no arguments?" Jake asked.

"No. I mean nothing. He's gone."

"Kevin is gone?" Birdie asked.

Francine Beadle heaved a great, exasperated sigh. "No. Pay attention. Mr. Edwards is gone. I collect rent on the 15th of the month. For all the trouble he causes, Mr. Edwards pays his rent on time. That's the only reason I've put up with things this long. He comes over, knocks on my door and hands me his check. Makes a big deal out of it. Always asking me why I don't do direct deposit or online banking. Because I don't, that's why. Well, he didn't come with the check. It's been four days now. He's never been late like this before. And he hasn't been home since the day before yesterday. His car's gone. He's supposed to let me know when he's leaving town for more than a day or two. He's been decent about that too. But nothing. No word. He's just gone. So what I want to know is, how long do I have to wait, legally, before I can start throwing his things out and renting that apartment? I've had enquiries."

"I'm not a lawyer," Jake said. "I can't advise you on eviction procedures. But I'd say a day and a half is probably too soon."

"He didn't pay his rent though. Isn't that abandonment?"

"Again, not a lawyer."

She waved a dismissive hand. "Knew it would be a waste of my time coming down here. You're no help."

"But you have been," Birdie said. "We really appreciate you letting us know all of this."

"You think it's got something to do with what happened to poor Kevin's mama?"

"I can't say," Jake said.

"Sure, sure," Mrs. Beadle said, rising. She clutched her purse in front of her. "Who do I see about getting bus fare back to my apartment?"

"I thought you said you had an appointment in town?" Birdie said.

"I gotta go home at some point," she said. "It's starting to snow again. I feel like spring's never gonna come at this point."

"I'll tell you what," Jake said. "If you wait in the lobby for a minute, I'll have one of the deputies drive you over to your appointment."

"Dr. Landis," she said. "Right across from the hospital."

"Perfect," Jake said. He made eye contact with Birdie. She nodded, taking the lead and Mrs. Beadle straight out of the room.

Jake's brain buzzed. Shane Edwards had gotten pounded on by someone. If Mrs. Beadle's story was to be believed, Burke showed up a couple of days later threatening him with worse. And Shane's girlfriend was spooked enough to finally extricate herself from a bad situation.

Jake walked back to the war room. He took the eraser and wiped away the red circle and line through Shane Edwards's picture. He pulled the picture down.

By that time, Birdie had come back. "I put her with Deputy Corbin," she said. "She feels like a real VIP now."

Jake tossed Shane's picture on the table. "He knows something," he said.

Birdie took out her cell phone. She went over to her computer and typed in a search. A moment later, she made a call. Putting her phone on speaker, she laid it on the table.

"Gansett Garage, how can we help you?" a gruff male voice answered.

"Is this Pete?" Birdie said.

"Who's asking?"

"Erica Wayne, Pete," Birdie said.

"Hey, Erica!" Pete Gansett said, his voice brightening.

"Hey, Pete. Quick question. I'm trying to track down Shane Edwards. Did he come in to work today?"

Pete let out an audible sigh. "Hell, no. That piece of crap hasn't shown up for two days. If you see him, tell him he can pick up his last paycheck at the end of the week."

"Wait a minute," Jake said. "Pete, it's Jake Cashen."

"Hey, Jake," Pete said. Pete was a fixture around town. Everyone brought their trucks in for tune-ups. There were seven Gansett boys. Pete was the only one of them who hadn't wrestled, but he was the biggest of them.

"You're saying you haven't seen Shane in two days?" Jake asked. "And he was scheduled to work?"

"Sure was. I'm already backed up as it is."

"He hasn't called or anything? Have you tried calling him?"

"Sure I have," Pete said. "We all have. Goes straight to voicemail. Hey ... nothing happened to him, did it? I mean, it was a hell of a shock seeing him with his face all messed up the other day. Just so you know, nobody in here believed the story he was trying to sell. We know you, Jake. We know you wouldn't just beat on him without a reason."

"Thanks," Jake said wryly. "And no. If anyone's asking. I had nothing to do with whatever happened to Shane Edwards's face."

"Oh, I knew that. Don't you worry. So, is Shane in some kind of trouble?"

Jake resisted the urge to answer "Probably."

"We just had some follow-up questions for him," Birdie answered. "Can you just shoot me a text if you see him, Pete?"

"Anything for you, Erica," Pete said. Jake swore he could hear the man blushing through the phone.

Birdie said goodbye and clicked off.

"Jake," she started.

"Something's wrong," Jake said. "Shane's AWOL."

"I'm heading over to the school," she said, grabbing her coat. "Let's see if Kevin's been going. I'm worried about him, Jake. If Shane's in over his head ..."

"If?" Jake said. "I think that's a given at this point. I'll go with you."

"Should we call Connie?"

"Not yet," he said. "Let's not worry her until there's a solid reason."

Jake grabbed his coat. As he began to follow Birdie out to the parking lot, his cell phone rang.

"Yun," Jake said. "Hold up."

He answered, putting Yun on speaker so Birdie could listen in.

"Hey, Jake," Yun said. "I just connected with my snitch. The one I was telling you hangs around with Edwards and Burke sometimes."

"Yeah?" Jake said.

"He's willing to meet with you. Can you be at the Waffle House off Exit 38 in twenty minutes?"

Jake looked at Birdie. She whispered, "You go. I'll head to the school."

Jake nodded and made a telephone gesture with his thumb and pinky on his free hand. "Call me after you know something," he whispered to Birdie. Then to Yun, "Sure thing. I'm on my way."

Thirty-Two

Billy Ogontz was a skinny, raw-boned guy with a chin so pointy it gave his face an odd, triangular shape. He fidgeted in his seat, adjusting its position so the legs scraped across the tile floor with an ear-splitting screech.

"No reason to be nervous, Mr. Ogontz," Jake said. Yun sat beside him in the tiny room in the basement of the Marvell County Sheriff's Department. It was a temporary space, not much more than a storage closet. The main interview room one floor above was being painted this week. After a brief meeting at the Waffle House, Ogontz agreed to come down to the station. He was twitchy, not wanting anyone to see him with two cops.

"You don't know my life," Ogontz said. The thing was, Jake did. He'd worked with hundreds of men just like Billy Ogontz. Scared. Always looking over their shoulders because they couldn't help themselves from associating with bad people. Or they had no choice.

"You know what I'm doing here," Jake said. "I appreciate your willingness to talk to me. You didn't have to."

Ogontz nodded but didn't say anything. He adjusted his chair again, moving it a few inches away from the table.

"Can we get you something, Billy?" Yun asked. "You want a Coke?"

"Yeah. Sure. You got some of those Corn Nuts from the vending machine? They had the ranch flavor last time."

"Sure," Yun said. He shot a quick wink at Jake then excused himself to scare up Billy's probable lunch.

When the door shut behind him, Jake took out his phone and laid it on the table between them. "Look," he started. "I said I don't want to waste your time. I don't want you to waste mine, either. Detective Yun tells me you hang around with Shane Edwards and Ian Burke sometimes."

Ogontz shrugged his shoulders and held them near his ears for a moment. It seemed a desperate attempt to make himself even smaller.

"I've got a murdered cop, Billy. That's why I'm here. I know you know that."

"Shane and Ian had nothing to do with that," he snapped.

Jake gave one short nod. "Right. I know they weren't in the house the night Detective Rathburn was killed. But I get the strong impression that at least one of them knows more than he's telling me. And whatever they're withholding ... it's gotten out of control. They're in over their heads. Somebody beat the crap out of Shane the other day. For some reason, he's lying about who did it. He wants people to think it was me. But we know that's not true. Don't we?"

Billy's eyes flicked away from Jake's. He squirmed in his seat.

"What's he hiding, Billy? Do you know who hurt Shane?"

"I don't know, man," Billy said, though his tone was less than convincing.

"How well do you know Shane and Ian?"

"We hang," he said. "Ian got me into the drywall business. So, we work on jobs together sometimes. Not lately though. I busted my knee a couple of months ago and went on disability."

"It's steady work though? Other than lately?"

Billy nodded. "I can usually work as much or as little as I want."

"That's good. Especially in this economy. Sorry about your knee, though. Hopefully, it won't sideline you for too long."

"Thanks. Took me forever to get the government to give me what I'm owed."

"I've heard that. Surprised you got what's coming to you so quickly. That's got to be a relief, having steady money coming in."

"It ain't even half what I can make on the job."

"Sure. Sure. Has Ian been understanding about that?"

"What do you mean?"

"Well, I mean ... do you think he's gonna start calling you again as soon as you're back on your feet? Or do you think he's gonna screw you over?"

A flash of anger hardened Billy's features. He recovered quickly. "I'm not worried about that now."

"You got any other prospects? Or were you getting most of your work through Ian?"

"Mostly through Ian."

"Then you might wanna diversify."

"What does that mean?"

"I mean ... do you think it's smart to hitch your wagon to somebody like Ian? If he's mixed up in some kind of trouble he can't handle, can't you see how that might affect you?"

"I've got nothing to do with whatever Ian does on the side. We hang sometimes. We work together sometimes."

"Billy." Jake leaned closer to him. "I need you to level with me. You wouldn't have agreed to come in and talk to me if you didn't have something to tell me."

"I came in because Yun asked me to."

"Detective Yun isn't in the habit of wasting my time, either. So let's cut to it. You know something. You know Ian and Shane are messing with something that's gotten out of hand. That got Shane's face bashed in. Do you know who did that to him?"

"I don't know."

"So, what do you know?"

"I asked him, okay? We hang out at the Rusty Bucket. He came in the other night looking like his face went through a meat grinder. He tried playing it off. Made some joke about how we should see the other guy. But he was scared. You could tell. And Ian got all stiff. Grabbed Shane by the arm and the two of them went outside together. When they came back, Shane was done joking. He was done saying anything at all."

"You think it could have been Ian who bashed Shane's face in?"

"It wasn't Ian."

Billy adjusted his seat again. He'd started to sweat.

"But you know who did," Jake said.

Billy looked away. Yun walked back in carrying a can of Coke, a bag of Corn Nuts, and a sandwich wrapped in plastic. He set all of it down in front of Billy. Billy tore into the sandwich, ravenous.

Jake let him eat for a moment. Yun took his seat next to Jake. Billy's hands trembled as he reached for the Coke and snapped open the tab.

"It was a warning," Jake said. "What happened to Shane? He's out there lying about it. His girlfriend is out there lying about it. Whoever worked him over, they were trying to send a message, weren't they?"

Billy put his sandwich down. He looked like he was about to throw it right back up.

Before he could answer, Jake's phone rang. Birdie's ringtone. Jake held up a finger then walked out into the hall. As he did, Yun picked up where Jake left off.

"You gotta help us help Shane Edwards," Yun said to Billy. "I know you know he's in bigger trouble than he can handle."

"Whatcha got?" Jake said to Birdie.

"Jake," she said, alarm in her voice. "Kevin Edwards hasn't been at school for two days. His teachers are saying they've tried calling his dad and get no answer. I reached out to the girlfriend. She didn't pick up either. I left a message."

"Dammit," Jake said.

"If Shane's hiding out and he's got Kevin with him ..."

"The kid's in the line of fire," Jake finished for her. He wanted to drive his fist through the wall. "That stupid son of a ... If anything happens to that little boy ..."

"I know," she said. "Are you making any headway with Yun's snitch?"

"Just getting into it. He's scared of something."

"What do you want me to do? Should I reach out to Connie Rathburn?"

"Not yet. Let's not freak her out if we don't have to."

"The teachers gave me some names. Some of Kevin's best friends. I can see if they know anything. Try to run down some of the places Shane hangs out a lot. And I can try to track down Ian Burke."

"Okay. Keep me in the loop. I shouldn't be too much longer here."

He clicked off with Birdie. When he walked back into the room, Billy had shifted in his chair, sitting almost sideways away from the table.

"We're out of time, Billy," Jake said, not even trying to conceal the anger from his tone. "You know who that was?"

Billy looked back at him. His eyes had gone bloodshot.

"Shane Edwards is missing. And you know what? If that were all it was, I wouldn't give a shit. I told you. I know he didn't kill Mary. But I think he was messed up in something that got her killed. Now he's gone to ground. Which again, don't care. Except he's got his kid with him. Kevin Edwards is four years old, Billy. A baby. Whatever Shane's mixed up in, he couldn't keep it from touching the mother of his child."

Jake held out his phone. He opened his camera roll and picked one of the worst pictures of the crime scene. Mary was lying on her side. From this angle, you could clearly see the grisly cut through her neck. Jake slapped his phone on the table right in front of Ogontz.

"Take a good look," he said. "That's the kind of trouble I think Shane and Ian are in. You gonna tell me I'm wrong?"

Billy practically convulsed when he looked at the picture. He lashed out and pushed Jake's phone away.

"That's got nothing to do with me."

"I know it doesn't," Jake said, taking a softer tone. "But if Shane and Ian are your friends, then you have to help me help them. I can put them in protective custody. I can make sure Kevin is safe. If something happens and you didn't say anything ... well ... you're gonna have to live with that."

"I don't know, all right!" he shouted. "I really don't. But ever since Ian started bringing this new guy around, things haven't been the same."

Jake sank into the chair beside Yun. "What new guy?"

"He's some friend of Ian's. Somebody he met when he was working a job in Circleville. He called me up but I couldn't come in because of my knee. Next thing I know, he's got this new guy with him."

"A name," Yun said. He grabbed a pad of paper off the table and a pencil from his pocket and shoved them both in front of Billy.

"Whitney," Billy said. "They called him Whitney. R.J. Whitney."

Whitney. Whitney. The name thundered through Jake. Rodney and Penelope Whitney were the names on the tax roll at the house he'd seen Ian and Shane come out of the day he followed them. Bernecki's neighbor.

"What did he look like?" Jake asked.

"Big dude. Maybe five ten, five eleven. Greasy brown hair."

Billy made a chopping gesture with his right hand just below his left shoulder.

"Long hair?" Jake asked. Billy nodded and made the same gesture. Shoulder length.

"Just a mean son of a bitch," he said. "Ian said he needed a place to stay. So he let him crash on his couch. Then he wouldn't leave. Ian was getting pretty pissed about it. R.J. wasn't kicking in for anything, you know? Ian got him work. Gave him a place to stay and the guy just took advantage. Shane told me about it. He didn't like the guy either but he said Ian wouldn't stand up to him. Which wasn't like Ian. He likes being top dog, you know?"

"This R.J." Jake said. "You think he's who beat Shane up?"

"Yeah. That's what I think. The two of them were always clashing. I don't know what it was about. Shane and Ian would clam up whenever R.J. came into the room. I'm telling you, they're scared of him. There's something going on. I don't know what. But Shane's been lying about what happened to his face. You're right about that. We all knew it."

"Do you know what R.J. stands for?" Jake asked.

"Nah. I tried to avoid talking to that dude. He threatened me."

"What do you mean?" Yun asked.

"I said something to Ian. Told him I just needed a few weeks for my knee to rehab. There's a big job over Arch Hill. I wanted to make sure Ian knew I'd be ready for it. Well, this asshole, R.J., overheard me. Told me Ian wasn't gonna need my weak ass anymore. Got in my face. Shoved me against the wall. Then he pressed his knee into mine and said how much of a shame it would be if I hurt myself again. Then he just pushed off me and started laughing. Ian did nothing. Didn't stand up to him. Just kind of skulked off. I don't know what's going on between those two. But

Ian and Shane are scared of him. So am I. And that's all I got. I swear to God."

"Did you ask them, Shane or Ian, what the deal was with R.J.?" Jake said.

"They shut me down anytime I tried. We're friends, but I don't need those guys. I cared because Ian was gonna hook me up with work. That's it. You should talk to Marissa."

"Shane's girlfriend," Jake said.

"I know she didn't like R.J. either. I don't know if he did something to her or what. But she and Shane were fighting about him a lot."

"She left him," Jake said. "Day before yesterday. She packed her stuff and moved out of his apartment."

"Yeah? Well, if that's true, I'd bet money it's cuz of R.J. I'm telling you. She was scared of him, too. The way he looked at her ... the way he looks at girls in general. He's got rapey eyes, you know what I mean?"

"Sure, Billy," Yun said.

"Look, I gotta go, man. People saw me come in here. I got things I need to do."

Jake took out his business card and slid it across the table. "If you think of anything else. You call me. If you see Shane. You call me."

"Yeah. Yeah." Billy took the card. He grabbed his bag of Corn Nuts and let himself out of the room.

When the door shut, Yun sat back in his seat. "Five ten. Long dark hair."

"You've never heard of him?" Jake asked. "R.J. Whitney? The name on the deed at 1478 Foreman was a Rodney Whitney."

"Yeah, but according to the neighbor, that guy's in his seventies, if he's even alive at all."

"A son maybe," Jake said. "Or a grandson."

"I'll see if I can dig anything up," Yun promised. "Jake … Shane Edwards's little boy. You don't think …"

A ball of heat formed in Jake's stomach. Yun couldn't finish the sentence. Jake wouldn't let himself form the thought.

"Just find out what you can," Jake said. "And hurry."

Thirty-Three

Ten minutes out from Oakton, Jake got a call from Deputy Amanda Carter. It took him a beat to realize the significance. She wasn't in the habit of calling him on his personal cell.

"Cashen," he answered.

"Jake," Carter started. "Hey, listen. I think you better come over to Connie Rathburn's house."

Jake's stomach twisted into a knot. "Carter, what's happening? I'm five minutes out."

Jake made a sharp right turn onto Palm Street. Connie just lived around the corner. In the background, he could hear a woman crying.

Then the call dropped.

"Christ," Jake muttered. A million things ran through his mind. Shane and Kevin Edwards were missing. Mary was dead. Shane's girlfriend, Marissa Nagy, was scared of something and every instinct in him told him she'd lied to him when he talked to her the first time.

Connie's house was just up ahead. Carter's patrol car was parked in the driveway. He pulled in behind it and ran up to the front door.

Deputy Carter opened it before he could even knock, her face grim.

"Is she okay? Where's Connie?" Jake asked.

"Jake?" Connie Rathburn bounded down the stairway to Jake's left. Her eyes were red from crying.

"I'll let you two talk," Carter said. She disappeared down the hall. Connie stopped on the landing.

"What's going on?" Jake asked.

"Shane was here," Connie said. "Something's wrong."

"When?"

Connie led Jake into the living room across the hall. She closed the French doors and motioned for him to take a seat on the couch.

"He showed up about an hour ago," she said. "Jake, he's a mess. His nose looks broken. His face was all purple. It looks like someone tried to beat him to death. He wouldn't tell me anything. I begged him to call you."

"Was Kevin with him?" Jake asked, trying to keep his voice calm. He didn't want to alarm her until he knew more. Connie's expression turned to one of surprise.

"Jake, that's why I had Amanda call you. Kevin's here. He's upstairs. I finally got him to settle down and take a nap. He was hysterical after Shane left."

"He's here?" Jake felt a tremor go through him. All his pent-up rage leached out of him at once, making him feel lightheaded with relief. Kevin was here. He was taking a nap.

Connie sat down in the overstuffed chair opposite him. "I don't understand it. Since Mary died, he wouldn't let me near him. Wouldn't even let me go pick him up from school like I did for Mary. He blocked my number from his phone. I don't know if I told you that. But then he shows up here. He wouldn't come in. He practically threw that poor sweet boy at me."

It was then that Jake noticed two suitcases leaning against the wall.

"Those are Kevin's?" Jake pointed.

Connie nodded. "I haven't had a chance to sort through it all. Shane said he packed Kevin's clothes and that he needs me to take care of him."

"For how long?"

"Jake, he didn't say. Kevin wouldn't stop crying. He threw his arms around my legs and hung on so tight. Like he was afraid I would disappear."

Tears streamed down her face. "That baby has been through so much in the last six weeks. I don't know if he's ever going to get over it. You know I've had my issues with Shane. But for him to just drop him off here like that. Kevin was terrified."

"Did he tell you anything? Where he was going? What happened to him?"

"No. Nothing. He got angry when I started asking questions. He threatened me. He said do you want him or not? Because I can send Kevin somewhere else and you'll never see him again. Jake … I can't let that happen. I won't. Something is very wrong with

Shane. I can't let Kevin be around that. If he comes back here, can I turn him away?"

"You let me worry about that for now. But if he does come back, I'm the first phone call you need to make, all right?"

"Is it safe? Jake ... he's involved in this. I feel it in my bones, don't you? I know you said he didn't kill my Mary. But ... she's dead. He shows up here after somebody beat the piss out of him. He's tried to keep my grandson away from me then all of a sudden he's dropping him off along with his things?"

"Connie," Jake said. "There are some things I have to do. I can't tell you everything yet."

"Am I safe? Is Kevin?"

As she searched his face, Jake knew he couldn't give her the answer she wanted. Not yet.

"It's good that Shane did the right thing and brought Kevin here," he said. "I'm going to ask Deputy Carter to stay close. As soon as I can tell you something, I will. For now ... you keep Kevin. Okay?"

"Jake," she said. "I'm not going to let that boy out of my sight ever again. I don't care what Shane tries to do. I'll go to court. Or I'll go ... somewhere."

Jake put a hand on her shoulder. "Let's not start planning any doomsday scenarios just yet. Just sit tight. Keep Kevin close. And wait until you hear from me."

Connie nodded. Jake gave her a quick hug and went to find Deputy Carter. She was hovering at the end of the hallway near the kitchen. From her expression, Jake knew she'd heard everything. He gestured for her to follow him back outside.

"She called me," Carter said. "I called you immediately."

"You did the right thing. She trusts you. So do I. Can you stay here the rest of the day? I'll clear it with Sheriff Landry."

"Of course. Connie's becoming like family. And Kevin? Jake ... she was downplaying it a little. That kid was scared out of his wits. He wet himself in the middle of the foyer when Shane tried to give him a hug. I think he was afraid his dad was going to try to make him leave with him."

Jake squeezed his eyes shut and let out a breath. If he got his hands on Shane Edwards, he wasn't sure he'd be able to restrain himself from finishing the job R.J. Whitney or whoever beat him started.

"Jake," Deputy Carter said. "What's going on?"

"I don't know yet. That's the God's honest truth. Just stay close to Connie and Kevin. If Shane shows up again, call me. I don't care about the courts. Don't let him try to take that boy."

"Is she safe here?"

"For now," Jake said. "But keep your eyes peeled."

Jake said a quick goodbye. Barnum Bagels was only ten minutes in the opposite direction. He hoped Marissa Nagy had the answers he needed.

Thirty-Four

When Jake pulled up, Marissa was right in front of him, carrying a garbage bag. She heaved it into the dumpster as Jake parked. She turned, startled to see him, looked left then right before realizing there was nowhere for her to go.

"Get in," Jake said, rolling down his window.

"I don't have to do that."

"Get. In." Jake reached over and opened the passenger door.

"You're going to get me fired."

"You really think your employment status is the biggest worry you've got, Marissa?"

She hesitated, looked toward the back door of the bagel shop, then dropping her shoulders in resignation, she climbed into Jake's car.

"Where is he?" Jake asked.

"I don't know what you mean."

Jake turned in his seat. "Let me help you understand what's happening. You lied to me the last time we talked. I know about R.J. Whitney. I know *you* know about R.J. Whitney. You wanna stick to your little story about Shane falling on the sidewalk?"

She stared straight ahead. Jake could almost hear the gears turning in her brain. Was it fear or stupidity driving her thoughts now? He realized he no longer cared.

"He gutted her," Jake said. "Let her bleed out on the floor. It wasn't quick, Marissa. It was slow, painful, and torturous. It was a message to Shane, wasn't it?"

Still, she stared straight ahead. Only the tiniest flicker in the corner of her eye signaled the torment going on inside her.

"You did the right thing leaving him," Jake said. "I have no doubt that if you'd stayed in that house, I'd be scraping your organs off the bathroom floor like we had to do for Mary."

It was an embellishment, but not too far off from the truth. Marissa began to tremble. She let out a sob.

"Where is he?"

"I don't know."

"You need to quit lying to me. I have enough grounds to arrest you for obstruction of justice based on your last lie. You wanna go for two?"

"I'm not lying."

Jake pounded his fist on the dashboard. Marissa jumped in her seat.

"I know you're not stupid. You get that I'm your best shot at not getting killed like Mary did. Shane got involved in something he couldn't handle. How many times did he promise you he could? Huh?"

She shook her head.

"He was mad at you for asking too many questions, wasn't he? But you were right. You knew. And you did the right thing getting the hell out of there before Whitney caught up with him again. Now do the right thing and tell me the truth. Where is he?"

"I can't help you."

"Did he tell you they'll hurt you if you talk to me?"

She buried her face in her hands.

"Every damn thing he told you was a lie, Marissa. Shane got Mary killed. I don't know why yet but I'm going to find out. And when I do, I'll make sure you're locked up right beside him if you don't tell me the truth. He killed a cop. Your window of opportunity to take the help I'm offering you is about to close."

"I don't know anything. I swear to God."

"They're gonna kill him. You get that, right? Shane's in over his head. Even he knows that now. He dumped Kevin off at his grandmother's about an hour ago. He thinks he can outrun whatever's coming. Suppose he's right. Who do you think Whitney's going to come looking for next? How long do you think it's going to take him to realize you know how to find him? Christ, he's probably watching you right now."

Another bluff. But this one had an immediate impact. Terror streaked across Marissa Nagy's face. She twisted in her seat and looked behind her.

"You set me up," she said.

"I'm trying to help you. Tell me where Shane is. That's your only play. The only thing that's going to keep you out of jail or the hospital if Whitney gets a hold of you."

"Okay. Okay. But I don't know anything. I swear to God. I don't know what Shane and R.J. were doing. I know it was bad. I begged him not to have anything to do with that guy. He's bad news. And I don't know what or if it had anything to do with Mary's murder. That's the truth. On my life, I swear it."

She pulled out her cell phone, unlocked it, then opened up her texts. She handed the phone to Jake.

It was a series of messages from Shane that Marissa hadn't answered. The last one came in just thirty minutes ago.

"We can start over," it read. "I promise it'll be different, baby. I swear it."

After that, he'd sent a link to an e-ticket for a Greyhound bus leaving ten minutes from now from the station on Main Street.

"He's got family in Tampa," Marissa whispered. "I've never met them. But maybe he's thinking they'll let him crash with them. I don't know. I really don't. You can see I didn't answer him. I'm done with him, Detective Cashen. But it doesn't mean I want him to get hurt."

Jake took a quick screenshot of Marissa's e-ticket with his own phone.

"Do you really think R.J. will come after me next?"

The truth was, Jake didn't know. "Finish your shift," he said. "Call me before you leave. I'll send somebody to follow you home and wait there with you."

He pocketed his phone. Still crying, Marissa got out of his car. He was angry. Not at her. She was one more victim of Shane Edwards's bad decisions. But Jake was running out of time.

He called ahead to the bus station on his way there. It was a twenty-minute drive even going lights and sirens and top speed. He gave them Shane's description over the phone, but there were no guarantees he'd make it in time.

He called Birdie and explained the situation.

"On it," she said immediately. "Even if he gets on the bus, we'll stop it before it even makes it across the county line."

He knew he could count on Birdie. He just hoped he wasn't already too late.

Thirty-Five

Shane Edwards had one foot on the bus step when Jake spotted him.

"Don't make another move, Shane," he said, walking up behind him. The bus driver, a middle-aged woman with white hair and tired eyes, took her hand off the wheel.

"Better listen to him," she said.

Shane dropped his head. He backed off the step and slowly turned around, facing Jake.

His face was worse than Jake thought. The bruising around his eye had deepened to a dark purple with black edges. His eyelashes were encrusted with yellow goo and his lower lip was still grotesquely swollen. He should have seen a doctor. He should have gotten stitches through that lip.

"I got nothing to say to you," Shane said.

"Good. That makes it easy. I've got plenty to say to you. Let's go."

"Am I under arrest?"

"We'll see how the day goes. For now, start walking."

Shane took a nervous glance left and right.

"I can't be seen with you," he whispered.

"Then walk faster."

Jake grabbed a hold of Shane's backpack strap and pulled him along. The bus driver closed the hydraulic door. A few passengers gave Shane and Jake a casual glance, but nobody cared. They were all engrossed in their own lives.

"Get in," Jake said. He'd parked his cruiser in the emergency lane near the curb just outside the terminal. Again, Shane looked around nervously. But he did what Jake asked. There was a darker part of Jake that wished he hadn't.

Shane sat silently, brooding as Jake drove them the short way back to the sheriff's department. He parked in the back, which seemed to relieve Shane. Until another car pulled up right behind them.

Bethany Roman walked out. She had her phone out. Jake could see her camera recording.

"Get out," he said to Shane through tight lips. "Keep walking. Don't say a word."

"Jake!" Bethany called out. He had a hold of Shane's arm.

"Jake, wait. Detective Cashen. Are you making an arrest? Can you comment on ..."

Jake practically shoved Shane into the building ahead of him. He turned around and faced Bethany.

"Go home," he said.

"Jake ... if you're arresting Shane Edwards, the public has a right to know."

"But you don't," he said, his anger getting the best of him. He closed the door on her and took Shane by the arm.

By the time he got him into interview room number one, Shane Edwards was practically in tears.

"Sit," Jake said. He took the chair across from him and turned it, straddling it backwards. Shane sat with his back to the wall, clutching his backpack as if it were a stuffed animal.

"Tell me about R.J. Whitney." Jake's voice boomed off the walls. "If you're lying, I'll know it."

Shane shook his head. His lips trembled, but no sound came out.

"He did that to your face. Your buddy Ian Burke's been going around town, threatening my witnesses. You're involved in something that got Mary killed. It's going to get you killed next. Tell me I'm wrong."

"I can't be here," Shane whispered, his voice breaking. "I can't be seen with you. You marched me right by a fucking reporter."

"Don't worry about her. She doesn't know anything. And this is about you and me."

"I didn't kill Mary."

"But you got her killed. Tell me why."

Shane kept shaking his head.

Something rose up in Jake. He saw Mary's lifeless, bloodless face staring vacantly at the wall. He saw her message to him, written in her own blood. The last act she took before she drew her last, agonizing breath. "They won't stop with Mary," he said. "Whitney's already told you that, hasn't he? Your face. It was a warning. I know you're scared."

"You don't know anything."

Rage poured out of Jake. It had weight. Shape. Darkness. He slammed his palm against the table. Shane jumped and held his backpack even tighter against his chest.

"Look at me!" Jake yelled. "You think R.J. Whitney's who you need to be afraid of?"

"I can't help you. I didn't kill Mary. I had nothing to do with it."

"Fine," Jake said. "Stay right here. That reporter is still out in the parking lot. How about I go on the record and tell her you're not under arrest, but you're in here cooperating fully with me? It'll take her five minutes to post it online."

"No!" Shane cried. "You can't do that. I'm not doing that."

"Doesn't matter. She saw you walk in. She recorded you. I can keep you here all damn day, Shane. Give a press conference. How long do you think you'll last as soon as I turn you loose?"

Terror filled Shane Edwards's eyes. He knew Jake wasn't bluffing. *It would be fitting,* Jake thought. Let R.J. Whitney or whoever he was mixed up with mete out their own punishment to Shane Edwards. Remove the layer of legal wrangling that would undoubtedly take place even if Shane decided to cooperate.

He thought of Mary again. Taken down for what? For this piece of slime and whatever he'd gotten himself into.

"You can't send me out there like this," Shane said.

"You're out of options. Tell me about R.J. Whitney. What'd you take from him? What do you owe him?"

Shane kept shaking his head. He started to rock back and forth in his chair. Tears fell down his cheeks.

His fear became Jake's weapon.

"Whatever Whitney said he'd do to you? Believe him. Did Burke tell you he had it under control?"

A bluff. Billy Ogontz said Burke was the one who brought R.J. Whitney around for the first time. It was Burke who'd taken the risk of terrorizing Seena Grimes. And Shane had yet to deny Whitney was the one who assaulted him. As far as Jake knew, Burke didn't have a scratch on him. Whatever was going on, it was Shane who was trying to get out from under it. Shane who had the most to lose.

"He doesn't though, does he?" Jake continued. "He sold you out, didn't he? Burke? Tell me what you're involved in. Tell me how it got Mary killed."

Shane crumpled forward, letting his backpack fall to the floor. He buried his face in his hands.

"He's gonna kill you, isn't he?"

"You have to help me," Shane said. "If you want me to help you, you have to help me. I want immunity."

The word cut through Jake. Immunity. This little weasel.

"Tell me what you know."

"I'm here," he said. "I haven't asked for a lawyer. But I know my rights. I can't go to jail. I won't."

"I think jail's the least of your worries, isn't it?"

Slowly, Shane raised his head and nodded.

"Get the prosecutor. I know he's the one who has to write everything up."

"It depends on whether you've got anything of value to tell me."

Something went through Shane's face. The fear evaporated for a split second, replaced by a kind of smug resolve. Jake felt his hand curl into a fist. He envisioned smashing it into Shane's good eye. Mary's wounds. The blade going into each of her lungs. It should have been Shane.

"I know who killed Mary," he finally said. "But I won't say a word until I have a deal."

A red haze clouded Jake's vision. Every cell in his body wanted to tell Shane Edwards where he could shove his deal. He didn't deserve it. He deserved whatever torture R.J. Whitney or his associates wanted to dish out.

But Jake knew he could never prove Whitney's involvement without Shane or Ian Burke to connect the dots. As far as he knew, Whitney was long gone by now.

Without a word, Jake rose from the table. He walked to the door and opened it. Birdie was right outside. Of course, she'd heard he was in here.

"Don't let him leave," he said, his voice sounding dark and foreign to his own ears.

Her jaw tightened. She gave him a nod.

Jake made the short walk back to his office and pulled out his phone.

Boyd Ansel, the county prosecutor, answered on the second ring.

"I need you," he said. "I've got a witness asking for immunity. I need him to tell me everything he knows."

Jake didn't wait for Ansel to answer. He clicked off. Landry came to his office door. Of course, she too had already heard through the grapevine who he had in interview room number one.

"Jake," she said. "Are you okay? Do you have this handled? Can you be objective?"

He looked her straight in the eye. "Absolutely not."

She read his face, lifted her chin, and stepped aside as Jake charged back into the hallway.

Thirty-Six

"It's unusual," Boyd Ansel said, thirty minutes later after Jake explained what he wanted to do.

"Unusual, but not illegal?"

"I'm just saying I'm not sure my office would be the one with the power to enforce it."

"If he'll agree to it, in writing, your office won't need to be the one to enforce it. Am I right about that?"

"Well ... yes."

"Good. Then let's get this done."

Ansel walked into the room behind him. Birdie had brought Shane a sandwich and a soft drink. He wolfed it all down. Some of the fear had left him. But he still had just enough to be useful to Jake.

"You understand what we're offering?" Ansel said. "And you understand your immunity from prosecution is contingent on the truth and value of your information?"

"Yeah," Shane said. "As long as you understand. I didn't kill Mary. I never wanted that to happen to her. I ... I still loved her."

"How sweet of you," Jake said. He grabbed a chair and sat down hard.

"Where do I sign?" Shane asked.

"First, you talk," Jake said. "That's how this works."

Shane looked at Boyd Ansel. A terse nod from him and Shane seemed to settle. He looked back. From this side of the wall, he could only see a mirror. But he was smart enough to understand there were people on the other side of it, watching and listening to everything he was about to say.

"Okay," he said. "I'll do it."

"All of it," Jake said. He'd jotted down his own terms on a yellow legal pad. "You'll do all of it. It's the right thing. And you'll be in jail anyway unless you tell the truth."

Shane snarled, but finally resigned himself to the fact Jake was right. He had no other options.

"Yeah. Okay. I won't be able to stay in Stanley after this anyway. I know what you think of me. I know what Mary told you about me. I'm not some monster."

Jake gritted his teeth. Over the next twenty minutes, Shane Edwards explained how he had let a monster into Mary Rathburn's life.

"It was R.J," he started. "R.J. Whitney. You're right about that. He killed Mary. I wasn't there. I had nothing to do with it. It wasn't what I wanted. Not at all. Not for a second. But ... he did it anyway."

"Why?" Jake asked.

"You have to let me start from the beginning. I was pissed, okay? Mary and her mother were turning my kid against me. My own kid. She was telling him all kinds of lies about me. He's little. A mama's boy. Of course, he was gonna take her side. And she kept at me. I paid for half his daycare. I bought him new shoes. Clothes. It was never enough. And then she wouldn't let me see him."

Jake knew Mary's side of it. He knew Connie's side of it. Shane rarely showed up for his scheduled visitation. More than once when he did, he was drunk. The court had sided with her. A court referee had done a home study. The only person who had taken Shane's side was Shane.

But Jake kept all that locked away in his mind. It didn't matter anymore. Not with Shane's written agreement in place.

"I bitched about her. I admit that. My friends knew where I was coming from. Ian knew where I was coming from. He'd had a sister-in-law do the same thing with his nephew. His brother's kid. He kept telling me I needed to get a lawyer. That I should fight it. And Mary treated him like crap, too. Like he was trash. Like she was better than him. She thought she was better than all of us."

"Get to the part about Whitney," Jake said.

"Fine. R.J. was Ian's friend. I don't know how they hooked up. But he started hanging around. Coming to the bar we hang out at. I didn't really care for him. But Ian thought he was the shit, you know? I could see right through that but it just wasn't worth my time getting involved. So one night, right before Christmas, we were hanging out at Ian's place over on Echo Lake. Actually, it's his grandma's old place. Ian's been doing some renovations there. He invited us out for the weekend. We went ice fishing. Drank some beer. Watched football. Whatever. Well, one night, we made a bonfire and were hanging out. We were drinking. Smoked some weed. You know, just blowing off steam. Ian started in on me about Mary. How I needed to grow a pair and take my kid back. I was pissed. I told him it was none of his business. This R.J. started chiming in. Busting my balls right along with Ian about something he didn't know anything about."

"Who else was there?" I asked.

"Just the three of us. Ian, R.J. Me. That's it. I swear. I was pretty hammered. I wanted to go to bed. But they kept on me. Poking at me. Finally, R.J. said he could take care of all my problems for me. Well, I didn't know what he meant. At first, I kind of ignored him. He'd been spouting off all kinds of shit all night. About what a tough guy he was. Stuff he'd gotten away with. I wrote it off. Thought he was just being a drunk asshole. Because he was. But then he got real serious. He said he could take care of all my problems for me but that I'd owe him. That me and Ian would owe him."

"Owe him what?" Jake asked.

"I thought he was full of shit. And like I told you. The two of them were just on me all damn night. I got sick of it. R.J. kept asking me if I was afraid. Said I was weak. All talk. I'm not proud. I said some things about Mary I shouldn't have. But it was just talk. I thought it was just talk. R.J. said it over and over. He said he'd take care of my problem but that I'd need to take care of one for him. And there was something going on. He and Ian kept passing these looks between them. Smirking. Like they were in on something and I was too stupid to catch on. It pissed me off. Finally, I told R.J. I thought he was full of shit. All talk."

Shane covered his face with his hand. He was sweating. Shaking.

"What did you do?" Jake asked. "What did you agree to?"

"Nothing! That's the truth. I swear it. I didn't agree to shit. I wasn't being serious. I didn't think R.J. and Ian were being serious. I said sure, you take care of my problem and we'll see about yours. He stuck his hand out. Wanted me to shake on it. So I did."

"You expect me to believe you didn't know what you were agreeing to?" Jake asked. "You're gonna have to say it, Shane. The words."

He grimaced. "Mary. Okay? Mary. I said Mary was my only problem. I said if she could just drop dead that'd fix all my problems. I wasn't serious."

"What did this R.J. do?" Boyd asked.

Shane drew his shoulders back. "He laughed. Just kept on cackling. Then he got real serious. He said she'd be fun to carve up. That he'd use a knife sharp enough to cut through her like butter, but dull enough it would hurt when he wanted it to. He asked me if I wanted him to make it so she'd have to have a closed casket. Said he could do either. Depended on whether I wanted her to keep her pretty face. Then Ian started chiming in. Said I could tell him where Mary kept her spare key. That we knew when she worked. When she got home. What weekend I'd have Kevin. They both got a big laugh out of it. I'm not proud. I was pissed, okay? She'd just tried to make a fool out of me in front of the judge. I said stuff I shouldn't have. But I thought we were just joking around. I didn't like the vibe. So I was done. I just walked away and went into the house. I went to sleep."

Jake went rigid. He waited for Shane to pick up the story. He rubbed his forehead. He looked at the wall. He looked anywhere but at Jake.

"What happened, Shane?" Jake said.

"He did it. Okay? R.J., he did it." Shane's voice broke. "I didn't think he meant it. I thought we were all drunk and kidding around. But then Mary was dead. Carved up with a knife, just like

R.J. said he would. I was scared out of my mind. I didn't think he was gonna do it."

"There was no forced entry. You told him her schedule," Jake said, his voice sounding flat, robotic to his own ears. "You told him where that key was. He knew exactly when she'd be home alone."

"We were kidding around!" he shouted. "I swear."

"But you told him."

"Yeah. I told him. He just kept trying to one up me, you know? All that crap about how I needed to grow some balls around her. I'll admit it. It felt good to fantasize about showing her. Putting her in her place. But I didn't want her dead. I didn't want that psycho to actually hurt her."

Jake felt sick. As Shane squirmed and spewed his tale, Jake thought about how good it would feel to slide a knife across his throat so he could feel what Mary felt.

"What did he want in exchange for killing Mary Rathburn?" Boyd asked.

"He didn't say, not that night," Shane said. "It was after. He showed up at my house the night Mary died. It was like midnight. He just showed up, pounding on the door. I opened it and he was holding this knife. It was covered in blood. He told me mission accomplished. That's what he said. Mission accomplished. Then he said it was my turn. He handed me this piece of paper with a name on it. Then he gave me a key. He said Ian and I had a week to return the favor. Then he left. I thought he was drunk or crazy or I don't even know what. Later that morning, when I found out Mary was dead ... I freaked."

"You knew he did it," Jake said. "You came into this room and lied your face off. You knew it was R.J."

"He was gonna kill me. He told me and Ian that he'd kill us if we said anything. We believed him. I saw the pictures. You showed me what he did to Mary. So did he. He said if we were lucky he'd just kill us."

"Shane, what was the favor you did in exchange for his killing Mary?"

Shane started to tremble again. "I couldn't do it. I'm not a killer. I couldn't do it. Ian said we had no choice. He said R.J. was out of his mind. That he'd make sure we either went to jail or disappear if we didn't do what we promised. I kept saying I never promised anything. Leave me out of it. But then he kept leaving things. A hunk of Mary's hair wrapped around my steering wheel. He sent me pictures of Marissa naked in the shower. Like he was taunting me. Proving he could get to anybody he wanted to. He ... he picked Kevin up from school one day. I don't know how he got past the teachers. But he dropped him off at my work. All smiles. Kevin was eating an ice cream cone. So I believed him. Then ... the other day, he confronted me. Kept saying tick tock. Time was running out for me to return the favor. Then he beat the shit out of me. I thought I was gonna die."

"What is the favor you did?" Jake said. Now he was beginning to sweat.

"His aunt," he said. "Some old bat who lives out in Marvell County. She's rich, I guess. His uncle's widow. Said she was gonna leave everything to R.J. cuz there's no other family left. Only she won't die. So R.J. wanted us to kill her. Said nobody would ever know because we have no motive, just like he had no motive to kill Mary. And R.J. could make sure he was out of town, so he'd have an alibi."

"You met with him," Jake said. "I saw you coming out of that house where R.J.'s been living. You and Ian. You were carrying a bag. What was in it?"

"A gun," Shane said. "Some piece of crap 9 mm with the serial number scraped off. I made Ian take it. It freaked me out."

"When is this supposed to go down?" Jake said, the adrenaline beginning to course through his veins.

"I don't know," Shane said. "Ian stopped returning my calls. I don't even know if he's still alive. He said he wasn't scared of R.J. at first. That if we kept quiet, it was all gonna blow over because nobody could prove we had anything to do with what happened to Mary. We weren't there. That R.J. made a mess of it. Eventually, his DNA was gonna do him in. Then he did this to me." Shane pointed to his face. "And Ian's AWOL. I don't know if he's dead. I don't know if he's on the run."

"Where is R.J.?"

"I don't know. If he finds me. If he knows I talked to you. You gotta catch him. You gotta arrest him. You have enough now."

"What's her name? The aunt?" Jake asked. But before Shane said it, Jake already had a hunch.

"Aunt Penny," Shane said. "He called her Aunt Penny. He gave us an address out in the south part of Marvell County. Way in the boonies. She lives alone. R.J. said it would be easy. Just put a pillow over her head. She's an invalid. She's like eighty-something years old."

"Why didn't he just do it himself?" Jake asked.

"Cuz then the cops would figure it out," Shane said. "He's gonna inherit all her money so of course they'd suspect him. This way, we'd get away clean."

"A murder swap," Jake said. "A damn murder swap."

"Yeah. Only I didn't do it. I'm innocent. I didn't want Mary dead and I sure as hell won't kill some old lady for that psycho. So you have to help me now. I did everything I said I would for you."

Aunt Penny. Penelope Whitney.

"The address," Jake said. "Write it down." He shoved the paper in front of Shane.

Shane's hand shook. But he wrote down an address.

"Do you have what you need?" Jake turned to Boyd. Boyd nodded.

"As long as you do. I can wrap up my part of it now."

Jake tore the sheet off the pad. Quaking with rage, he charged out of the room, practically running smack into Birdie and Landry.

"My office," Landry said. "Before you do anything else, Jake."

Jake nearly pushed past her. He wanted to move. He wanted to punch something. She saw it in him. Landry was forcing him into a mental ten-count whether he wanted to or not. Gritting his teeth, he followed Birdie into Landry's office.

"Do you believe him?" Landry asked. She paced in front of her desk, hands on her hips. "He's been lying since day one."

"I believe R.J. Whitney probably killed Mary," he said. "Everything else fits. If we can find him."

"You need his DNA," Birdie said.

Jake held out the scrap of paper on which he'd written Aunt Penny's address.

"I'll start here. She needs to know she's in danger."

"What do you need from me?" Landry asked.

"I'm gonna head out to Marvell County. See if I can track the aunt down. In the meantime, we need to find Ian Burke. I have a hunch he's not in as much danger as Shane thinks. If R.J. Whitney's smart, he's as far away from the state of Ohio as he can be. But on the off chance Shane's right, we need to find Ian and bring him in. Can you take charge of that?"

"I'll start making phone calls and knocking on doors," Birdie said.

"Check with Detective Yun. His snitch, Billy Ogontz, might know where Burke is hiding out."

"What are you going to tell this woman?" Landry asked.

Jake looked at the address again. "I'll make it up as I go."

"Okay," Landry said. "Both of you. Be careful out there. No cowboy crap. Let's see if we can wrap this case up by the end of the day. Any resource you need, you call me."

"Bethany Roman," Jake said. "She's been prowling around the parking lot. I need her out of my hair. I need her off the scent of this for the next twenty-four hours. At least until we have Burke in custody and I can get Penny Whitney to safety."

"You leave that to me," Landry said. "Just watch your back."

Jake assured her he would. He folded his note and slipped it into his back pocket. Birdie was already on the phone with Dave Yun by the time he slid behind the wheel of his cruiser.

Thirty-Seven

The address Shane gave him for Penny Whitney couldn't have been more out in the boonies. He'd gone so far south and then west, he wasn't even sure he was still in Marvell County. He missed the turn-off twice. It was an old dirt road that didn't look like it had been plowed all winter. Jake found himself wishing he had Grandpa Max's pickup. His tires spun as he made the turn and headed up a steep incline.

The house was at the top of a hill surrounded by oak and maple trees. He counted at least twenty that had fallen over in the last ice storm. The woman needed to call a tree service. There was one rotted old maple partially obscuring the driveway. Jake drove around it. From old tracks in the snow, several cars had been up and down this road in at least the last week.

Penny Whitney had a gravel driveway. Her dingy gray ranch house had a wraparound porch but several of the posts had broken in half. The thing looked like it might not survive another good storm. As he put his car in park, he counted at least a dozen cats scurrying under the porch and into an open detached garage to the left of the house.

Jake walked up the rickety porch steps. A fat tabby cat stared at him through the window. A smaller gray cat came from nowhere and rubbed herself against Jake's leg.

Jake knocked on the screen door. There was no doorbell he could find.

"Mrs. Whitney?" he called out when he got no answer. It was dark in the house. No lights in any of the front windows. The cat at Jake's feet purred and curled her tail around his ankle.

He knocked on the door again, louder this time. "Mrs. Whitney? I'm from the sheriff's department. I just need a couple of minutes of your time."

No answer.

Jake stepped off the porch and headed toward the open garage. Three cats followed close behind. There was a blue Buick parked in the garage. It had been backed in so the hood was closest to him. He put his hand on it. The car still felt warm. He saw a plastic grocery bag on the front seat, filled with bags of cat food.

Jake walked around to the back of the garage. The woods stretched out behind it. He saw an overgrown trail leading down to the road.

"Mrs. Whitney?" Jake shouted. Three cardinals took flight from a low branch of the oak tree in front of him. Grotesque clay faces peered at him, cherub sculptures nailed into the trunks of four trees leading up to the house.

She had a covered grill on the deck at the back door. Jake walked up the steps to it and peered in through the glass sliding door. The kitchen was at the back of the house. The sink was filled with sudsy water. Dirty pots and pans were stacked on the counter beside it, waiting to be washed. She was home. Somewhere.

"Mrs. Whitney!" he called out.

He took a step back, trying to get a look through the glass block windows to the basement. There was a light on down there. Something flickered in front of it.

That's when he heard it. A crash. A thump. Breaking glass.

Jake's moves were automatic. In one fluid movement, he unsnapped his service weapon from its holster and drew it.

Three cats scurried for cover under a nearby bush. From inside, Jake heard a thud. Something very heavy had fallen to the ground.

Jake tried the slider. It was unlocked, but crooked in the track. He had to lift it up to move it sideways. He opened it just enough to slip through it.

Silence in the house now save for the drip, drip of the leaky faucet into the soapy water.

Jake looked left, then right, keeping his back against the wall. He moved to the right, toward the living room. Four cats darted soundlessly across the kitchen floor then out the now open sliding glass door.

The living room was clear. He could see all the way into the laundry room. He held his weapon pointed forward but tight to his chest. He headed toward the front of the house.

He came to a closed doorway. Jake hugged the wall, staying clear of the fatal funnel directly in front of the door.

He tried the knob. The door swung open with just that slight touch. Jake dropped low, weapon out. There were two gray cats on the bed, but the room was empty.

He moved back into the hallway. Another closed door, Jake guessed led to the basement. That's where the sound had come from. He heard another one. Muffled.

Then something else. Jake heard the unmistakable sound of a pump-action shotgun racking a round. He knew it immediately as the shotgun he was brought up with, a Remington 870, not a Mossburg or some cheap knockoff.

Adrenaline shot through his veins. Twenty years of training kicked in as he headed into the danger. For him, there was no worse place in the world, but he had no choice but to advance.

One step down. Two. He kept his back plastered against the wall.

He heard someone breathing heavily. There was an open doorway to the right at the bottom of the stairs. That's where the light was coming from.

A thousand visions flashed through Jake's mind in the three seconds it took him to get to that threshold.

Mary, lying in her own blood, trying desperately to write him her death message. White male. Five foot ten or eleven. Long dark hair. Shane Edwards's eyes filled with terror, his nose exploding in blood when R.J. Whitney's fist made contact.

Then, appearing disembodied at first, Jake saw the blackened gleam of a shotgun advancing through the open doorway.

"Drop it!" Jake shouted. "Police! Lower your weapon slowly!"

"No!" a male voice shouted in terror. Jake hadn't expected that. It came to his left at the bottom of the stairs. Two legs crab crawled backward in front of him.

Then the old woman emerged from the doorway on the right, her shotgun aimed straight at the chest of the man on the ground. Jake's shoulder made contact with a light switch. With lightning quickness, he flipped it on.

The woman, Penny Whitney, had murder in her eyes as she advanced on the man on the ground.

"Mrs. Whitney?" Jake said, holding his weapon steady. "I'm Detective Jake Cashen. I need you to put your weapon down. Now!"

She looked at him, cocking her head slightly to the side. She regarded him.

"Took your time getting here," she said. "He thought he could sneak up on me. Didn't you, R.J.?"

Jake took a step toward her, keeping his weapon trained on her. R.J. was on his back, his knees drawn up. He bled from a swelling gash on his forehead.

"She's crazy," he said. "She's got Alzheimer's. She's off her meds. I just came here to check on her and she butt-stroked me."

"Shut your lying mouth!" Penny yelled. "No-good ungrateful piece of trash! He came in here thinking he was gonna shoot me while I slept. Didn't work out like that, did it?"

"Penny," Jake said. "Put the gun down. I don't want to have to hurt you."

"You know what he did?" she said. "Tell him, R.J. Tell this nice detective what you did."

"I know what he did," Jake said.

"You're both crazy," R.J. said. He flicked his head back, brushing the hair out of his eyes. His hair. Long. Brown. Wavy. Exactly the color of the clump of hair found in Mary Rathburn's fist.

"Tell him what you did," Penny demanded. "Or I'll blow a hole straight through your chest. The first one is buckshot, the second is a slug."

"I'm under duress," R.J. said with a snarl. "You see it."

Jake took a step closer. Just out of the shadows near the wall, he could see a black lump. He took another step. It was a cheap, semi-automatic handgun lying on the floor about eight feet out of R.J.'s wingspan.

"I see it," he said.

"Yeah, you do," Penny said. "I heard this idiot the second he stepped onto my porch. Came in here thinking he could get the jump on me. He thinks I'm some addled old lady. Thinks I don't know what he's after."

"Penny," Jake said, trying to keep his voice even. "I'm going to need you to drop your weapon. I've got it from here."

"I knew it," Penny said. "The minute he started hanging around those two lowlifes from Stanley. I knew it. I heard him talking to one of 'em on the phone. Saying how he lived up to his end. He brought 'em out here telling me they were gonna fix my porch. This deadbeat wouldn't even change a lightbulb for me when I asked him to. I heard you. You think I'm dumb. You think I'm just old and addled. Well, who's the dumb one now?"

"Mrs. Whitney," Jake said, taking another slow step toward her.

"He killed your partner," Penny said. "I heard them talking about it when they came out here. R.J. carved her up, didn't you?"

He knew it. Jake could see it in R.J.'s stone-cold eyes. The DNA would be a match. R.J. wore a thin white tank top. The muscles in his neck bunched and corded. Even from here, Jake could see the freshly healed scar across his neck. Three jagged lines the exact distance apart as three fingernails. He could almost feel Mary in the room, pointing it out to him. Her testimony from the grave.

"He pulled a gun on me," Penny said. "You understand what I'm telling you, son? I was alone in my own home. You saw his gun over there. I had him drop it on the ground. His prints are all over it. You shoulda stayed outside. Called for backup or something. You still can. Just go up those stairs. Wait in the kitchen."

"She's crazy!" R.J. shrieked, realizing what his aunt was trying to do.

"Let me do it," she said. "Let me end him. You know what he did to that poor girl. He doesn't deserve to live."

Jake could see it. At that range, Penny Whitney couldn't miss. It would blow a hole through R.J. Whitney the size of a melon.

"No one would know," she said. Or at least he thought she did. Perhaps it was just his own conscience.

Easy. One shot. An instant. No one would know. It would hurt. Maybe R.J. wouldn't die instantly.

"He'll see it coming," Penny said. "He deserves to see it coming. Don't you think?"

Jake felt his own hand tremble on his weapon. He could almost smell R.J. Whitney's blood already. It mingled in Jake's imagination with the scent of Mary's.

She was dead. He killed her. Hunted her.

"He might get the death penalty," Penny said. "But how long's that gonna take? Huh? You rotten son of a bitch. I did everything for you. Gave you a roof over your head. Took you in when even your own mother wouldn't have you."

"Aunt Penny, please," R.J. said.

"That's right," she said. "Beg for your life. Did that girl beg for hers? She has a little boy, you piece of shit."

Kevin. Jake thought of Kevin. Then Connie. The trial would be a fresh horror for her. The crime scene photos. The autopsy. Mary's bloody robe would be entered into evidence.

"Let me end him," Penny Whitney said, her voice clear and strong. "I know you want me to."

He did. God help him, Jake did. He could see it. Taste it. No one would know. The blood would be on Penny's hands, not Jake's. R.J. Whitney meant for her to be a victim, too.

One second. One shot. And everything could be over for Connie Rathburn.

"It's justice," Penny said. Maybe if she hadn't, Jake would have made a different choice.

Maybe.

Justice.

Jake took the last step.

"R.J. Whitney," he said. "You're under arrest for the murder of Mary Rathburn. You have the right to remain silent ..."

He said all the words. Penny Whitney let out a sigh and pulled up her shotgun. She stepped aside as Jake took out Mary Rathburn's handcuffs and clamped them around R.J.'s wrists. He hauled R.J. to his feet. Penny leaned her shotgun against the wall as he led R.J. upstairs and into the light of day.

Thirty-Eight

For a woman who'd just learned she was the center of a murder plot, Penny Whitney took it remarkably well. She sat across from Jake in interview room one and asked for two things. A diet Dr Pepper and a bendy straw. She'd managed to handle her Remington 870 just fine, but needed help prying back the pop tab. Jake did it and slid the can back toward her.

"What do you want to know?" Penny asked. The woman had a large, square face with bushy eyebrows and a thick head of gray hair she wore layered. Her straight bangs only added to the right angles of her face.

"Anything you can tell me," Jake said. "But let's start with your relationship to R.J."

"I want it known ... and I mean, write this down in your little book there. I share no blood with that boy. His father and Rodney, my late husband, were brothers. I'm only his aunt by marriage."

"I'll make sure that goes in the report."

"Good. Make sure it goes in the paper too. I don't even like that we share the same last name. Nothing I can do about that now."

"Mrs. Whitney, did you have any inkling that your nephew was plotting to kill you?"

"Not until the last day or so. Not for sure. But I can't say it came as a shock."

"You can't? Because it would have shocked the hell out of me. You're pretty poised for someone ..."

"My age?" She cut him off. "Because I'm an old lady?"

"I wasn't going to say that at all." She reminded him a little of his Grandma Ava. A similar fire to her temperament. Jake knew it was the thing that had saved her life today.

"He's after my money," she said. "See, Rodney and I never had kids of our own. We tried, but he had the mumps when he was a kid and shot blanks. What are you gonna do?"

"I'm sorry to hear that."

Penny waved a dismissive hand. "We lived a full life. The animals are my babies now. And I get to take care of them how I want to now that Rodney's gone. If I want 'em sleeping in the bed with me, who's gonna say something?"

"Nobody." Jake smiled. He imagined his grandmother would have done the same if Grandpa Max had gone before her.

"We had money, me and Rodney. On account of the fact we both worked hard all our lives, lived frugally, and never had kids. Well, Rodney was a softy for that boy. For R.J. And so you know, he's a Randall, not a Rodney. R.J. stands for Randall Junior."

"Got it," Jake said, writing it down in his notebook.

"Randall Senior was Rodney's little brother. They were twelve years apart. Rodney always felt kind of responsible for Randall. Then his kid by extension. Oh, it nearly broke Rodney when his brother, Randall, died. Colon cancer. R.J. was only eighteen at the time. Randall made Rodney take a deathbed vow to keep looking after that boy. Like he wouldn't have anyways. So he did. Always bailing him out of trouble. Finding him jobs that he could never seem to keep. Over and over again. I put up with it because that's what you do for your husband. And when Rodney passed on ten years ago, I looked out for him as best I could. Invited him over for holidays and such. He said he was gonna help me around the house. And he did for a bit. I'll admit that. But then there he'd come with his hand out soon enough. Some new scheme he'd get roped into. Some debt he'd need paid off. It was like that when Rodney was alive, but it got worse after he died."

"You have a will?" Jake asked.

"Sure do," she said. "Rodney and I had 'em drawn up together maybe fifteen years ago. I wasn't thrilled about it, but Rodney believed you take care of your family no matter what. So I went along."

"You left everything to R.J."

She heaved a great sigh and nodded. "That's the way Rodney wanted it. And we didn't have any kids. I was an only child. I didn't have anybody else to leave things to and it meant so much to Rodney. So sure. Figured what difference would it make where my money went after I was gone? So I signed the papers and forgot about it. I had no idea Rodney told R.J. about it. If he hadn't done that, I don't think you and I would be sitting here."

Jake swallowed past a lump in his throat. He wondered whether Mary would still be alive if Rodney hadn't shown that will to R.J.

"Anyway," Penny continued, "Rodney died. As you know. And I just didn't want to think about it. But over the years, R.J. got worse and worse to deal with. Only showing up when he wanted something. And he's just rude. Disrespectful. He was supposed to manage my rental properties but you've seen what's become of that house on Foreman. Then he started living there himself without my permission. Without the courtesy of paying rent. Well, I told him enough is enough. That I was gonna go talk to a lawyer about making some changes. He told me I'd better not. That he'd take me to court and put me in a home."

"You believed him?"

"I believed he believed he could. But I talked to a lawyer anyway. And he told me it was up to me entirely as far as what I want to do with my money. Even the stuff that used to be Rodney's. Because he left everything to me. It's mine free and clear to do with as I please. So that's what I was planning to do. I was gonna take R.J. off my paperwork and leave everything to the Oakton Animal Shelter. I've got a final appointment to sign all the papers on March 15t^{h}. Took me three months to get that appointment."

"Did R.J. know that?"

"I didn't think he did. But he said something a couple of days ago when he was over here fixing my storm door. Or trying to. He did a piss-poor job of it and I've got somebody else coming out next week. But he said something that got me thinking. I heard him talking on his cell phone. It sounded like he was arguing with somebody about getting paid for a job. He kept saying he held up his end. That he took care of his business. And he said something that kinda stopped me cold. I heard him say you shoulda told me she was a cop."

"I'm sorry?" Jake said.

"He said you shoulda told me she was a cop. It seemed such a weird thing to say, you know? And I'm sorry that I didn't put it together sooner. But then, he started saying that this job had to be done by the fifteenth of March. Over and over he said it. The fifteenth of March."

"The same day as your appointment with the lawyer," Jake said.

"You betcha."

"So what happened today?"

"R.J. just showed up. I was in the basement organizing my canned goods. I saw him through the window. He had that cheap ass gun in his hand. Stormed up the front porch and barged right in. He knows I don't like that. He doesn't have no-knock privileges. Well, I had a bad feeling. I mean, what good could he have been up to, right?"

"Right."

"So, I grabbed my Remington and I stayed where I was. He was up there banging around, swearing up a storm. Yelling for me. Saying come out come out wherever you are, Aunt Penny. I wouldn't have done anything. I figured he'd just leave when he couldn't find me. I was worried he'd steal some cash I have in a cookie jar in the kitchen but I wasn't looking to have an argument. He sure was. Calling me all kinds of vile names I won't repeat. Then he came downstairs. I told you, I knew he had that Nine in his hand so I decided it wasn't good to take any chances. So I knocked him in the head with the butt of my shotgun. Just like he told you. Boy, he wasn't expecting that."

"I don't suppose so."

"Well, he changed his tune pretty quick. Begging me to let him go. Telling me he loved me and just wanted to look out for me. I told him I knew he was lying. Then I lied. I told him I already went to that lawyer and wrote him out of my will. Oh, he got real nasty after that. I asked him what he'd done. Because I remembered what he said. About the cop. And I saw him hanging around with that Shane Edwards loser. I read the news, Detective Cashen. I knew that boy was married to the cop that got killed. So I bluffed and told him I knew what he and his friends did. He didn't deny it. Can you believe that? If you were innocent of something like that, you'd deny it, wouldn't you?"

"Yes. Yes, you would."

"The rest, you pretty much know. You showed up right after that. Good thing. Because I was gonna blast his head off. He killed that poor lady cop, didn't he?"

"I believe so."

Penny let out a choked sob. It was the only time she lost her composure. She quickly recovered.

"I'm sorry," she said. "I should have called the police the second I suspected something."

"You did just fine. Where'd you learn to handle a shotgun like that?"

She smiled. "You probably wouldn't guess it by looking at me now. But I was a champion trap and skeet shooter when I was younger. My daddy raised me around firearms. He was with the 101st Airborne. Screaming Eagles. Operation Overlord. Survived Normandy."

"He'd be damn proud of you today."

"He wouldn't have waited," she said. "He'd have ended that bastard for what he did to your partner, Detective Cashen. And if you hadn't shown up when you did, I would have killed him."

"Part of me wishes I hadn't shown up when I did." Part of him wished he hadn't said it out loud.

"But you did," she said.

She got up and did something else Jake wouldn't have expected. She walked around the table and gave him a hug. He froze, not knowing how to take it.

"I suppose you did the right thing. I just hope you can learn to live with it, honey. Do you need anything else from me? I need to get home and feed the cats."

She let go of him. Jake closed his notebook. "No. You've given me everything I need. I'll have one of the deputies drive you home."

"That'd be nice," she said. Penny Whitney didn't wait for Jake to stand. She opened the door and looked back at him. There was something odd in her expression. She got misty-eyed. For a moment, she looked exactly like his grandmother.

"She'd be proud of you, you know," Penny whispered. He didn't know who she meant. Mary? Or was she channeling spirits? Grandma Ava always said she could hear them. Jake didn't ask. Penny's face melted into a mysterious smile. Then she let herself out and headed for the lobby.

Thirty-Nine

Twenty-four hours later, Jake walked into Sheriff Landry's office. He hadn't slept, ate, or been home since the morning before he apprehended R.J. Whitney from his Aunt Penny's house.

"He's still not talking?" she asked.

Jake slapped a fresh file folder on her desk.

"He doesn't need to."

She reached for the file folder and opened it. One by one, she flipped through the printouts of the photos Jake took at R.J. Whitney's house on Foreman Street, her eyes widening with each successive shot.

"This is Mary's house," she said, her voice cracking.

"He cased it," Jake said. "These were all taken two days before the murder with a high-powered lens."

There were photos of Mary at her kitchen table. Photos of her answering her back door when Jeff Hammer came to visit. The two of them embracing once he was in the living room. Kissing. Later, Mary was alone. Whitney snapped pictures of her washing dishes at the kitchen sink. In two of the photos taken through her bedroom window, he caught her undressing. Landry flipped through those quickly, then gasped as she stopped at the most disturbing of the pictures.

Whitney had taken pictures of Kevin as well, sleeping in his bed. A few were in extreme close-up.

"Jake," Landry said.

"I know."

"If Kevin had been home that evening ..."

"I can't let myself think about that too much."

"Is this all you have?"

"No. Cheek swab got sent off to Ramirez and the BCI lab twenty-four hours ago. Mark says he'll have an answer for me tomorrow or the next day at the latest. But his phone forensics are damning in and of themselves. His phone pinged the tower closest to Mary's at nine o'clock the night she died. He was there for almost forty minutes."

"God."

"The timing overlaps when Sarah Hammer's phone pinged the same tower," Jake continued. It took a beat for Landry to appreciate the magnitude of that fact.

"She pulled into the driveway when Whitney was still in the house?"

"Yes," he said.

"What if she'd knocked on the door?"

"We can't get sucked into the what-ifs. As it is, I've got enough to make an arrest even without the DNA. With Shane Edwards's testimony, what we found on his phone and hard drive, we've got our guy."

"You've got our guy," she said, closing the file folder.

"Sorry to interrupt," Birdie said, poking her head in the doorway.

"No, no. Come in."

"We've got Ian Burke," she said. "I tracked him down to an old girlfriend's house. She let him crash on her sofa for the last couple of days. He's in the interview room but his lawyer just showed up. He says he'll refuse to answer any questions."

"Who's he got representing him?" Jake asked.

"Tim Brouchard," she said.

A flash of anger went through Jake. "Why doesn't that surprise me?"

"How is that not a conflict of interest?" Landry asked. "Brouchard's been stage managing Ed Zender's campaign. He's the one out there pulling the strings and second-guessing how we've led this investigation."

"Doesn't matter," Jake said. "Ansel's not going to offer up any more immunity deals. Shane beat Burke to it. He'll end up charging him with conspiracy. Burke's gonna be looking at the death penalty right alongside R.J. Whitney. He'll talk. The only angle Brouchard has is keeping a needle out of Burke's arm and he knows it."

"I think he knows," Birdie said. "Brouchard's had to practically sit on him to keep him quiet."

"Cooperation now is the only card he's got to play," Landry said. She'd gone from horror to anger in the span of the last sixty seconds. "I want to talk to Boyd Ansel. Let's make sure we're all on the same page. No deals unless he talks to me first. Those dirtbags should have come to you the second they found out Mary was killed. All these weeks, they've sat quietly by while the time and resources of this office were expended. They've been acting like guilty men. In fact ..."

Landry stood up and strode toward the door. Birdie just got clear of it before Landry charged out. "Zoe," she hollered. "Can you get Boyd Ansel on the phone for me? I want a meeting. I want him in my office in the next fifteen minutes."

"Sure thing, Sheriff."

Landry whirled around and shut the door. "Whitney's a cop killer. Edwards and Burke aided and abetted, lied and tried to cover their tracks."

"They did worse," Jake said. "Burke tried to intimidate a witness."

"He thought if Seena Grimes gave him an alibi, he'd have nothing else to worry about," Birdie said.

"What about Edwards?" Landry asked. "Are you sure he's been forthright about everything? Is his immunity deal solid?"

"I want that bastard to fry right along with Whitney," Jake said. "But the truth is, without his testimony, I'm not sure I would have been able to get to Whitney."

"And Penny Whitney might be dead too," Birdie offered.

The image her comment conjured in him made Jake smile for the first time in weeks. Penny Whitney was never going to go down easy.

"I wish she'd have just blown his head off," Birdie muttered. "Man, I'd like to have seen him sprawled out on her basement floor like that."

"She's a tough old bat," Jake said. "Whitney was right that Aunt Penny's not in the mood to die anytime soon."

He went quiet after that. It had been a close thing. How easy it would have been to just let Penny Whitney have her own retribution and blast R.J. Whitney off the face of the earth.

"I need to schedule a press conference," Landry said.

"Give me an hour," Jake said. "I have to go talk to Connie Rathburn. She should hear all of this from me, not on the news."

"Of course," Landry said.

"Do you want me to go with you?" Birdie asked.

"I think I have to do this myself. Can you oversee the search warrants at Burke's apartment and his phone?"

"You bet," Birdie said.

Landry dismissed them both. Birdie headed for the parking lot. Jake took a different hallway, putting him in front of interview room number one. Tim Brouchard stepped out just as Jake went by. His back was turned. He didn't see him. Jake came to the doorway. Ian Burke looked like hell. Dirty. Ragged clothing. Unshaven.

Jake said nothing. He just filled the doorway and stared at him. Slowly, Burke lifted his eyes. For the first time, Jake noted real fear in Burke's expression.

"I didn't ... I wasn't ..."

Jake put a hand up. "You better stop talking, Burke. Your lawyer wouldn't appreciate it."

"He says the same thing. But you have to know. I never wanted that girl killed. Whatever Shane's telling you, it's a lie. I won't go down for it. She wasn't my problem. She was Shane's."

"You're too late, Burke. There aren't going to be any deals."

"He's crazy. You gotta know that. A psychopath. You saw Shane's face. R.J. did that. He was gonna do it to me, or worse. We were trying to figure out how to tell the truth ..."

"Detective Cashen!" Tim Brouchard's booming voice bounced off the walls. Jake didn't move so much as a muscle.

Burke mouthed the words, "Help me!"

"The way you helped Mary?" Jake said.

"Cashen, that's enough," Brouchard said.

Jake took a step back, letting Tim get through the doorway and into his client.

"You two deserve each other. That's all I'll say."

Then he left Burke to his lawyer and to his fate.

Forty

Connie Rathburn wore an apron with red hearts on it when she answered the door. She had flour in her hair and a rolling pin in her free hand.

"We're making Valentine's cookies," she said. "You're just in time to help us frost them."

"Thanks," Jake said. He walked in and followed Connie to the kitchen. Kevin was busy spreading red frosting over heart-shaped cookies. He got half of it on the countertop.

"Hey, Kevin," Jake said. "Those look delicious."

"Maybe we'll have you on sprinkle duty," Connie said. She pulled two jars out from under her kitchen cabinet. One had white sprinkles, the other red.

"And those red hearts that make my mouth burn," Kevin said.

"Red hots," Jake said. "Those are my favorite."

Kevin smiled, revealing a bright-red tongue. He'd clearly been sampling the frosting while Connie turned her back.

"Can I trust you not to destroy the kitchen, kiddo?" Connie asked her grandson.

Kevin was already intensely focused on the jar of white sprinkles.

"Ah, the hell with it." Connie laughed. "Let him make a mess." She wiped her hands on her apron and led Jake into the living room out of Kevin's earshot.

"I wanted you to hear it from me," he said. "We caught the guy."

Connie had a smile on her face. She held it there, frozen. There was just the faintest twitch in her right eye. Then, slowly, her shoulders dropped.

"Shane?" she asked.

"No. But he was involved."

Jake took a breath. As simply as he could, he told Connie Rathburn about the plot that had taken her daughter from her. She bore it. She clutched Jake's arm at one point. But she listened to every word he said. Finally, she took a step backward and sank into the couch behind her. Jake guided her down then sat beside her.

"You're safe," he said. "Kevin is safe. This guy is never getting out."

"But Shane," she said. "He's not going to jail for this?"

This was the hardest part of the story for Jake to tell.

"No," he said. "He has full immunity. It was the only way we could build a case against the real killer, Connie."

"Kevin won't understand that. I don't care how old he gets, how is he supposed to handle the fact that his dad helped get his mother killed?"

"I don't know," Jake answered. Then Connie blanched. She put a hand over her mouth. "Oh Jake. I'm sorry. You're the last person I should have said something like that to."

Jake found a smile. "No. Maybe I'm the only person you can say something like that to. This won't define him. You won't let it. Kevin's going to have something I had. He'll have a grandmother who will raise him in a house filled with love. Who will put him first. And over time, things will feel normal again. He'll feel the ground beneath his feet again. And through it, so will you. Just ask my grandfather."

Tears filled Connie's eyes. She hugged him.

"She loved you so much. Never forget that. You and Gemma were Sonya's world. But you were your father's world, too. I believe that in my soul. Because I saw it with my own eyes."

Jake felt as though thunder cracked somewhere inside him. He went rigid, breathing past it. No. Not here. Not ever. There were some things he could never let himself feel. So in that, he'd told Connie a lie. Kevin Edwards would feel that thunder someday too.

"Wait," she said. "Raise him? You said I would raise Kevin? But Shane's not going to jail. He could ..."

"No," Jake cut her off. "Shane agreed to give up full custody of Kevin to you. He's already signed paperwork. It will be filed with the court later this week. Talk to your lawyer. Shane's going to consent to you being made Kevin's guardian. Shane will have no visitation unless you want it or Kevin does someday. While he's a minor, it'll be your call."

Connie nodded rapidly. "Oh Jake. He gets to stay? I get to keep him?"

"You get to keep him."

She flung herself at him, enveloping Jake in a bone-crushing hug. She muffled a sob of joy into Jake's shoulder.

Later, Jake went into the kitchen with her. Kevin was covered in red frosting, but he was laughing. He was happy. The thunder might come, but for now, the skies were clear.

Forty-One

Ten days later…
Schottenstein Center
The Ohio State University

"Circle! Circle!"

Jake crouched in the corner of the mat. Two gladiators faced each other, sweat pouring from their lithe, muscular bodies. One had the advantage of size and brute strength. The other, a preternatural quickness that couldn't be taught.

Jake saw himself in him. Hungry. Mean. The darkness might come to him in waves of rage that seemed to have no cause, only an outlet. Both of them fatherless. Both of them intense.

But Ryan Stark had something Jake never did. Even in the thunderous din of the crowd, he could hear Ryan's mother's scream of encouragement all the way up the stands.

"Get him!" she yelled. "Get. Him!"

Ryan was down by three points with ten seconds left. McManus stepped out of bounds, stopping the clock.

Ten seconds. That's all it would take and Blake McManus would be a four-time state champion. In ten seconds, he would shatter Ryan's dream. Ryan looked to his corner and locked eyes with his uncle. The boy knew Jake was the only person in the world who understood what he was feeling at that moment. The only one who could show him what to do.

No words. They would not help.

Jake was on his feet. The crowd melted away. The frozen clock melted away. The noise melted away.

Jake jerked both arms up, then twisted his torso to the right. Double underhooks to a headlock.

Ryan nodded. He understood. He went back to the center of the mat, lowered his stance and faced Blake McManus in the neutral position.

The whistle blew. Ryan advanced. It was seconds. It felt like hours. It felt like nothing. It happened. Ryan got his arms under Blake's and executed his double underhooks. Jake saw the fear pass over McManus's face. He knew he was in trouble even before Ryan knew what he'd done. McManus tried to back out of bounds. But it was too late. It would always be too late. Ryan ripped the picture-perfect Frazier headlock.

Jake saw the shock and disbelief go through Blake McManus's eyes. His superior strength wouldn't help him now. Gravity and inertia took over as his body flipped under the weight of Ryan's.

Jake leapt to his feet. He saw it even before the referee did. There were three seconds left. "Squeeze!"

A different referee stepped onto the mat, holding the rolled towel he would use to pat his colleague on the back when the clock ran out.

But he would never get the chance.

The mat referee raised his arm in a slow arc. Then brought it down, slapping his palm against the mat.

All four hundred people on the west side of the arena rocketed to their feet at once. A deafening cheer went up. Blake McManus rolled to his stomach, burying his face in his hands. He would relive those final three seconds for the rest of his life. He would stand on the second step of the podium and take his medal. But Ryan Stark would always be at the top.

Ryan launched himself to his feet. In Jake's right ear, he could hear Gemma screaming through her tears.

Ryan didn't look for her. Not yet. Instead, he turned and ran toward his Uncle Jake. He threw himself into Jake's arms. Jake lifted him off the ground.

"You did it," Jake whispered. "It's real. You did it. I love you." He realized he was saying the words he wished his father could have told him all those years ago when Jake Cashen won his own state championship. He hoped they were the right ones.

Later, Ryan did look for his mother. She hugged him. Gemma wasn't one to break down in public, but she did that day. Ryan hoisted his little brother, Aiden, onto his shoulders. Aiden would marvel at Ryan's medal. He would find Uncle Jake and ask him if he could make him into a state champion someday, too.

But as Ryan celebrated, Jake felt a weight on his chest. He couldn't breathe. His vision clouded. He needed air. He needed ... something.

Quietly, he walked away from the others. They didn't notice. Between the other parents, Ryan's teammates, and half the town that had traveled to watch Ryan become a hometown hero, it was easy to slip away.

Jake found himself alone in a dark corridor just outside the locker rooms. It was snowing again. The buses would have a treacherous ride back to Stanley if they chose to leave tonight.

A text came through. He felt his phone vibrate in his back pocket. Instinct told him who it was even before he looked. Slowly, he pulled his phone out and read the text. It came from an unknown number.

You did it, kid. Enjoy this moment. It's yours as much as Ryan's. I remember when you stood on that podium like it was yesterday. I'm proud of you. For all of it. Frank.

Jake looked back toward the stands. They'd begun to empty, the Stanley High School fans making way for another school's fans to take their places. Hundreds of people streamed toward the exits. Was he there? Had he been watching the whole time? Would he have risked it?

The answer came to him, as sure as his own name. Of course, Frank was here somewhere. Of course, he would risk it. And Jake also knew he'd never find him. Not today. He slipped his phone back in his pocket.

A moment later, it all came crashing into him. Mary's last moments. Her funeral. Connie's tears. Kevin's trusting eyes. Penny Whitney's fingers on the trigger of that shotgun. Mary's handcuffs as he placed them around R.J. Whitney's wrists.

"You've done enough." The gruff voice seemed to come from nowhere. Then Grandpa Max stepped out of the shadows.

How had he found him? He could barely see two feet in front of him. And it was dark down here. But somehow, Max Cashen had known where to find his grandson. And he had known what he might need.

Jake said nothing. Grandpa walked to him. He put an arm around his shoulders.

"You did good, kid. For everybody."

Still, Jake could find no words. He couldn't let go. If he did, he knew he might drown.

But Max Cashen wouldn't let go either. He pulled his grandson to him, hugging him tightly.

"You did enough," Grandpa whispered. "You always do."

"No."

"Yep. Now it's time to go home. There's work to be done in the woods. Spring's coming. I'm getting too old to run that chainsaw all day, and that fence needs fixing."

"That fence always needs fixing," Jake said.

"Now you're getting it," Max said.

Max let him go. Jake felt the weight lift a little from the center of his chest. He knew. The old man always knew. And he had been there through the worst of it.

For Jake.

"Come on," Grandpa said. "The rest of 'em are waiting. How about we go home and get good and drunk tonight? We've earned it."

Jake smiled. He took Grandpa by the hand. They walked back into the arena together. Ryan was still surrounded by his teammates.

His mother snapped pictures through her tears with her phone. Aiden danced around the edges of the crowd.

This was family. All of them. Kevin Edwards would have this too. Jake would help make sure. He looked skyward. He didn't always know what he believed in, but he felt Mary Rathburn there that day. Watching. Waiting. He made a promise to her like he'd made to so many other people he had lost.

But he was still here. And he would look out for those who were left behind.

Until his last moment.

A vacation getaway at a remote cabin becomes the scene of a gruesome double murder. Detective Jake Cashen is called in to investigate the chilling deaths of a young couple in the heart of Blackhand Hills. What he uncovers threatens to turn a thriving rustic tourist haven into a breeding ground for fear and suspicion.

One-Click So You Don't Miss Out!

Turn the page and keep reading for a special preview...

Interested in getting a free exclusive extended prologue to the Jake Cashen Series?

Join Declan James's Roll Call Newsletter for a free download.

Sneak Preview of Secrets of Blackhand Creek

Secrets of Blackhand Creek
by Declan James

Five Months Later

She hated the water. Ever since she was five years old in a flamingo floaty at her aunt's pool. Her older brother had come down the slide and landed on top of her, flipping her over. She'd stayed there, upside down, staring into blue nothingness, chlorine burning her eyes, the muffled sound of her own scream as the water rushed in and filled her lungs. She remembered her brother's goggled face appearing in front of her, bubbles coming out of his nose.

It had only lasted a few seconds, but to Kayla, it had seemed forever. They'd all laughed about it later. It became a family joke. Her parents' "material" at later Christmas parties and reunions. Remember how ridiculous Kayla looked with her legs flailing above the water, clinging to that overturned pink flamingo inner tube? And how she'd screamed bloody murder when her brother finally pulled her out?

Today, fifteen years later, Kayla gripped the sides of another inner tube. This one big and yellow with cup holders. She reached for her can of watermelon vodka seltzer and downed it. It was her third one. Her tube spun around as the current flowed faster. The creek got deeper here and just around the bend. She'd hit a small drop that would jerk her sideways and spill her out of the tube.

But Kayla didn't know that yet.

"You empty, Kay?" Aubrey yelled. She was in the tube right behind Kayla. Three more of her sorority sisters brought up the rear but Aubrey had the cooler tied to her tube. She'd been tossing cans of White Claw to whoever needed them as nine members of the Zeta Kappas floated the length of Blackhand Creek on that sweltering Saturday in July.

"I'm good!" Kayla shouted back. She was more than good. Her brain floated as much as she did. It was a good buzz. The kind that could almost make her forget how much she hated anything to do with swimming.

It was peaceful here. The creek cut through the deepest gorge in Blackhand Hills. She leaned back, letting her butt hit the water. Large black birds circled overhead, spinning and diving. The cliff face looked so high. Kayla saw a waterfall spilling out of the rock and followed it all the way down.

They'd just rounded the so-called Devil's Pass. For tens of thousands of years, the water carved its way through the sandstone cliffs, forming this very gorge that would later give the region its name.

It meant Kayla could relax. Devil's Pass was the only treacherous part of this path. There, the water churned in three directions. Beneath it, slick rocks littered the creek bed, making it impossible to navigate the shallow water on foot. You just had to hold tight to the sides of your inner tube and hope you didn't capsize.

She hadn't. Aubrey had. It got a big laugh. Kayla wasn't proud that she'd chimed in. But it was over now.

She leaned back and focused on the black birds overhead. She trailed her fingers over the water. Maybe swimming wasn't so bad this time. Maybe the answer was more vodka.

"I'll take one more, Aubs!" Kayla shouted back.

She tried to sit up higher on her tube. Aubrey gave her a thumbs up. She pulled at the green rope tied to the side of her tube, bringing the Styrofoam cooler closer.

"Here it comes!" Aubrey shouted. She arced the can through the air. Kayla would have preferred if she'd just thrown it in the water. It would have been easier to just pick the thing up as it floated by.

Aubrey had a good arm. Too good. Kayla twisted in her tube, realizing the can was about to smack her in the face if she didn't get out of the way.

Her foot fell through the middle of the tube. One side dipped and the other hit a small rock. Kayla's foot got tangled in the rope threaded through the side. It was then she hit the drop that turned her sideways.

She was going over. She was at the bottom of that slide all over again. Behind her, Aubrey and the others were already laughing. Kayla pitched forward, landing face down in the water. She felt her left palm split open and got a face full of dirt and sand.

She swore. Her inner tube floated down the creek without her. She'd have to run along the shore to try to catch it.

Wiping the dirt from her eyes, Kayla got to her knees. She landed beside a rotted log that had fallen halfway into the creek. She grabbed it for balance and started to pull herself up. The bark was covered with green slime and the waterlogged wood crushed under her grip. She lost her balance again and fell forward, landing on her chest. She sank into about three inches of muck.

"Gross!"

Kayla tried not to think about all the leeches or other creepy crawlies that could be hiding in that slime. She got herself up on her elbows.

That's when she saw it.

It took a moment for her brain to register what her eyes were seeing. The log had hidden part of it. The girls might have floated right on by without even realizing what was there.

A dead body.

A woman. She had long dark hair embedded with muck and leaves. She was lying on her side, topless, her legs buried beneath the water. But her eyes were open. Milky and sightless. Her blue lips slightly parted. To Kayla, it looked as though the woman's face had been frozen in a perpetual scream. A crawfish crawled out of her mouth.

Adrenaline shot through Kayla. She tried to scream but no sound would come out. Instead, she slipped in the slime and got a mouthful of the creek water just inches from where the dead woman was submerged. Kayla got her legs under her. Somehow. She bolted out of the water and finally let out a scream that echoed through the gorge.

Don't miss Secrets of Blackhand Creek, Book #6 in the Jake Cashen Crime Thriller Series.

➡ https://declanjamesbooks.com/SBC

About the Author

Before putting pen to paper, Declan James's career in law enforcement spanned twenty-six years. Declan's work as a digital forensics detective has earned him the highest honors from the U.S. Secret Service and F.B.I. For the last sixteen years of his career, Declan served on a nationally recognized task force aimed at protecting children from online predators. Prior to that, Declan spent six years undercover working Vice-Narcotics.

An avid outdoorsman and conservationist, Declan enjoys hunting, fishing, grilling, smoking meats, and his quest for the perfect bottle of bourbon. He lives on a lake in Southern Michigan along with his wife and kids. Declan James is a pseudonym.

For more information follow Declan at one of the links below. If you'd like to receive new release alerts, author news, and a FREE digital bonus prologue to Murder in the Hollows, sign up for Declan's Roll Call Newsletter here: https://declanjamesbooks.com/rollcall/

Also by Declan James

Murder in the Hollows

Kill Season

Bones of Echo Lake

Red Sky Hill

Her Last Moment

Secrets of Blackhand Creek

With more to come...

Stay in Touch with Declan James

For more information, visit

https://declanjamesbooks.com

If you'd like to receive a free digital copy of the extended prologue to the Jake Cashen series plus access to the exclusive character image gallery where you can see what Jake Cashen and others look like in the author's mind, sign up for Declan James's Roll Call Newsletter here: https://declanjamesbooks.com/rollcall/

Made in the USA
Las Vegas, NV
24 August 2024

94375235R00215